PULL
THE
THREAD

M A R K O   S A N S

PAGE PUBLISHING, INC.
Conneaut Lake, PA

First originally published by Page Publishing 2020

ISBN 978-1-6624-0233-3 (pbk)
ISBN 978-1-6624-0234-0 (digital)

Printed in the United States of America

ACKNOWLEDGMENTS

I want to thank my review crew: Paula, Roger, Louise, and Karen for their help and untold number of hours spent in the creation of this story. I listened to everything you told me. Your insights, honesty, and eagle eyes contributed to the success of this book. Thanks also to Paula, Maureen, and Pat from the Triple Dubs for their honest feedback, excitement, and encouragement.

"It is with deep sadness that we have to tell you all that Marko has passed before his book was published. Writing was one of his passions and he had many stories to tell! This earth has lost one of the good guys!" With loving memories, his wife and family.

Find a thread to pull
And we can watch it unravel
But this is just the start
We'll find out who we are

From the song "Thread" by Now Now

I'm tired of keeping it together
I'm tired of lies disguising who I really am
There's pain that's hiding under the surface
I'm tired of keeping it on the inside

From the song "Threads" by Dave Leonard

PROLOGUE

I'm sitting here in a bar at a swanky hotel, waiting on a new lady friend, agreeing to meet for drinks. She's running very late and hasn't called or texted me. I'm wondering at this point if she will stand me up.

As I nurse my beer, a guy comes into the bar and sits a couple of stools away from me. He appears happy and greets me with a big smile and a nod. He orders a drink, and I make an observation about his happiness. He tells me that he is meeting an old friend he has known for many years.

I introduce myself to him, extending my hand to shake his, "Hi. My name is Jack. What's yours?"

Returning the handshake, he responds, "I'm Anthony."

"Please to meet you, Anthony." I then ask him if he really knows this person.

He looks at me incredulously and tells me, "I have known this guy for over twenty years, and we have been through everything together. I even know what drink he's going to order when he gets here."

I respond, "You know, it's great that you two are that close. But what do you know about his past?"

He looks at me with furrowed eyebrows and responds, "I know everything about his past."

I lean in. "Are you sure?"

"Yes," he says. "Why would you ask a question like that?"

"What you know about him is based upon what he has told you, right?"

His eyes narrow some. "Yes, of course. What are you getting at?"

"Perhaps you need to pull the thread of what you know about your relationship with your buddy."

Anthony looks a little confused. "What do you mean pull the thread?"

"It's a phrase that means as you pull on a thread, like on a sweater, the whole thing could unravel and uncover what is beneath."

"So you're saying if I decide to delve into my friend's past, the whole relationship could unravel?"

"Since we are here waiting on others to show up, there is a story you need to hear."

Discovery

Josh Bishop returns to the laydown yard late in the afternoon on a frigid January day. The sun is going down as he sits in his truck, cold to the bone from a day of working on a rebuild of an electrical transmission line. He tries to thaw out with the heater on full blast before making his way in to the construction trailer. The laydown yard he enters holds all the material for the job, plus parking for the crew's vehicles and a trailer for them to get ready for the day's work.

Josh eventually gathers up the stuff in the seat next to him to take in and gets out of his truck. He leaves the truck running to keep it warm in the now-minus twenty-five-degree air. Being the last one back from the work area, which is usually the case, there is only two other crewmen in the yard getting ready to leave for home. Josh waves to the men and decides to use one of the porta-potties next to the trailer. As he takes care of business, he reminds himself to thank Roger Simmons, the project manager for renting porta-potties with heaters, which is a blessing in this weather. The crewmen think this is the most important piece of equipment in the yard.

As he exits the porta-potty, he notices that the two crew members are now gone and alone now in the yard. It is very quiet now, especially since the laydown yard is in the middle of nowhere, several miles from any town. He reminds himself that he will most likely need to heat up the lock on the gate to the yard so it will lock in this cold.

Josh has been working for Badger Power Company that is based out of Wisconsin for more than nine years and has worked up from being an apprentice to where he is now—a general foreman. He is very knowledgeable and gets right to the point and isn't much for politics. Plan the work and get it done, that's his mantra.

He scans the yard again and stops when he notices the gray GMC pickup truck in the back of the yard, the same one he saw this morning belonging to Roger Simmons, his best friend. It seems like the truck had not moved all day, and in the dimming light, he does not see his friend. *What the heck is he still doing here? Didn't he say he had a meeting in Madison to go to earlier? Maybe he came back to get more pictures of the screwed-up pole sections. But it's getting dark out, so why would he take pictures in this light?* He doesn't see any lights from the truck or a beam from a flashlight back there. Josh gets his phone out and dials Roger's cell. It keeps ringing until voice mail picks it up and senses something isn't right here.

He quickly scans the yard but sees nothing out of the ordinary. Red flags go off in his head that there is something wrong; he puts the stuff back in the truck and drives back to where the other truck is sitting. He pulls up behind and to the left of the GMC truck and gets out of his vehicle. Josh stops and listens; there is no noise coming from Roger's truck or any other sound for that matter.

With his boots crunching in the snow, he makes his way around his truck and goes to the driver's side of the GMC and peers through the driver's window. No one is in the truck, and he notices the key is still in the ignition and in the On position, but the engine is not running. The passenger seat holds some papers and Roger's cell phone. The front passenger door is open, but because of the height of the truck, he can't see what's on the other side. Josh's heart is now pounding in his chest, dreading what he may find on the other side of the truck. Almost in a panic now, he quickly goes around the front of the truck to the other side.

When he clears the front of the vehicle, he stops in his tracks, slipping in the snow and almost falling. There, no more than a few feet from him, he observes his friend Roger lying facedown in the snow with his arms outstretched to his side and his legs are spread apart. It's almost like he was doing snow angels but lying facedown.

CHAPTER 2

Rescue?

Josh's first responder training kicks in as he scans the immediate area around Roger for hazards that would make him a second victim. Satisfied that there is no danger, he reaches his friend, and as he does, he calls out to him but gets no response. Josh kneels and shakes the man and calls out to him again, asking if he's okay. Again, no response. At this point, it is dark out, so he runs to his truck and retrieves a large flashlight, taking his gloves off so he can operate the flashlight. Upon returning, he shakes the man again with his now almost-frozen hands and calls out to him with no response. He scans the back of the man's body and doesn't see anything out of the ordinary. Josh sets the flashlight down on the other side of the Roger and points it to himself. He tries to straighten out the legs, but they are stiff from the cold. He gets on the other side and grabs the shoulder and the hip and slowly starts to roll the man over onto his back.

Once he has Roger on his back, he scans his body again, and two things jump out at him right away. First is the mixture of dirt and snow on the front of Roger's jacket and, secondly, that his face is very red. He quickly thinks that it could be due to lying facedown on the snow on this very cold day. He checks for breathing and hears some gurgling which he takes for labored breathing. Roger's eyes are closed, and Josh opens an eyelid and sees that the eye is rolled up into his head. With that, he calls for help.

The Waushara County 911 center took Josh's call, and after playing twenty questions with them, they dispatch a sheriff's deputy and an ambulance, and given the severity of the situation, they dispatch a MedFlight operating from the university hospital in Madison. The dispatcher tells Josh that help should be arriving in fifteen to thirty minutes.

Josh is then told to wrap the patient in a blanket. He puts the cell phone down on the hood of his truck and goes through his first responder's bag for something to wrap him in. His hands are very painful now that they have been exposed to the extreme cold this long, but Josh is operating on adrenaline and has ignored the pain. He finds a thin, shiny mylar blanket and puts it around Roger. Now Josh notices that Roger is not making those gurgling noises anymore; in fact, he's not making any sound at all. He checks for breathing by placing the side of his face close to Roger's mouth to feel for breathing.

It is hard to discern whether he is breathing since the wind had kicked up about ten minutes ago. In his optimism, he feels Roger is breathing but knows that he is far from being all right. He returns to the cell phone on the hood of the truck and tells the dispatcher that the man's condition is getting worse and to tell the responders to step on it. At this point, the cell phone chirps at him to let him know it is critically low on battery life. He gets into the warm truck and plugs it into his car charger fumbling as he does so because his fingers are numb and then decides to move his truck around to put light on Roger.

He can hear the dispatcher trying to talk to him. He puts the phone on speaker in time to hear the dispatcher tell him to meet the deputy out by the road. He tells her, "No can do. I'm alone out here, and I'm not leaving my man." He instead gets up and runs to his truck to turn on his flashers and his yellow emergency rotating lights. He tells the dispatcher what he has done, hoping she relays the information before the deputy unknowingly goes past his location. He gets out and checks on Roger; nothing has changed. He tells him to hang in there and that help is coming. He starts rubbing Roger's arms to help the warming process but seems futile in the frigid temps. He goes back to his truck and pulls out extra jackets and places them on

Roger's legs and upper body. His mind is whirling, trying to figure out what happened to his friend. *How long has he been out in the cold? Has he been here since he left him this morning?* He didn't see anything that pointed to an injury, so what happened? Just as he is wondering when help will arrive, he hears a siren in the distance and getting closer.

After the air ambulance took off to the hospital, the responding sheriff's deputy wants to get a statement from Josh, but he tells him he will do it later, that right now he needs to get to the hospital. He tells the deputy that since this accident occurred on company property and being a ranking manager, he needs to go with the victim. The deputy acquiesces and asks when he can make a statement, which Josh responds with "I dunno."

Josh jumps into his truck and grabs his phone, calling Roger's home number, hoping to reach his wife, Sarah. He didn't have her cell number and hopes he could catch her at home. Like him and his wife, Roger and Sarah still had their landlines since cell coverage was spotty at times out in the country. The phone rang and rang, then went to voice mail. He starts the truck and begins to leave, then it occurs to him that his wife, Marsha, may have Sarah's cell number. He stops the truck with a jolt just before leaving the yard and calls Marsha's cell phone. The call didn't go through, so instead, he calls her on the home line, hoping she was already home from work. Marsha picks up on the third ring. "Hey, dear, coming home soon?"

"No. As a matter of fact, I've got an emergency right now."

"Oh my god, are you all right?"

"Yes, I'm okay, but Roger's been hurt. Do you have Sarah's cell number?"

"What happened?"

"Not sure. I found him in the yard, and he's being airlifted to university hospital in Madison."

"Oh my god, Josh! I've got her number. Got something to write on?"

"I tell you what, you call her and tell her to meet me at the hospital emergency room. I've gotta get going!"

"Okay, I'll call her right now. What do I say to her?"

"Just tell her what I told you. Roger has been hurt and he is being airlifted to university hospital."

"Okay, bye."

Josh presses the End key on his phone and shoots out of the laydown yard on the county road, heading south to Madison, going as fast as he can on the icy roads.

C H A P T E R 3

Notifications

Shortly after treatment began on Roger in the ER, Waushara County Sheriff Steve Cantor receives a phone call from the university hospital in Madison that a man has died of suspicious means from his jurisdiction. The person from the hospital indicates the patient came in DOA. He is then asked when they will pick up the body. He thinks about it for a moment and tells the hospital that the Waushara County medical examiner out of Wautoma will pick up the body. He tells the hospital to make sure they bag and tag everything they took off the body in the course of treating the deceased.

The county has dealt with homicides before, especially vehicular homicides, since there is an enclave of Amish in the middle of the county. There are frequent car versus buggy accidents, and the Amish usually lose. His next two calls go to the medical examiner's office to have them go pick up the body and then to Eric Halvorsen, one of two detectives under his authority.

The phone rings twice and Halvorsen answers, "Halvorsen. What's up, Sheriff?"

Cantor informs him of the homicide and wants him to start looking into it. "I'm putting a deputy at the entrance to the company's laydown yard where the body was found. I want you to go to the university hospital to start asking questions. Let's not get lackadaisical about this, Eric. This is a murder investigation."

Halvorsen let the dig roll over him and acknowledged the sheriff's request. His relationship with Cantor wasn't the best, and they had several conversations about his detective work. This was an important case, and he knew that the other detective didn't get called to work this one because he was pretty green. Eric thought this would be a good opportunity to increase his stock with the sheriff. He got into his cruiser and starts his drive to Madison.

C H A P T E R   4

The Hospital

Marsha drives from her home in Montello and picks up Sarah at the Simmons's home east of Portage, about halfway between Portage and Marcellon. They get to the hospital about thirty minutes after Josh did, and he meets them as soon as they came through the emergency room doors. Josh tells them, "They are working on Roger but won't tell me anything. They are waiting for family to arrive to give us some news." Josh directs the women to the reception desk where Josh introduces Sarah to the receptionist.

The receptionist looks at Sarah and says, "You are Roger Simmons's wife?"

Sarah nods and says, "I want to see my husband. I was told he was brought here."

"Yes, I'll have a nurse come and take you to him," the receptionist says flatly. "Please have a seat while you wait."

Josh thought it odd that a nurse would take them back to see him; he thought they would be allowed through the doors and look for the bed he was at. He dismissed it as new security procedures to keep the number of people in the trauma bays to a minimum. So they sat in the ER waiting room for the nurse to come. Ten minutes go by, then fifteen minutes and, finally, after waiting twenty minutes, the door to the inside of the ER swings open and a nurse calls out,

"Sarah Simmons?" At that, Sarah gets up along with Marsha and Josh, and all three moved toward the nurse.

When they get to her, Sarah identifies herself. The nurse says to Marsha and Josh, "And who are you?"

Sarah answers, "They are very good friends and I would like them to come along."

The nurse hesitates as she is deciding whether to allow them, and then says, "Okay, follow me." The nurse leads them past the trauma bays where there was a boy in one and an elderly man in another, but no Roger. Josh thought that he should be in one of the bays unless he was in surgery or has been admitted to the hospital and is up in his room already.

The nurse stops at a door and opens it and motions the group to go in. The carpeted room has a sofa, two overstuffed chairs in it, along with a big silk plant in the corner and a couple of nondescript landscape prints hanging on the wall. Alarm bells start going off in Josh's head now. *What kind of room is this? And more importantly, where is Roger?* He is about to say something, but he sees a woman in a white coat and a stethoscope around her neck come into the room. She introduces herself all around, shaking hands with all three.

"I am Dr. Paula Winters, trauma surgeon from the emergency department. Please sit down. Which of you ladies is Sarah Simmons?"

Sarah says, "I am. Where is Roger? I need to see him."

Dr. Winters turns to the other two and asks, "You are family as well?"

Sarah responds, "This is Josh and Marsha Bishop, very good friends of ours. I asked them to be here with me."

The doctor turns to fully face Sarah and with a sad face and says, "I need to tell you that your husband has passed away. I'm so sorry for your loss."

It is as if Sarah was hit in the chest with a sledgehammer, lurching back in her chair, hands to her face, and finally yelling, "No! That can't be!" Marsha has a similar reaction to the terrible news. Josh, on the other hand, just sits there with no expression, dazed, confused. He is trying to process what the doctor just said and could not believe it. He could swear that Roger was alive when he left the laydown yard. He just sits there, shaking his head, not saying a word or comforting the women.

Josh looks up at the doctor, "What happened? He was alive when he was airlifted. I would know, I was the first responder!"

The doctor responds, "That may be, but I doubt it. Mr. Simmons was dead before we started to work on him here in the ER. He may have passed on the way to the hospital, but more likely, he was dead long before that."

Sarah manages to speak and asks, "How did he die?"

The doctor looks at all three of them and says, "I'm sorry to say, Mr. Simmons was shot and stabbed." With that revelation, Sarah begins to sob loudly, and through her own tears, Marsha tries to console her.

Josh becomes agitated and says, "I don't know how that could be. There was no blood where I found him!"

The doctor responds, "How cold was it out there today?"

Josh says, "It was minus twenty degrees and started to get colder once the sun set."

Dr. Winters explains, "Given the extremely cold temps today, there would be very little bleeding from the wounds since the body usually draws blood back to the core and the vital organs. Mr. Simmons began bleeding here once he was in a warm environment. Most likely it was blood that was already pooled in the body cavities and in the clothing."

Josh shakes his head. "I didn't know that! Had I known, I would have done something different to save him." Josh now feels as though he failed Roger.

"Given the wounds Mr. Simmons has, there would not have been much you could have done for him," informs Dr. Winters.

"Wounds? I didn't see any wounds when I worked on him," Josh continues, not sure if that piece of news makes him feel better about failing Roger. "I need to call this into work as a fatality accident. I'll be back in a minute."

C H A P T E R   5

Badger Talk

Josh heads to the emergency waiting room to get a better cell signal. As he enters the waiting room, he sees that Stan Brockdale and Joe Halsted from Badger Power are coming into the waiting room. Stan is the director of construction and Joe is the safety manager. Josh was a little surprised to see them here since he didn't call them. Stan and Joe saw Josh and went right to him. Stan asks, "How is he doing?"

Josh responds, "I was just about to call you, Stan." Josh is hesitating because he is still struggling with the news himself. "We just got word that Roger did not make it." Just saying that made him sick to his stomach as though saying those words made it really happen. This news caught both Stan and Joe off guard.

"What do you mean he died? What the hell happened out there, Josh?" asks Stan. Josh heard the accusatory tone in Stan's voice and immediately resented the implication that he somehow caused or contributed to Roger's death.

Sensing the emerging tension between the other two, Joe explains, "Josh, save it for now. I will have an investigation team set up by morning and we will need to get a full statement from you."

Looking at both Stan and Josh, Joe says, "This is the first Badger Power employee who died on the job. I will have to contact OSHA about this."

"But if he was murdered as Josh said, then will OHSA need to be involved?" Stan asks.

Joe thought about that a moment and says, "I'm not sure. I'll have to find out."

Thinking they are more interested in who to notify than Roger or his family, Josh interjects, "Look, I need to get back in there," pointing to the door behind him.

Stan asks, "Who else is here with you?"

"I had my wife get a hold of Roger's wife and drove her down here to the hospital. I came down straight from the laydown yard after the air ambulance left. My wife and I are good friends with the Simmons," Josh explains.

"All right, Josh, keep me posted personally on developments," Stan informs Josh. With that, he and Joe leave the hospital and Josh heads back to where Marsha and Sarah are.

When Josh made it back to the room, the doctor was gone, and Marsha was consoling Sarah and making a list of relatives to call about what has happened. Marsha gets off the sofa, where she and Sarah were sitting, saying in a hushed tone, "The doctor said the hospital has contacted the sheriff's department and they are sending down a detective to talk to us. She also said we can stay here as long as we want to." Marsha then adds, "Did you get ahold of your boss?"

"Actually, I met them in the emergency waiting room as I was trying to call him. He and the safety manager showed up wanting to know how Roger was doing. I broke the news to them. They are going to start a safety investigation tomorrow, but I'm not sure what the result will be given how Roger died," replies Josh.

Marsha nods. "Where are they now?"

Josh shrugs his shoulders and simply says, "They left." Marsha gives him a puzzled look. He explains further, "I told them you and I are here with Sarah and maybe they think they didn't want to horn in on it. I don't know."

They stop talking when they heard Sarah speak. "Guys, I need you to promise me something." They both come back to the couch where Sarah sat. "I need you two to promise me that you will walk with me through this. I can't do this alone!"

"Of course, Josh and I will help you. Just say the word," responds Marsha.

"Yes, whatever you need, we'll help you," Josh adds.

CHAPTER 6

Hospital Questions

Eric Halvorsen arrived at the university hospital and made his way to the emergency room and stopped at the receptionist. He flashed his credentials. "Hello, I'm Detective Halvorsen from the Waushara County Sheriff's Department. We received a report that a Roger Simmons came to this hospital and passed." He paused and continued, "I would like to speak to the attending physician that worked on Mr. Simmons."

"Yes, that would be Dr. Winters. I will page her," replied the receptionist.

Eric thanked her and then asked, "Is the family here yet?"

"Yes, the wife and two friends are here already," added the receptionist.

Eric went and sat down in the waiting room for the doctor to come up. He made a mental note to talk to the family after talking to the physician.

When Dr. Winters entered the waiting room, Eric stood up and walked up to her, flashing his credentials. "I'm Detective Halvorsen from Waushara County. Are you Dr. Winters?

"Yes, I am. Are you here about Roger Simmons?" the doctor replied.

"Yes, ma'am. I would like to ask you a few questions if you don't mind."

"Sure. Let's go to my office and talk." She led him through the emergency room double doors and then took a left, and halfway down a hallway, she stopped and opened a door to her office. Eric followed her in, and as she settled into her chair behind her desk, he closed the door and sat in a guest chair in front of the desk, taking out his notepad and his pen.

"Okay, Dr. Winters, can you run through what happened when Mr. Simmons came to the hospital?"

"Well, our MedFlight was dispatched to a location in your county with unknown trauma," Dr. Winters began.

Detective Halvorsen interrupted, "Is that normal for an air ambulance to be dispatched for unknown trauma?"

"Yes, it happens a lot actually. You need to remember the 911 dispatcher makes the call whether the helicopter is brought in and usually it is done with little information from the scene."

"Thanks, please tell me more," Eric added.

The doctor continued, "When the air ambulance landed, the patient was taken directly to a trauma bay here in the ER. The flight nurse mentioned to us that he observed the patient began to bleed toward the end of the flight. Once in the bay, we began monitoring his vitals and began cutting and removing the patient's clothing. The patient was flatlining, and we were in the process of intubating the patient to get air into the lungs. We gave the patient a shot of epinephrine to get his heart started. We also noticed that the patient's temperature was in the lower seventies."

Eric raised his hand toward the doctor. "Excuse the interruption, but I have a couple of questions. First one. So the deceased was not bleeding when they loaded him into the helicopter?"

"Yes, that is what the flight nurse told us," the doctor responded. "There is typically a flight doctor and a nurse along with the pilot on the aircraft. Some jurisdictions will have a flight nurse and paramedic instead of the doctor. In this case, this hospital utilizes the nurse and paramedic combination."

"And the patient started bleeding when they were almost to the hospital?"

"Yes. I asked the flight nurse to note that in his report, which we should have by morning," said the doctor.

"Doesn't that seem odd to you? I mean, I would expect someone to bleed the whole time."

"True, given normal circumstances, but in very cold weather, bleeding can be inhibited until the body warms up again," responded Dr. Winters.

"Second question. If his temperature was in the upper seventies as you indicated, wouldn't he have been frozen?"

"That was a peripheral reading and didn't necessarily reflect his core temperature, which could have been warmer," explained the doctor. "May I continue?" The doctor was showing her impatience with his questions.

"Yes," said the detective, raising his hands in surrender.

"By the time we were going to shock the heart, we had removed all the clothing and we saw the extent of the injuries. There were three gunshot wounds to the chest from a large caliber weapon, and we did not see any exit wounds. Besides those injuries, the patient had two stab wounds to the heart. We decided to go ahead and shock the heart on the outside chance he would respond to it."

The detective asked, "Did he respond?"

"No. Regardless of the efforts we made, there was no response. We pronounced him dead at that point."

"One last question, Doctor. Did the patient's outer clothing show any evidence of the wounds the victim received?"

The doctor paused and thought about that. "Not that I remember, but we were too busy trying to save him and didn't take the time to investigate that. Perhaps that is something you need to follow through with."

With that, Eric stood up and thanked the doctor and started out of her office. In the doorway, he inquired where the family was, and the doctor directed him to the bereavement room down the hall.

CHAPTER 7

Family Interrogation

The detective walks down the hall to talk to the family, gets to the room, and loudly opens the door without knocking. He sees two women and a man sitting on a couch. He asks if they are the family of Roger Simmons. Josh gets up and challenges the detective, "Who wants to know?" Eric identifies himself, showing his credentials. Josh continues to put himself between the detective and the women, crossing his arms.

He remembers this guy from five years ago when his brother was falsely accused of robbery. Once it was clear his brother was not the suspect, this detective and the sheriff's department didn't even apologize. The animosity Josh felt about Eric welled up again. It seems now that the detective did not recognize Josh or at least pretended not to know him.

Josh didn't like how the detective refused to give anyone respect as he came into the room, supposing they need to fear him or something. He should have knocked before coming in, been politer given the circumstances. Well, he came barking up the wrong tree tonight.

Sarah notices the change in Josh and indicates to Halvorsen that she is Roger's wife and that he and Marsha are close friends. Eric then tells Josh and Marsha to leave the room, saying that he wants to talk to the wife alone.

To Sarah, Josh says, "We'll be right outside the door if you need us." With that, he and Marsha leave the room and close the door gently.

Sarah has not left her place on the couch, and Eric moves to one of the chairs closer to her and sits down. "Mrs. Simmons, I need to ask you some questions about you and your husband. Are you aware of anyone who wanted to harm him? Anyone who had issues with him?"

After thinking about it for a moment, Sarah responds, "I can't think of anyone in recent memory that Roger had a serious issue with, and he didn't mention anyone wanting to harm him."

"Okay, Mrs. Simmons, what about you?" Eric queries. "How was your relationship with your husband?"

Sarah is starting to get miffed with Eric. "We had a normal relationship as a couple of ten years would have, plenty of ups and downs but nothing to drive me to do that."

"He never beat you, abused you verbally or psychologically? I mean, you don't look too broken up about the death of your husband."

She has been tolerating him to this point and concludes that he has the bedside manner of Attila the Hun, but that would be insulting the Hun. He does not even care about the fact she is in shock over the death of her husband. He didn't ask what kind of person Roger was and probably doesn't care. But the last insult was the tipping point.

Sarah shoots off the couch and is on the detective before he realizes what happened. She slaps him hard across the face and steps back. She points to the door, "Get out of here! *Now!*"

With Sarah's shout, Josh quickly enters the room and gets between Sarah and the detective. Josh notices how angry Sarah is and the surprised look on the detective's face, who hasn't left the chair, along with a red mark on the cheek. He quickly deduces what happened, and fearing that Sarah could be arrested, he turns to the women and tells Marsha to take Sarah home. The women nod, grab their coats, and abruptly leave without saying another word.

"I'm ready to give you my statement," Josh says evenly as he turns to the detective, who is looking angry at the moment.

"Why do I need your statement?"

"Because I am the person who discovered Roger earlier today. I assume the account of what I saw would be of some importance to you." The last dripping in sarcasm.

Josh sits down in the other chair across from the detective and begins to tell him what happened at the laydown yard. He starts with his interactions with Roger that morning, thinking it was relevant to the discovery. As he was telling the story, Josh realizes he was the last person he talked to that day outside of the killer. He walks the detective through how he found Roger, what he saw of the scene, and his efforts to render aid.

When Josh was done, the detective asks, "What did the front of his jacket look like when you turned him over?"

Josh thinks about that for a moment and then says, "First of all, the jacket was dark blue in color, and with the low light I was working with, I could only see a mixture of snow and dirt on the front."

Eric makes a mental note to talk with the medical examiner about the jacket. "I understand you were friends with the deceased? How close?"

"We have been friends for about eight years, so I think we are pretty close."

"So who do you think did this?" asks the detective?

Josh shakes his head. "I can't think of anyone he and I know that would have a beef like that against him."

"What about you? Was he stepping out with your wife and you found out about it?"

Josh's facial features narrow considerably. "Not likely, Detective."

"We'll see, we'll see," comes the response from the detective.

CHAPTER 8

Remembrance

Josh is back at the laydown yard early the next morning, let in by the sheriff's deputy at the entrance. The area in the back of the yard is roped off with crime scene tape. It is another sunny and frigid day as the previous one. He is struggling with the fact that Roger had died, losing his best friend that he knew so well. Right now, he feels numb and he didn't sleep much last night, trying to process all that happened. *Who would do that to Roger? And why?* In all the years he knew Roger, Josh never saw him really get into it with someone and always seemed to get along with everyone. What could Roger possibly have done to make someone shoot and stab him? It was almost like they wanted to make sure Roger was dead. *Why would someone do that to Roger?* What happened to Roger doesn't seem to line up with what Josh knew of him, and that got his curiosity going.

Josh can clearly remember his last conversation with Roger.

Josh rolls down the window on the passenger side and hollers to Roger, "Hey don't stay out here too long. You'll freeze."

Roger looks up, "Oh, don't worry, I've got a meeting to go to back at the office." The office is in Madison, one of four offices they have around the state.

Josh asks him why Ralph didn't show up. Ralph Peterson is new to the company and is the design engineer on the project and usually he comes to the construction meetings with Roger.

"Oh, I don't know why he's not here. I tried calling him and it went right to voice mail," Roger responds with a shrug of his shoulders. "Maybe he's out sick."

Josh tells Roger to stay warm and they'll talk later.

"You stay warm too. You and your guys take warming breaks, okay?" Roger tells him.

"Hey, I work out in this every day and I'm used to it. I'm not an office puke like someone I know," saying the last with a smile of his face.

"Really funny," Roger retorts. "See ya later."

Josh tries to come to grips with the thought of that being their final conversation. He sits in his truck and shakes his head in disbelief.

CHAPTER 9

Detective Work

After his encounter with *Defective* Halvorsen, Josh is convinced he will need to find out what happened to his friend. He is certain that Halvorsen is incapable of solving this case and it will be up to himself to do it.

Before coming to the laydown yard, Josh waved off the crew for the day since the yard is a crime scene now. Company policy dictated that an operator is at the yard whether the crew is working or not, mainly to handle any incoming material and offload it. Today, that operator was Earl Watson, a journeyman operator, who has done this kind of work since he graduated from high school. Earl has an opinion about everything and isn't afraid to express it, often very loudly. He is now camped out in the office part of the trailer, checking his cell phone. Show-up trailers, for the most part, have two sections. The smaller section is the office where the general foreman usually is set up complete with a laptop, printer, all the engineering drawings related to the job, and, of course, a coffeepot.

The larger section is where the crew comes and gets their personal equipment ready to go in the morning and remove it at the end of the day. In the winter, there is a phalanx of boot dryers lined up on one wall to keep work boots dry.

Every crew member has their own nickname, and Earl Watson's was Tagger. No one seems to know what the origin of the name was, and Josh suspects Earl doesn't either. Earl has had the nickname since he was an apprentice. Rumor has it that he got it when he put graffiti on the side of a material trailer, but no one knows for sure. Josh's handle is Gif, mainly since he is the general foreman and every GF has this handle.

As Josh drives his truck to the company's show-up trailer, he sees that there is some activity where he found Roger. There is a white van and three people walking around the location as well. They taped off the area where the truck is still sitting and where the body was. They are taking pictures and using a steel tape measure to determine distances. They seem to be fixated with the area inside the yellow tape.

Then he notices a wrecker coming into the laydown yard, stopping to check in with the sheriff's deputy. The wrecker then drives to the back where Roger's truck is and starts to pull it up on the flatbed trailer. Josh makes the conclusion that the truck is being impounded. By now, he is out of his truck and walking up the steps to the show-up trailer and enters his office. He pours himself a cup of coffee, thanks to Tagger, and sits at his desk, trying to warm up.

Tagger is sitting in the other chair in the office and looks at Josh. "When ya gonna tell me what happened last night, Gif? I kin see a bunch of cops out der and dey got part of da yard taped off like some crime scene on TV."

"Well, Tagger, that's because there is a crime scene out there," Josh further recounts the events of last night.

"Are ya kiddin' me! I can't see um gettin' wrapped around da axle that bad wit anybody."

"I know. When you came back to the yard yesterday, did you happen to see Roger's truck in the back?"

"Can't remember. I was too worried about startin' my car in dis cold."

"Did you see anything out of the ordinary," asks Josh.

Tagger thought about it for a moment, then says, "No. Don't remember seein' any headlights or anythin' dat didn't look like it belonged."

"I should check with the other guys to see if they saw anything."

Josh waits until the sheriff's crime scene people leave, which seemed like they weren't there long at all. He then drives his truck out to the scene and looks over the scene in the daylight. In the light of day, it doesn't seem like a murder could take place here. He replays the events of the night before; reality sets in, and he begins to sob for the loss of his friend. *Was there something more he could have done to save Roger? Would he be alive if I returned to the yard earlier?*

After he gets himself under control, he gets out of his truck and walks to the front of the truck, looking around, this time beyond the place where he found Roger. Then he spots it, and it is plain as day. He observes something in the snow he didn't see the night before, mainly because it was dark, but this caught his attention.

There are footprints in the snow that he thinks Roger might not make since they trail off into the woods. *Roger was taking pictures of steel poles. Why would he go into the woods? Too far from the porta-potty and just relieved himself in the trees? That would make sense since it is secluded back here and there are one set of tracks going to the woods and one set coming from the woods. But what if he didn't? It was very cold yesterday, so why expose himself like that? The cops didn't even look at those tracks; they just concentrated on the area around where Roger was and around his truck.* Josh gets an idea, grabs his radio, and raises Tagger. Into the radio, Josh says, "Hey, Tagger, take one of the 120-foot bucket trucks and drive it to the back of the yard and set it up about thirty feet north of the crime scene tape."

"Sure, Gif. Any of 'em in particular?"

"It doesn't matter. Just one in working order in this frigid weather will do."

Tagger gets the equipment running and makes his way back to where Josh wanted it. Seeing this, the sheriff's deputy, there to make sure the scene is not disturbed, comes out and asks Josh what he was doing. Josh responds that they needed to test the boom on the truck coming back to that part of the yard since it was causing problems the previous day.

Of course, this was a lie and the deputy didn't quite buy it. The deputy asks why they are going to test it there and not where it was parked. Josh had a quick answer for that. He tells him that if the boom were to fail, it would be catastrophic and others could be injured and potentially damage costly material for the job.

Tagger just walks up and hears the exchange and is just staring at his boss as he talked to the deputy, not sure what to make of raft of crap he is shoveling at the deputy. The deputy acquiesces and goes back toward the front of the yard. Tagger deploys the outriggers on the bucket truck, and Josh gets into the bucket with a pair of binoculars he took out of his truck.

With Tagger on the ground, he takes the rig up to eighty feet and surveys the ground around Roger's truck and then moves his eyes to the east. He spots the footprints in the snow he has found and keeps tracing them eastward into the trees. He sees an area that looked like someone was standing there, stamping their feet around. That could be consistent with taking a leak in the trees. He continues panning the binoculars to the east and saw that the footprints continued through the woods.

He then raises the bucket to one hundred feet and now notices that the footprints ended at a clearing on the other side of the woods. Josh also notices that there was a field road, coming from a nearby township road, running along the backside of the stand of trees. He takes pictures of the trial in the snow and the road on the other side. He decides to drive up that road once he is done in the yard and maybe find some other things of interest. One thing he was certain of, those tracks did not belong to Roger.

Josh had another idea and gets down off the bucket truck. Josh keeps a somewhat sophisticated metal detector in the back of his truck. As a hobby, he likes to go to various places and see if he can find anything. The model he purchased can discriminate between types of metals by emitting a different tone when the metal detector is passed over it. It can detect metals that are up to eighteen inches deep. He isn't as interested in finding a lot of money, but he is more about finding old things, which he usually collects.

He grabs the metal detector, sets it up, which takes a little longer given the temperature today. He is not sure what he will find, but in his mind, it will be worth doing nonetheless. While he is waiting for the metal detector to warm up, he takes out his Pin Pointer and powers that up. A Pin Pointer is a small handheld metal detector used to quickly find objects that may be found in a shovel full of dirt.

Once the metal detectors are ready to go, Josh starts scanning where the truck was sitting, moving the detector slowly back and forth just over the snow. Tagger, not knowing his boss had a metal detector, watches Josh start to work with it. He doesn't find anything right around where the truck was, so he moves toward the east to where the steel pole sections are. He scans now in wide arcs to cover more ground and still nothing, even as he moves north and south. As he moves more to the east, he goes closer to the steel poles, hoping the discriminator will show him something other than the steel. As Josh gets right up to the steel poles, he only gets a chirp from the nearby steel. He moves along the pole sections north and south, and still nothing.

Looking around, Josh observes an opening between the rows of pole sections that heads east and decides to check out that area. This is where the trail of footsteps is located that he observed on the bucket truck. Walking toward the mouth of the opening, Josh stops for a moment. If he walks down that path, the footprints would be obliterated. To use the metal detector and not to disturb the footprints or anything that is in the snow and above the ground, Josh jumps up on a pole lying on the ground closest to the path and gets on his knees so that the metal detector coil can reach the top of the snow. He begins his back-and-forth motion, and as the loop gets near the steel poles, he gets a chirp, but the discriminator tells him it is the steel. He keeps moving along the steel pole east along the opening, still nothing except the steel.

At a little more than halfway down the length of the steel pole, the metal detector emits a two-tone warbling sound in the center of the path. Josh looks at the discriminator which is showing the words *brass or bronze* and is hopeful that he found something of interest.

Tagger breaks his silence, "Ya found somethin', Gif?"

Josh looks up at Tagger, "Well, maybe. We'll see." Josh changes his position on the steel pole and is now lying on his stomach. He removes the Pin Pointer from his jacket pocket and begins to wave it just under the snow. The Pin Pointer's alarm goes off to indicate it found metal. Josh very carefully isolates the snow that contains whatever metal is there. He reaches down with his gloved hand and grabs the isolated pile of snow and metal and brings it up to him on the steel pole he is perched on. The process of blowing gently on the snow to dislodge it reveals three shell casings. After staring at them in disbelief for a moment, Josh looks up, "Tagger, go in my center console and grab a clean plastic bag. I have a bunch in there. Bring it to me, but walk on the other side of this pole."

"Comin' right up!" Tagger finds a small plastic resealable bag and brings it out to Josh. "Whatcha find, Gif?"

Josh puts the shell casings in the plastic bag and seals it, then shows it to Tagger. "Shell casings. Looks like 9 millimeters or for-ties to me, not sure." Forty is a reference to .40-caliber ammunition, which is a little larger in size than the 9-millimeter ammunition.

"Lemme see." Tagger takes the bag and looks closely at the end of one of the casings, "It's definitely a 9 mil. All day. I can tell by the markins' on da end. Anyway, it's not big enuf fer a forty."

"You sound certain of that. Why?" asks Josh.

"'Cus it's da same ammo I got in my Glock in my car."

Josh lowers his head and begins shaking it and raises it, and sounding irritated, he says, "Don't tell me you have a loaded Glock 9 mil in your car right now."

"Okay, I won't tell ya I gotta Glock 9 mil in my car."

"Oh, for the love of Mike, how many times do I got to tell you guys not to bring your guns to the jobsite! And it doesn't matter why you have it your car. You could get fired for that, you know!" Josh sounds really pissed now. "So right now we are getting into my truck and I'm driving you to your car. Then you are going to unload the gun and put it in your trunk.

Acting put out, Tagger says, "What good is it if I gotta unloaded gun in my trunk?"

"It will keep you from getting arrested for having a loaded con-cealed weapon, that's what!" comes Josh's retort.

Once Tagger stowed his weapon, they take Josh's truck and leave the laydown yard heading south. He quickly finds the township road that leads to the field road he saw from the bucket truck. Turning east, he finds the field road that he saw up in the bucket and slows to a halt on the road. Looking up the field road, they can see two sets of fresh tracks in the snow and no other activity. They pull in toward the field road, but Josh pulls in just to the east of the tracks in the snow to avoid driving over them. They stop and get out, looking at the tracks.

Tagger comments, "It don't look like truck tires made these tracks. Day be too skinny and too close t'gether." Tagger points to Josh's tires. "See, dem tires are wider and day be furder apart too."

Josh nods his head. "So maybe a smaller SUV made those? The vehicle would need all-wheel or four-wheel drive to get down this road." Josh takes out his cell phone and takes close up pictures of the tracks.

They get back into the truck and drive down the field road alongside the tracks already in the snow. Almost a half mile from the entrance of the field road, the tracks stop. Tagger and Josh get out again to look around. Josh notices the tracks stop where the footprints come out of the woods. He takes pictures of the tracks and the footprints coming out of the woods. Tagger observes something else, "Gif, git over ta my side of da truck, careful like. Ya need to see somethin'."

Josh makes his way around the back of his truck, careful not to step on the tracks in the snow left by the SUV, and comes up alongside Tagger on the passenger side. "What do you have, Tagger?"

"Look," he points to the footprints that would be on the passenger side of the SUV crossing in front of where the SUV stopped and went into the woods. "Whoever went inta da woods was ridin' shotgun, not drivin'."

Josh looks closely at what Tagger was pointing to. "So that means there were two of them. The driver and the one who went into the woods." Josh takes pictures of what Tagger found.

Josh then walks to where the front of the SUV stopped and backed up a few paces. He looks at the contour of the snow, looking south down the road. After a moment, he gets a puzzled look on his face. He then squats down to have his view closer to the ground. "Tagger, come here and tell me what you see." Tagger comes over to where Josh is and crouches down to be level with Josh. "Look at the contour of the snow between the tire tracks. What do you see?"

He looks intently for a couple of moments. "Gif, if I was a bettin' man, I'd say dat's a low spot in da snow where da car sat."

"That means the snow was melted there, right?"

"Yep. Tween da engine and da catalytic converter, day ud have melted da snow some. Musta been runnin' da engine while dey were waitin'."

"But wouldn't that have taken a long time in this weather?"

"Yep, no tellin' how long, but yeah, a long time."

Josh takes pictures of that area with his phone but isn't too happy on how they turned out. "Okay, I'm getting cold. Let's get some lunch." Josh stands up and starts for the truck.

"Well, it's about friggin' time you came t'your senses. I thought I had to freeze to death before ya stop playin' Dick Tracy." Tagger straightens up and heads for the warm truck.

After lunch, Josh and Tagger head back to the show-up trailer, stopping to ask the deputy how he was doing. The deputy was getting ready to go to lunch himself and said he would be back in an hour. Once inside, Josh asks Tagger, "Are there any deliveries today?"

Tagger grabs the material intake sheet, which shows what material is being delivered and when. "Nope. Nothin' t'day."

Josh suggests, "Why don't you go home then? I'll clock you in for the whole day."

"Ya sure?" Tagger asks.

"Sure. No problem. Hey and thanks for the help today."

"Well, if ya insist, den yeah, I'll go. I kinda liked what we did today, wasn't da usual stuff."

"Oh, and don't forget to take your Glock in your house and leave it there. Got it?"

"Sir, yes, sir!" responds Tagger, giving Josh a mock salute as he got his coat on and walked out the door.

CHAPTER 10

Deduction

Josh waited for Tagger to leave and noticed the deputy had already left as well. He is alone now. He has an hour to do what he needs to do alone without interruptions or someone discovering what he was about to do.

Josh quickly prints off the photos he took on his phone with the printer in his office. Next, he takes those and the bag of shell casings and goes into the big room and lays everything out on the table by the whiteboard that is hung on the side of the trailer. On the whiteboard, Josh writes at the top, on the side, "Last see Roger around eight to 8:15." Then about midway down, and just under the one above, he writes, "Find Roger between four and four thirty." He stops and looks at the times he put on the board. That is a long time to commit a murder. Next, Josh writes on the other side of the board:

1. Two people drive up field road in SUV.
2. Passenger gets out and goes into the woods.
3. Person stops in small clearing in woods.
4. Person stabs and shoots Roger.
5. Person reverses his direction and heads back to the SUV.
6. SUV backs out of field road onto township road and leaves area.

Josh steps back and considers the order of events he just wrote. He concludes that the sequence is accurate. Instead of answering questions, it seems to create more. *So why go through all this trouble? It would seem there would be easier ways to do this. Did they do it this way so they would not get noticed? But the laydown yard is in a remote area. Easy in, easy out.*

So why does it look like somebody was standing in that clearing? Were they waiting for the opportune time? For the yard to clear out? Yes, for the yard to clear out because once the person comes out of the woods, they would be exposed. Josh has a chilling thought. *What if the killer was already there waiting when he went out to talk to Roger?*

So where is the element of surprise? After all, the killer couldn't run very fast because of the snow. Maybe it didn't matter since they knew Roger was unarmed. And where would Roger go to get away from the killer? Josh concludes there is not much in the way of escape routes.

Josh remembers seeing the passenger door to Roger's truck open last night. *So why would that be open? When he talked to Roger in the morning, the door was closed and the engine running to keep the interior warm. Did Roger make for the truck and get the door open when he saw the killer? To what, get his phone? Or did he also have a gun under his seat?* No, that would be on the driver's side. It was the passenger door that was open. What if he had the gun in the console between the seats? It would be easier to get to. *Why would Roger have a gun?* He told Josh he wasn't a hunter. *Did he have it for protection? From who? Or did he think he could jump into the truck and drive away?*

If the SUV was running while the driver waited on the killer, wouldn't Roger have heard the car running? Maybe the woods and distance muffled the sounds. Or it could have been mistaken for a vehicle out on the county highway or in the laydown yard? Could he have heard it but ignored it?

So why stab the man if you already shot him with three 9 mm bullets? Did they miss? No, the doctor last night said Roger was shot three times in the chest. So much for missing him. Or did they want to make sure he was dead? That seems very likely. That tells Josh that the murder was no accident. Somebody wanted Roger dead.

After an hour goes by, Josh is not done with his analysis and looks out one of the small windows in the trailer to see if the deputy has returned. Right on schedule, the deputy pulls into the yard. The next thing Josh sees sends him into a panic. Instead of taking up his usual spot in the yard, the deputy is driving over to the show-up trailer! Josh quickly takes the big project map and tacks it over the whiteboard. He then runs to the office and grabs one of the books of drawings and brings it back into the main room and opens it up, placing it on top of the copies of the photos he took and unfolds a drawing.

The deputy makes use of the porta-potty by the trailer and then Josh can hear him coming up the aluminum steps. The deputy enters, and Josh greets him, "Coming in to warm up?"

"Yeah, if you don't mind. Hey, I noticed you guys have heaters in the porta-potties. Nice!"

"Yeah, in this weather, they are standard equipment. Help yourself to a cup of coffee. There are Styrofoam cups next to the coffee maker."

"Hey, thanks! Don't mind if I do." The deputy looks at the map on the wall and the drawing on the table and asks, "So what are you doing?"

Josh freezes for a moment while trying to think of something. "Well, when this line was originally built, the design called for a couple of transpositions along the length of the line. A transposition is a change in the order of the phases from top to bottom. So phase A would be on top, phase B in the middle, and phase C at the bottom. A transposition would be having phase C on top and phase A on the bottom." Josh further explains, "The new design doesn't need these transpositions, and so I need to figure out where they are located on the existing line so when we put in the new line, they won't be there. And of course, those locations were never noted anywhere." Josh is pleased with his explanation. He has determined those locations last week, but the deputy wouldn't know that.

"Wow, there sure is a lot that goes into constructing these lines," notes the deputy.

"Yeah, when dealing with this high a voltage, there is no room to screw up," quips Josh.

"Well, I'll get that coffee and get back out there. Thanks again!"

Josh manages, "You take care."

After the deputy leaves and gets into his car and assumes his usual place, Josh breathes a sigh of relief at the close call. He takes the project map off from covering the whiteboard and returns it where it was and pulls out the photos from under the book of drawings. *Okay, let's see if I can finish this without any more interruptions,* Josh thinks to himself.

Based on all that Josh finds, he deduces that this was a hit and a well-planned one at that. *How did they know Roger would be in that part of the laydown yard on that day or even at the laydown yard at all? How did they know the lay of the land? To know where to go and where in the woods to come out? Someone who knew where Roger was going to be and what he was going to do gave the information to the killer. So that means there was someone within the company who had it in for Roger. So his death was either partly or wholly an inside job.*

Josh thinks he just figured out the how, but why? What could have Roger done that warranted an assassin waiting to strike in sub-zero temperatures? There was nothing he could think of that would lead him to answer that question. And who would want to do this? Was there a disgruntled employee he didn't know about? The thing is, everyone got along with Roger. But if it was an inside job, then the answer to that question is yes, then someone had a beef with him. Was it an angry landowner? No, they usually get upset when you go on their land. They wouldn't come after you on your turf. It seems that we don't have an answer to *who* either.

Josh looks at his watch—almost four thirty in the afternoon. He is drained from lack of sleep and the events of the day. He decides to go home and see how Marsha is doing. He'll call her on the way home. He takes a picture of the whiteboard with his cell phone and erases the information on the board with a rag, making sure no one can see what was on it. He then puts the pictures he printed out in his backpack, dumps the pictures that are on his laptop, gets his coat on, turns off the lights, and heads to his truck.

On the way to the truck, Josh realizes he didn't call Ralph Peterson today, something he wanted to do earlier. Once in the truck, he dials Ralph's cell phone. It goes right to voice mail and now gets a notification that his mailbox is full. "Where the heck *is* he?" Josh mutters to himself. He concludes that, apparently, he isn't the only one looking for him since the mailbox is full.

He next calls Marsha. When she answers, he says, "Hey, babe, how are you doing?" Then he adds, "Yeah, I'm in the truck and heading home." As Josh pulls out of the laydown yard, he doesn't see a nondescript black SUV parked in a driveway just down the road with heavily tinted windows and its lights off. As Josh passes the SUV, it pulls in behind him and follows at a distance.

CHAPTER 11

Interviews

While Josh is at the laydown yard looking at footprints and tire tracks, Detective Eric Halvorsen is also busy. He is driving down to the Badger Power office in Madison, where the victim worked, calling ahead to make sure he has a conference room to work from in order to talk to other employees and maybe find someone that has it in for him. His goal is to talk to those who worked closely with Simmons and to look at the victim's office for any clues.

Halvorsen walks into the reception area of the Badger Power office and flashes his credentials to the receptionist. Also standing in the lobby is one of Badger Power's corporate security investigators, Ron Palchek. He introduces himself to the detective and asks the receptionist to give the detective the visitor's badge that was made for him. Halvorsen protests, "I don't need a visitor's badge. This is all the badge I need," pointing to his credentials.

Ron says evenly, "Detective Halvorsen, we operate under federal law that is regulated by the Department of Energy. As such, all visitors to a Badger Power facility need to have a visitor's badge and be escorted by an employee. That is my function today, to be your escort."

The detective puts on the badge but lets him know that he is unhappy about it. Unfazed by the detective, Palchek continues, "I have set up this conference room for you to use today." Palchek points to a small conference room off the lobby, which is outside the secured door to the office. He continues, "Please make yourself at home. Can I get you a cup of coffee?" The detective requests a cup of black coffee and removes his coat and takes a seat in one of the conference room chairs. Palchek leaves and, in a few minutes, returns with the coffee, which he sets in front of the detective.

Halvorsen makes a request, "I would like to look at Simmons's office before I start my interviews."

"Well, Detective, some of the people are pressed for time, and I moved them up in the list to accommodate their schedule. Let's look at the office later."

Halvorsen feels like this security guard is stalling him and wants to push the point, but Stan Brockdale walks into the room and introduces himself to the detective, "Stan Brockdale, director of construction, good to meet you. I understand you are investigating the death of Roger Simmons."

Detective Halvorsen introduces himself, "Yes, I am the lead investigator." Of course, he didn't mention the fact that he was the *only* investigator working the case. He adds, "I would like to ask you a couple of questions about Mr. Simmons."

"Sure, whatever you need," Brockdale continues. "Roger was a very good project manager for us."

"Did Mr. Simmons have any issues with anyone here?"

"Are you kidding? He got along with everyone here, and when there was an issue, Roger made a point of trying to work out a mutually beneficial result."

"Okay, was he ever passed over for a promotion or denied a choice project to work on?"

"Well, in the past couple of years, he had applied for several management positions but was turned down each time."

"So how many is several?"

"Seven to be exact."

"Why was he turned down for these positions?"

Brockdale hesitates with his response, "Ah well. You see, we felt he was not management material. He didn't have the right mix of skill sets to be part of our leadership team."

Halvorsen smells crap and isn't sure how to react to that statement but asks, "So did anybody sit down with him early on and tell him to lay off the applications?"

"No, we felt that he was very advanced in his career here and that it would not be worth the effort to create a path for him into management."

Halvorsen hears enough. "Okay, thank you, Mr. Brockdale. I will be in touch if there is anything else I need." He stands and shakes Brockdale's hand, and the manager leaves the room.

Halvorsen then heard from someone in their real estate department, an environmentalist and someone in their project controls group. Eric wasn't sure what the person in the last group did and really didn't care. All three were currently part of the victim's team for the construction underway in Waushara County. All three said the same things: Roger was easy to work with, listened to everybody, and kept his project on track. They were stunned by the news of his death and could not fathom who would want to kill him.

Palchek comes into the room and tells the detective it will be about twenty to thirty minutes before his next interview, this time with Roger's direct supervisor. Palchek also tells him that one of the people on this list cannot be found, so an interview with them will need to be rescheduled.

Halvorsen asks as he picks up the list of names, "Which person would that be?"

Palchek looks at his list. "That would be Ralph Peterson. Apparently, no one has been able to contact him since yesterday."

Halvorsen thinks, *Bingo, we got a hot one*, then asks, "What can you tell me about Mr. Peterson?"

"He joined the company about a year and a half ago as a design engineer working in this office. He was part of Simmons's team on the project up north."

Eric asks, "Did they get along?"

Palchek says, "All indications say yeah, they got along."

"What does Mr. Peterson drive? Do you have an address for him?"

"No, I don't know what he drives, but others that work here may know. As for as an address for him, I don't have that here and would have to contact HR to get it."

"Okay, get that information for me. Also, when can I see Simmons's HR file?"

"I do not have Simmons's HR file here. They are held in our office in Milwaukee. I'll call them to send me that file and see if they can give me an address for Peterson as well."

"Thanks. While you are making your calls, I have a couple of my own to make."

Palchek leaves the conference room and leaves Halvorsen alone. Eric gets on his cell phone and calls back to the sheriff's department. He gets ahold of a deputy and asks him the run a check on Ralph Peterson and instructs the deputy to call him back about what he found. Next, he calls Alan Regan, the assistant district attorney for Waushara County. "Hey, Alan, Eric here. I need your help with a search warrant and two subpoenas for this murder case I'm working on."

"Yeah, Eric, I heard you picked up that case. What do you specifically need?" In Wisconsin, the district attorney's office usually goes before a circuit court judge to get warrants and subpoenas since, by law, the police cannot perform this function alone.

"I need a search warrant for the home of Roger Simmons and a subpoena for his bank records and another for his phone records. I'll need to get the address to you as well as the name of the bank and telephone provider."

"Wait, you want to search the victim's house and pull his phone and bank records? You sure you want to do that?"

"Yes, I believe there may be information from all three sources that can point me in a direction to look for the killer. Right now, I don't have much of anything. I will potentially need another search warrant for the residence of a Ralph Peterson of Madison. He may be a person of interest."

"Getting a search warrant for the victim's home is a big ask. I'm not sure a judge will grant that, but I'll give it a try if you really think you need it. I assume you will need to pull records for the person of interest as well?"

"Yes, I really need to get into that house. And yes, I want to be able to pull records for Peterson too."

Regan promises he will do the best he can, and Eric texts the address and other information to him after he looks in his notes.

Palchek returns and tells Halvorsen that he checked and Ralph Peterson drives an older white Ford Taurus and gives the detective the partial license plate number. Robert also indicates that Peterson's address is still a work in progress but should have it shortly. The detective requests a photo of Peterson, and Palchek shows him the security badger photo he has in the system.

Halvorsen takes a picture of it with his cell phone. He then asks Palchek, "Is the supervisor available yet?"

"Sure, I will bring him up to the conference room." With that, Palchek disappears through the security door to retrieve Simmons's supervisor while Eric sits back and waits.

Palchek returns with the supervisor and introduces him to Eric, "Detective Halvorsen, please meet Chad Ramsey, Roger Simmons's immediate supervisor." Both men shake hands, and the first thing Halvorsen notices is how young the guy is, maybe no older than thirty.

Eric starts right in, "I know you are pretty busy, so I will keep this short. Do you know of anybody that had a beef with Mr. Simmons?"

"You know, since I heard the news, I have been thinking about that. I can't think of anybody around here that had a beef with Roger. He got along with everybody."

The detective is getting tired of the same words be used and leans over to Ramsey and says quietly, "Well, there is at least one person that had an issue with Simmons, don't you think?"

"Well, yeah, but not anyone from this company."

"So there might be someone from another company you do business with that had an issue with Simmons?"

"Roger ruffled the feathers of one contractor we used on another project of his."

"How did he ruffle their feathers?"

"Roger used a new innovative construction method to speed things up, but the contractor saw it as taking money out of their hands."

"So how bad did it get between them?"

"Roger got in a big argument with one of their people at their office, and they told him to leave. Afterward, Roger fired the contractor and found another one to do the work. I heard about this through that company's management."

"Did you talk to Simmons about this? What did he say?"

"He said they were not seeing the big picture and how it could benefit them as well. As far as the firing, Roger said we can't have the tail wagging the dog."

"Can you give me the name and address of the other company and who he had the argument with?" Ramsey gives the information to Halvorsen, who makes a notation to contact this person later.

Halvorsen further asks, "So this innovation he came up with, how did it go over here? Did people embrace it?"

"You have to remember, Detective, we are a utility. We don't innovate, and we're not set up to innovate either. There were some that embraced it, but for the most part, no. He was rocking the boat. Personally, I think it was something he used to stay relevant. After all, he is an old guy."

Eric feels he got the answers to why Badger didn't promote him. Everyone who worked with Simmons loved him, but management just tolerated him, maybe even wanting to push him out. "Mr. Ramsey, I think I have what I need here. Thank you for your time." The two men stand and shake hands again, then Ramsey leaves the room.

After Ramsey left, Palchek asks the detective if he wanted to see Simmons's office. Eric says yes, and the two men walk through the security doors into the offices of the utility. They walk down a corridor into a larger room with offices, and Ron stops at an office midway down a row of them. "Here is Roger's office," motioning with his arm for the detective to go in. The first thing Halvorsen notices is how neat and clean it was, as if it were sanitized. He mentions to

Palchek. "Wow, this guy was a real neat freak. I mean, you could perform surgery on his desk. It's so clean."

"Yes, that's Roger for you." Just then, Palchek's phone rings and he answers it. Lowering it, he says to Eric, "I've got to take this call. Feel free to look around that office." With that, Ron walks down the hallway with his back to Halvorsen.

Taking advantage of the situation, the detective walks across the hall to the office directly across from Simmons's and talks to the occupant, "Hi, my name is Eric and I was supposed to meet Roger Simmons today. Man, that guy is neat. I wish I was like that."

The occupant looks up from reading something on his computer and smiles. "Yeah, usually, there would be small stacks of paper on his desk. Then I saw someone come and clean it up those piles fifteen or twenty minutes ago."

"Hey, thanks!" Eric goes back into Roger's office and continues to look around, knowing that he won't see anything worthwhile.

Palchek comes back, off the phone now. "I have the address to Peterson's house for you." He gives the detective a piece of paper. "Are you all done here?"

"Yes, I'm all set. I need to get back to my office. Thanks for all your help."

"Thank you, Detective. It was a pleasure to help you. Here is my card if you need anything else. Let me escort you out."

Once inside his car, Eric is thinking he does not like the vibe he is getting from the people in there. They are either hiding something or are worried that they are in trouble and kept everything close to the vest. Regardless, he gets the impression that this was no Shangri-la. He gets on his phone and calls Alan Regan and gives him the address to Ralph Peterson and that he is a solid person of interest. Alan told him that he was preparing to go before the judge in about an hour and a half.

Eric then gets on the phone and calls Sheriff Cantor and gets him on the third ring. "Hi, Sheriff, it's Eric. Just checking in with you. I had our technicians process the scene this morning, and I just finished interviewing coworkers at Badger Power. I have a solid person of interest that I am following up on."

"What make this person a potential suspect?" asks the sheriff.

"Mainly because no one has seen him since the day before the murder, and a lot of people in that company are trying to track him down for work-related questions. I'm in the process of getting a search warrant for his house." It seems the detective omitted the fact he also requested a search warrant for the victim's home.

"Where you at now?"

"I'm in Madison and starting to make my way back to Wautoma to talk to the ME."

"Okay, call me later today with progress." With that, Cantor hangs up and Eric starts his car.

CHAPTER 12

CSI

Just as Halvorsen was about to leave the Badger Power parking lot, he gets a phone call. Eric picks up the phone and answers it, "Halvorsen."

"Eric, this is Todd." Todd is one of the crime scene technicians that processed the scene at the laydown yard.

"What do you have for me, Todd?"

"We processed the scene and impounded the victim's truck and have it in our garage right now."

"What did you find at the scene?"

"Not much. There were no prints, no hairs or fibers, and very little blood. We are processing what blood we did find and should have results very soon. We also found the victim's cell phone and will start processing that next. The reason I'm calling you is not about what we found at the scene but what we found in the truck."

Eric has a bad feeling about what he is going to hear next. He pulls off to the side of the street and puts the car in park. "What did you find?"

"We found a loaded 9 mm semiautomatic Sig Sauer handgun in his console between the front seats. We're not sure yet if it has been fired recently. It has been wiped clean and has a full clip and one in the chamber. It is registered to him and we checked. The victim had a concealed carry permit. We traced the gun back to a gun shop in Madison where he purchased it legally about a year and a half ago."

It seems that Mr. Simmons is afraid of someone, after all, thought Eric. "Well, that puts a new twist on things. What else did you find?"

"We're still processing the truck, but right now, we see nothing else other than work-related papers and his laptop."

"What about shell casings?"

"We could not find any, so maybe the perp policed his brass."

"Have you looked at what is on the laptop?"

"No, mainly because the computer is encrypted, and we can't get in it. We will have to obtain a warrant from a federal judge to defeat the encryption. It may be easier to have Badger Power open it for us."

"Okay, keep me posted on what else you find. Thanks, Todd." With that, Eric ends the call and resumes driving north to meet with the Waushara County medical examiner. Based upon his visit with Badger Power just now, he thinks they wouldn't be so inclined to pop open that laptop for him.

Eric now calls the sheriff's department dispatcher. When she answers, Eric responds, "Hi, Linda. It's Eric. Hey, I need to get out a BOLO out on a person of interest on the Simmons case." A BOLO is an acronym for *be on the lookout*. He continues, "The person's name is Ralph Peterson and he is driving an early 2000 white Ford Taurus with a partial plate starting with the letters *SHD*. He is to be considered armed and dangerous."

"Okay, Eric, I will get that out right away."

"Thanks, Linda."

Halvorsen next calls Alan Regan to let him know he issued a BOLO on Peterson just now.

CHAPTER 13

Before the Judge

As Halvorsen makes his way back to the medical examiner's office, Alan Regan goes before Phillip J. Rowles, the circuit court judge for Waushara County, in his chambers at the courthouse in Wautoma. Alan first indicates the applications he is presenting are related to the investigation of the murder committed in rural Waushara County yesterday. The first application he presents to the judge was for the search of the victim's home to obtain information that would aid in the investigation. Along with the warrant request, Regan presents the subpoenas for bank records and phone records, again to determine in what direction to move the investigation in.

The judge looks at the applications and set them down on his desk. Looking up at the ADA, he says, "So you want me to sign off on a fishing expedition at the home of the murder victim?"

"Yes, sir, the investigator does not have any solid leads, and they hope to find something that will be useful."

"Is that so? Did the sheriff's department go and ask the man's family if they could look around?"

"Sir, I have the impression that the investigators could not gain access through those means." Regan wasn't really sure that was the case and actually did not ask Halvorsen why he didn't just ask.

"Well, Mr. Regan, do you think it is a wise decision to execute a search warrant against a family that just lost their husband and father? Have you thought of the consequences of doing just that? I do not believe the optics look very good on this request. I am going to do you and the sheriff's department a favor and deny this warrant request along with the subpoena requests for the Simmons's home and records."

"But, sir, I—"

Judge Rowles interrupts Regan, "They are *denied*, Mr. Regan. Have the sheriff ask the family nicely to look around, and if the say no, then you are out of luck. What else do you have for me?"

"Well, sir, I have another search warrant request related to the same case. We are requesting a search warrant on a residence of a person of interest in the case. He is of interest since he was last seen the day prior to the Simmons murder. He is a coworker of the victim, sir. The sheriff's department feels that there is a connection between Mr. Peterson and the victim. We are also seeking warrants for phone and bank records."

"So this person is in the wind?"

"Yes, sir. The employer, Badger Power, cannot locate him and has given information to the sheriff's department to find this person. The sheriff's department has issued a BOLO for Mr. Peterson and his vehicle."

"Mr. Regan, I will grant this request for the search warrants for Mr. Peterson's residence as well as the accompanying subpoenas for his phone and bank records." With that, he signs all three applications for searching the premises, cell records, and bank account and hands them back to the ADA. "Any other business for me?"

"No, sir, and thank you, sir."

As the ADA leaves his chambers, the judge makes a mental note to give the district attorney a call about the request for search and seizure at the victim's house.

CHAPTER 14

Medical Examiner

When Detective Halvorsen gets to the Waushara County medical examiner's office, he finds out who is working the Simmons autopsy. He is happy to hear that Dr. Derek Vaughn has been assigned to this case. Eric and Dr. Vaughn have worked together in the past and know each other. Eric makes his way to Dr. Vaughn's office only to find that he is not there. He goes downstairs to the autopsy rooms to see if he could find him there. Sure enough, Eric finds him in one of the rooms and assumes he is working on Simmons. Eric knocks gently on the windowed door and waits for Derek to look up from his work. Derek waves him in and mentions to Eric that he is working on Mr. Simmons. Eric asks, "What have you discovered so far?"

Dr. Vaughn briefly refers to his notes. "The victim suffered three 9 mm gunshot wounds, all at a close range. One entered the victim and went through the right lung and came to rest on the spine. The other two, as you can see, were close together and went through his heart, killing him, and lodged in the spinal column. I sent the slugs to the lab for analysis already."

Halvorsen says, "Okay, what can you tell me about the knife wounds?"

"Yes, I was about to get to that. The knife wounds to the chest were delivered postmortem, and the assailant did it standing over the victim."

"So the knife wounds were inflicted from the front?"

"Yes, that's right." Observing the puzzled look on the detective's face, he asks, "Why, is that a problem?"

"Well, it's just that the initial report indicated the victim was lying on his stomach. So that means the perp stabbed the victim and then flipped him over. But why?"

"I'm not sure. I think it will be something you need to figure out."

Eric nods. "So if I got this right, the perp shoots the victim from the front, then walks up to the body and stabs him twice to make sure the deed is done, then flips the body over for an unknown reason and leaves the body where it lays to be found later."

Derek responds, "Yeah, that is a very plausible order of events."

"Okay, so there is one other thing that is bothering me. When Ted processed the scene, he said he didn't find much blood. I would think that there would be plenty of blood given the wounds the victim sustained."

Dr. Vaughn points to the body of Roger Simmons on the table. "My opinion is that given he was working out in minus-twenty-degree weather for a period before he was killed and the fact that he was there until found, the blood drew back to the core. Then you would say, so what, that would just make him bleed more given the wounds. But since he was out there, he froze along with the blood that pooled in the chest cavity and stayed frozen until the body was warmed up at the hospital. The ER doctor's report indicated that he started bleeding in the air ambulance just before they landed."

As Halvorsen leaves the medical examiner's office, he gets a call from the Madison Police Department regarding the search warrant for Ralph Peterson's place. They want to execute it later that night at seven thirty if Halvorsen wants to be there. He indicates he wants to part of it and will meet them at the address on the warrant at 7:15 PM. It is already 5:30 PM, so he would need to leave Wautoma soon to get there on time. But before he leaves, he needs to check in with his boss.

Steve Cantor hangs up from a call from the district attorney regarding the attempt to get a search warrant for the victim's house. The DA fills in Cantor about the call he got from Judge Rowles.

Neither he nor the DA is happy about this and, between the two, decides they would review any search warrant Halvorsen requests. Cantor has seen this before—Halvorsen pissing people off and, in the process, not getting any cooperation. So to make any headway, he requests search warrants for information he should have just asked for nicely. Well, he is going to have to put the hammer down on Halvorsen.

As he begins to figure out how to approach this problem, his phone rings. He sees the familiar cell phone number of Halvorsen on the caller ID. What timing! He picks up the phone, not even saying hello. "What the *hell* do you think you were trying to do getting a search warrant for the Simmons's house? What happened? You piss off the widow so much that you can't ask her for cooperation? Gee, that sounds familiar, doesn't it? It's nice to see you are consistent in your methods, Halvorsen. You're gonna get your ass down here in the morning to explain to me what you have done on this case. Do you understand?"

Eric is shaken by what he has heard and merely responds, "Yes, sir." Cantor then hangs up on Halvorsen.

The Stash

It has been a rough past few days, to say the least. Sarah has been numb for the most part, trying to make sense of what happened to Roger. The thought of her husband of ten years being murdered was not something remotely on her radar. She literally can't think of anyone she knows that would be capable of doing this to Roger. Sleep doesn't come easy either, especially trying to sleep in an empty bed. She doesn't even try to sleep there anymore, opting for the couch in the family room instead, where she catnaps through the night.

Her college-aged son and daughter are home now. They have stepped in to handle the day-to-day things needing taken care of. They both try to comfort their mother, but it's hard considering they are feeling their own pain. All three are feeling as though they are just going through the motions. Marsha has been there a lot and makes a point to support all three of the surviving Simmons. She can relate to the pain they are feeling since it has been a couple of years ago when her mother and father passed away six months apart. So she has a good idea of what they are going through.

Sarah is washing her face in the sink of the master bathroom. When she lets the water out, nothing happens. The sink doesn't seem to be draining properly. The lack of sleep leads to frustration, and she shows it out loud to nobody in particular. Marsha is down the hall, talking to Sarah's daughter, when she hears the outburst. She excuses herself and goes down to see what is going on.

She pops her head into the master bedroom and asks, "Is everything okay, Sarah?"

"Oh, that stupid bathroom sink is backed up. It won't drain."

Marsha offers, "You know, I can have Josh come over and take care of that for you."

Sarah comes back with, "I don't want to impose on him."

"Nonsense, Sarah, he will feel like he is really contributing if we ask him."

"Well, if you put it that way, it would be great if he could."

Marsha grabs her cell phone and calls Josh. "Hi, honey, where are you at?"

"I'm down in Madison, talking to the higher-ups about what happened. Do you need something?"

"Well, on your way home can you come to Sarah's house to fix a stopped-up drain?"

"Yeah, sure. But I don't have any of those kinds of tools in my truck. I need to go home first to get them."

Marsha asks Sarah while she still has Josh on the phone if Roger has any tools here to work on it. Sarah tells her that yes, Roger has tools in the basement he could use. Marsha gets back on the phone. "Josh, Roger has tools in the basement you could use and save yourself a trip."

Josh now remembers Roger's workbench that had almost every tool known to man. Josh answers Marsha back, "Okay, I'll see you there soon."

Josh makes it to the Simmons's house in about an hour. When he goes into the house, he makes a point to say hi to the kids along with Sarah and, of course, Marsha. To the kids, the Bishops are considered Uncle Josh and Aunt Marsha. He spends a few more minutes talking to everyone, then he says to Marsha, "Okay, show me the uncooperative sink."

Marsha leads him to the sink in the master bath, and he opens the vanity cabinet door to look at the plumbing. He hopes to find newer PVC pipes with an easy-access drain trap that makes this job faster. Today is not his lucky day; the pipes are old metal pipes, and as an added bonus, there is no trap in the drain.

Armed with the knowledge of what faces him under the bathroom sink, Josh heads down to the basement to find tools he will need. He stops in front of the workbench and notices, besides nothing being out of place, a lot of Roger's hand tools are mounted neatly on pegboard, logically laid out. All the wrenches are mounted left of center, and all the screwdrivers are mounted to the right of center. Along the back of the workbench, he spots several small bins of various types of fasteners. There is a freestanding metal cabinet next to the workbench. Josh opens one of the two doors on the cabinet and observes power tools neatly placed on the shelves. Although it may seem Roger was suffering from OCD, Josh was not surprised by the extent of the neatness of the workbench.

Josh returns to the front of the workbench and searches for a pipe wrench and spots it halfway down the pegboard and left of center. In a hurry to get started on this job, he grabs it and pulls it down, forgetting to lift up to get the wrench off the metal pegs holding it in place. Instead of lifting, he just pulls on it harder than before. As he does this, a section of the pegboard around the wrench comes loose from the wall. The wrench, pegboard, and pegs are now in his hand. He mutters, "What the *hell*." He stares at what is in his hand like it is some kind of alien life-form. The edges of the section are straight, evidence that it was cut and not torn. He then looks up to where the pegboard came from and observes a recess in the wall. He leans forward to get a better view while placing the wrench and pegboard section on the workbench. He peers into the recess and can see something, but it's dark in there. He searches for a flashlight but can't find one that works. Instead, Josh uses the flashlight function on this cell phone to shine light into the recess in the wall. As he examines the recess, he stares at what's inside.

Josh reaches into the opening to retrieve the contents. The first thing he brings out are two memory sticks. He looks at them closely and notices that there is something about them that seems out of place. They look big and clunky. It finally dawns on him that they are older, like a lot older, not looking like memory sticks you can buy today. Next, he pulls out, rather gingerly, a Smith and Wesson snub nose .38 revolver that, after inspection, appears to be fully loaded. Looking over the weapon, shaking his head, he wonders why Roger would keep a gun in that recess. Most people put them in a drawer or other places they can easily get their hands on it. He places the handgun next to the memory sticks on the top of the workbench.

He then turns his attention to the recess and removes the rest of the contents. Josh is looking at two eight-by-eleven manila envelopes. After examining them, turning them over to see all sides of them, he notices that the envelopes are not only clasped, but they are also sealed with a heavy red tape. The other thing he notes is that there is no writing on the outside of both envelopes. Josh considers opening the envelopes but thinks better of it; he wants to get Sarah's permission to do so.

He returns to the opening in the wall and shines the flashlight at the back of it to make sure there is nothing else in there. It looks like there is a picture up against the rear wall, but he can't see an image. He reaches in and must get on his tiptoes to be able to get in to retrieve the picture. Pulling it out and staring at the picture, Josh notices a somewhat younger Roger posing with a group of four other men, no one smiling. All, including Roger, are wearing black uniforms with no insignias, holding automatic assault rifles, and sporting green-and-black face paint. Josh looks at the image of Roger again. Roger never told him he was in the military or even the paramilitary, which this photo shows. He puts Roger in his thirties in the picture, which makes the age of the picture at about twenty years. The others in the picture Josh does not recognize. He turns the picture over and notes there are two words written there: *The Team*. Josh does not understand the significance to those words and takes them at face value that the group in the photo worked together. But what kind of work did they do? They surely didn't sell Girl Scout cookies. This is clearly something he was not aware of about Roger, which makes him think there will be more surprises as he goes. He places the photo on top of the manila envelopes on the workbench.

Instead of climbing all the stairs to the second floor, Josh texts Marsha for her and Sarah to come to the basement. He didn't say why, mainly so as not to alarm them but also the fact he wasn't sure what to tell them. In a few minutes, he can hear them coming down the basement stairs, talking between themselves. They spot Josh and walk over to the workbench where he was still standing.

Marsha notices that Josh has a worried expression on this face and asks, "Are you okay? What's the matter?"

"Well, I'm not sure if I'm okay. Here is what the matter is." He holds up the wrench and pegboard and then he points to the opening in the wall above the workbench. "I accidently found a hidden compartment in the pegboard here." Josh continues by telling the women how he found it. He then proceeds to show them the envelopes, old-school flash drives, and the gun that he found in the compartment. He then asks Sarah, "Did you know this was here?"

Shaking her head, Sarah says, "No. I never knew that was there. I never seen those things before. Why would Roger hide anything in a wall? And why hide those things, especially the gun? I just don't understand."

"Have you seen this picture before or recognize anyone in it," Josh asks Sarah.

After studying the picture, Sarah states, "No, I haven't seen this picture. Roger is younger in this picture, but I can't even place it. This was long before I met Roger." Sarah becomes a little melancholy, thinking of her and Roger when they first met. That was the very happy time in her life, and now her prince is gone. With a clouded look on her face, she hands the picture back to Josh without a word.

Marsha interjects, "Josh, how long do you think those things have been in there?"

Josh shaking his head, Josh replies, "I really don't know. Maybe we could get an idea if we knew the vintage of the memory sticks. If we open the envelopes, we could get an idea there but if the documents are older, then maybe not."

Marsha turns to Sarah. "When did you and Roger buy this house?"

"We bought it shortly after we got married, so ten years ago."

Josh offers, "So they may have been there for that long." He turns to Sarah. "Would you mind if I take the memory sticks and the envelopes to see what information they have on them?"

"Yeah, sure, but let me know what you find."

"Of course. Okay, so I am going upstairs to fix the sink." Josh leaves the items from the recess on the workbench and picks up the pipe wrench and an old raggedy towel and puts them in an empty plastic bucket and makes his way upstairs. The ladies follow him up, wondering why Roger had a hidden compartment.

CHAPTER 16

Super Stash

Josh Bishop is not a small man. He stands six feet, two inches, has broad shoulders, and well muscled. Looking at the small opening in the vanity, he wonders if he can fit in there and, maybe more importantly, if he can get out. He lies down on the bathroom floor in front of the opening, looking in, to see what the best way in would be. The plumbing is not in line with the opening but is more to the right. This, Josh figures, will make him have to twist his body to get the wrench on the pipe fitting. Resigned to his fate, Josh flips over on his back and moves his upper body into the vanity opening with the wrench and the cell phone on his chest. Getting in as far as he can, he flips on the flashlight function and looks at the drain pipe as it exits the sink and tries to put the wrench on it. No deal. So with a sigh, he twists his body such that he is facing the front of the vanity. He tries the wrench again, and this time, he not only can get the wrench on it, he can get some leverage as well. The flange is not giving up so easily, not moving much at all. He puts more muscle into it and the flange moves.

After copious amounts of swearing, which, at one point, Marsha comes by saying, "Hey, Josh, the longshoremen out here are starting to blush. You might want to tone it down a bit."

He manages to free the pipe that is clogged and puts it into the bucket. Now his exit is a little trickier; he needs to twist in the other direction so he is facing the back of the vanity to get out. When he does so, he comes face-to-face with something he did not expect to see in this location.

He blinks a couple of times, but nothing changes. Within a couple of inches of it, Josh is staring at another rectangular access panel cut out of the wall in the rear of the vanity. In this position, he can't get his hands up to it to open it. He backs out of the vanity and tries again, but his arms and hands are too big to be able to get it open. At this point, he backs out all the way and lies on the floor, enjoying the fact that he is free from the confined space. He shines the cell phone at the access panel and wonders, *What did Roger put in there? What was so important and secretive that he put something in that tight place? What was he doing that he felt compelled to do that?*

He shakes himself out of his thoughts and gets up off the floor and cleans up any water that leaked out of the pipe with an old towel he picked up in the basement. He walks out of the bathroom and heads in the direction of the Sarah's and Marsha's voices. He finds them with the kids in the son's room, and he stands in the doorway.

Sarah and Marsha have their backs to him, and the daughter spots Josh. "Hey, Uncle Josh, I have to say I haven't heard that much swearing since Dad slipped and fell on the ice out on the driveway a couple of years ago. There was a couple I haven't heard in a long time."

Josh quips, "What can I say? I have my talents." With that, the four in the room have a good laugh. With the older women now turned around, Josh asks, "Can I steal you two for a moment?"

"Yeah sure," comes the reply from Sarah.

Both women follow Josh down the hall to the bathroom. He lets them in and then closes the door behind him. Both women look at Josh, and Sarah speaks up, "What's going on, Josh?"

He begins by telling them what he did to remove the clogged pipe and then he says, "I think I found another of Roger's hidey holes." The women just stare at him, unbelieving. With that, he bends down, beckoning them to do the same, and shines his light on the access panel on the back of the vanity. Both women just look at each other and then look at Josh, then back at the access panel.

Marsha asks, "Did you open it?"

"No, I'm not small enough to get in there and open it. Perhaps one of you can get in there and open it."

Marsha, being the smaller of the two women, volunteers to do it. She crawls into the opening in the vanity and cranes her neck up to look at the door to the recess in the wall. She looks back at the other two. "I need some light in here." With that, Josh passes his cell phone to Sarah, and she moves in close to Marsha and gets the light into the opening and points it in the general direction of where they saw the access panel. Marsha then grabs the front end of the cell phone in Sarah's hand and points it so that it shines right on the panel. She asks Sarah, "Can you keep it there?"

Sarah replies, "Yep, let's see what's in there."

Marsha starts to work along one of the edges of the panel. She can get her fingernail in the gap but can't seem to pry it open. Maneuvering her other hand to work along another edge, she pries with both fingers, but the panel doesn't budge. Finally, she gives up and turns so that she is looking behind her. "Josh, you have your pocketknife with you?"

"Yeah, here." He fishes it out of his pocket and opens it, handing it to Sarah, who, in turn, hands it to Marsha.

Moving the blade of the knife to the edge closest to her, to get as much leverage as she can, she pushes it into the gap and is able to insert it all the way to the hilt of the knife. Next, she moves the blade up and down the opening, encountering resistance but it still moves. Using it like a pry bar, Marsha then pushes the handle of the knife toward the wall, hoping to pop off the panel. For her efforts, she gets a crunching noise wood makes, but not a lot of movement. She moves the knife to a long edge and repeats the process. She gets more crunching and a little more movement of the panel. Encouraged by the progress, she moves the knife to the other long edge and again moves the knife up and down the edge of the opening. She starts her prying motion again but puts a little more into it, even letting out a grunt. With a louder crunch, the panel explosively flies free and hits Marsha in the face.

"Shoot!" Marsha exclaims.

Sarah tries to get her head in the opening. "Hey, Marsha, you all right?"

"The thing hit me in the face!"

"Come out of there and let me see your face." It is Josh this time.

Marsha crawls out of the vanity and looks at Sarah and Josh. She has a small stream of blood running down her face from a small puncture wound on her forehead.

Josh gives her a hand up. "Well, let's take care of this cut." Marsha has the access panel in her hand and gives it to Josh. He notices the wood that made up the back of the vanity and a chunk of the drywall, glued together, make up the access panel. He puts that on the sink and motions Marsha to sit on the toilet while holding a washcloth to her face while he looks for the first aid kit. Sarah, knowing what he is looking for, directs him to the linen closet. He returns to Marsha and opens the kit.

A little frustrated, Marsha remarks to Josh, "Oh, I suppose I'm going to get a safety lecture like the guys at work. Let's see, I should have worn safety glasses and a face shield? Oh, I almost forgot. I needed a hard hat too, right?"

Josh smiles big. "Don't you know, guys dig chicks with scars?" Marsha rolls her eyes and shakes her head. Josh tells Marsha, "Now hold still. I have to make sure this leaves a *huge* scar." He takes the washcloth away and notices that the bleeding has stopped. He then applies an alcohol wipe to the area and then finds a small round bandage and applies it to her forehead. "There, that should hold you."

While Josh is tending to Marsha, Sarah grabs the cell phone and starts to explore the opening in the wall. She observes there are things in the opening and pulls them out with some effort. There are three manila envelopes just like the ones in the basement. They even have the heavy red tape on them. But these look older based on the condition of the envelopes. She turns them over to see if there is any writing on them. On each of the envelopes, there is a name that appears to be put on with a stamp with red ink. One has the name Javelin, another has Blue Horizon stamped on it, and the third, the thickest of the three, has the name Lightning Rod.

Sarah then shows the envelopes to Marsha and Josh, telling them, "I've never seen these before. It seems to me that these are older than the ones we found in the basement. Just look at the edges."

Marsha inquires, "What do the words on the envelopes mean?"

Josh shrugs his shoulders. "I'm not sure. It looks like the same kind of tape used on the other envelopes. It seems to me that this stash was put here to keep out of sight and not to be accessed at all. The stuff at the workbench was put there to access when he needed it, especially the fact he had a gun in there."

Sarah, crossing her arms and with a pained look on her face, asks, "Do you think Roger was expecting trouble?"

"I think the bigger question is why Roger kept all this hidden." Josh now looks at Sarah. "What did Roger tell you about his past?"

"Well, Roger was married once before, but it ended in divorce and there were no children. He said that after the Navy, he worked as a project manager in different places until he came to Badger Power."

"What? Wait." Josh is clearly surprised. "You said he was in the Navy?"

"Yes, he was a lieutenant for four years stationed on a submarine."

"I had no idea he was in the Navy. He never told me about it. Did he tell you the name of the sub he worked on?"

Sarah pauses for a moment, then shakes her head. "If he did, I can't remember it right now."

"Would you mind if I took all this stuff we have found and sort through it to try to make sense of it?"

Sarah nods. "Yeah, no problem. I want to know what you find out though. Oh, and please leave me the gun you found in the wall too."

"I'll keep you posted on what I find. It might take a couple of days."

With that, the conversation has ended. The ladies go downstairs to the family room and Josh finishes his plumbing job. After he is done, he thinks he would tell Sarah that he will come back and put in a proper trap so that it will be easier in the future to unclog the sink. He cleans up his mess and retrieves all the manila envelopes and memory sticks. He cleans and wraps the gun in a clean shop rag that he found on the workbench and brings it up to Sarah, who then places it in a drawer in an end table in the family room. He asks Marsha if she is staying or not, which she tells him that she is coming home. They put on their coats and go out the door to get in their respective vehicles and drive off toward home.

CHAPTER 17

Gathering Storm

The black SUV had been parked in a field access road close to the Simmons house in the opposite direction from where Josh came to the house so that he would not pass and notice the SUV. With the engine turned off and no lights on, two men were sitting in the front seats of the vehicle. Each one had high-power binoculars as well as night-vision goggles. They both carried Chinese-made pistols which were high velocity, small caliber weapons that, with the right type of ammo, were well suited for assassinations. In the trunk were two Chinese assault rifles, the most powerful small assault rifle in the world. They brought this with them in case things went really south.

Both men traveled as agents of the Ministry of State Security of China to the Chinese embassy in Tokyo, Japan. From there, they traveled as part of the diplomatic mission to the Chinese embassy in Washington, DC. Once there, they found other members of their group permanently located in the United States and were provided the initial intelligence, and weapons, they needed to get started.

They had been chatting in their native language about what to do next when they spotted Josh coming out of the Simmons house. They knew who Josh was based upon the information they were given. In fact, they were given information on everyone that Roger came into contact with on a regular basis.

The driver noted to the other that Josh was carrying items out of the house he did not bring in. The other man, by using night vision glasses, confirmed that their target was indeed carrying five manila envelopes. They looked at each other and then returned their gaze to Josh as he climbs into his truck. They now believe that what was kept in that house was being moved. Items they were sent to take.

This was not the first contact they had with Simmons and his associates. They were near the laydown yard the day Roger was murdered and witnessed who done it. They did not interfere, so they would remain hidden. Their mission was not to murder Roger Simmons but to steal information their employer wanted. The murderer made their job more difficult, and now that someone else has the information they are seeking, their mission just got more complicated.

The driver started the engine and pulled out onto the road with just the running lights on initially and began to follow the truck. They were not concerned about losing Josh in the darkness since they had installed a GPS tracking device on his truck while it was parked at the Simmons house, and for good measure, they installed one on Marsha's car as well.

These men are not operatives of the Chinese government as their forged papers would have you believe. No, both of these men are working for the Hong Kong Triad, an Asian organized crime family, which have been known to be ruthless in their criminal activity.

CHAPTER 18

Commence to Pulling

Once at home, Marsha and Josh have a late dinner, a dish that Marsha started in the slow cooker that morning. They sit at the dining table, quietly at first since both are tired from their respective days at this point. Josh goes to the fridge and takes out two beers and opens them, coming back to the table and gives one of them to Marsha and sits back down. They both take a long pull on the beer.

He breaks the silence, "So what do you make of the stuff we found tonight?"

Shaking her head, Marsha replies, "Honestly, I don't know, but it seems to me that it is kind of odd to hide stuff. I mean, yeah, you bring work home and it sits on or in a desk. But to hide it in a wall just seems bizarre, and with a gun no less. It almost seems that Roger wasn't supposed to bring those envelopes home, but he did, and he hid them. But why? And not tell Sarah about it? I don't get it."

"I don't know either. Maybe he hid the stuff so no one else would get ahold of it. It could be a case of the less people to know about it, the better. It seems so unlike Roger to do something like that. He usually is open about things. You wouldn't think he would be hiding something. Yes, you're right, it is peculiar to hide stuff in a wall."

They finish dinner and put the dirty dishes in the dishwasher. Josh asks Marsha, "Hey, you want to come downstairs with me and help me look through those envelopes?"

"No, I think I'll take a pass on that tonight. I would just like to relax and maybe even go to bed early. Don't stay up too late."

"Yeah, I won't be making an all-nighter out of it." With that, he picks up the envelopes, flash drives, and his laptop from the top of his desk and heads downstairs to the basement.

The basement at the Bishop house is half finished with a rec room complete with a large flat-screen TV and couches on one end. At the other end of the finished area is an air hockey game, which is Marsha's favorite, a Foosball game, a favorite with the now-grown Bishop children and one of those mini basketball games where you try to get as many baskets in a set amount of time. Josh can remember several times having to fix the basketball game because of overzealous children trying to get off one more shot before the buzzer sounded. This was the center of the universe for the kids and their friends growing up. Many a party and sleepovers occurred down here and, at times, was a noisy place to be. Now that the children have gone on to college, the room is very quiet as it is throughout the house once, one by one, the kids left. The Bishops have three children, two daughters and a son, that were born a year apart from one another. All were active in school and were popular, even the youngest who was the more sensitive of the three. Before she left for college, she expressed her worry to Mom and Dad they would be left home alone and that they wouldn't have anything to do. Marsha assured her that they would figure something out.

Next to the stairs that lead to the upstairs is a door which leads to the unfinished area of the basement that, at one end, has all the home's mechanicals. Most of the rest of the space, according to Marsha, is where the magic happens. Indeed, Marsha and Josh figured out something they can do together with their newly found spare time. The centerpiece of this area is a larger-than-normal metal worktable that Josh fixed up to raise and lower by pressing buttons on one side of the table. There are drawers on two sides of the table that hold tools and small parts. Along one wall is a table saw, planer, and lathe for woodworking. Next to that is a sheet metal break and a setup for welding. There are also a couple of freestanding cabinets that housed smaller specialized tools. Opposite this wall are the workbench, drafting table, and rolling tool chest. In the center of the back wall is a double door that opens up to the outside, which allowed larger items to be brought in or taken out of the workshop. Together they decided to get into upcycling items they have salvaged and selling them online. Marsha is the one with the design vision, and Josh has the know-how to put their ideas together.

Josh walks into the workshop and sets the envelopes down on the big worktable. He then drags the stool in front of the drafting table to the worktable and sits down. The area is illuminated only by the big light over the worktable. He opens his laptop and turns it on. While it is booting up, he takes out the two memory sticks recovered from the workbench's hiding place and looks at them again. The storage capacity of each one is stamped on the outside and indicates they were thirty-two megabytes. Thirty-two megabytes? These had to be old since, nowadays, you can get them from eight gigabytes to four terabytes in size. He plugs in one of the memory sticks into his laptop.

On the computer's desktop, he double-clicks on the folder representing the memory stick. Immediately, a dialogue box appears, requesting a username and password. Josh tries to ignore it and clicks OK only to have the box reappear. He then types in Roger's last name for the username and puts in Roger's birthdate for the password. Nothing happens. Josh tries a few more iterations of Roger's last name, first name, and important numbers. Still nothing. Stymied, he wonders why the memory sticks would be password protected. Josh tries the other memory stick and gets the same results. "Well, that's a dead end," Josh says to himself. He sets the memory sticks aside, wondering if there is a way to bypass the password protection.

Josh now turns his attention to the envelopes. After selecting one of the newer ones, he walks over to the workbench and opens one of the drawers and selects an X-Acto knife and returns to the table. Josh uses the X-Acto knife to carefully cut open the red tape on one of the envelopes.

Slowly he pulls the stack of papers out of the envelope so as not to tear anything. The stack of white computer papers is about three quarters of an inch thick made up of eight-and-a-half-by-eleven-inch pages and larger ones folded to fit that dimension. The document on top looks to be a summary page that contains information about a project such as the name, the location of the project, the requested timeline, the budget, and what the customer ordered.

Josh reads the page. This project was called Shalom and was located in Israel, as the name implies. It looks like Roger installed some equipment at a port in Ashdod and at another in Tel Aviv. Based on the dates in the summary, this installation took place in 1992 through 1993.

He turns his attention to the first folded page and opens it up. It appears to be a drawing of the wharf at Ashdod, or at least that is what the legend indicates. The drawing shows the location of a building in red, presumably the new building Roger installed there. It depicted how cargo containers would be moved through the building. Josh wonders, *Why would cargo containers be moved through a building?* He goes back to the first document and notices the customer purchased a port cargo scanner. "So the contents of cargo containers are scanned without being opened," Josh is talking to himself. As he is thinking about why this needed to be done, it dawns on him why they are looking for contraband.

He sits up straight as his mind begins to connect the dots. So the government of Israel was concerned that the Palestinians were smuggling in contraband through the ports of Ashdod and Tel Aviv? *Well,* Josh thought, *that could really piss somebody off if their shipments get confiscated.*

As Josh studies the other drawings in the stack, he comes across a layout of the building that conducts the scanning. Based on the information on the drawing, it appears that the container is scanned not only for contraband but also radioactivity and explosives. The drawing also indicated that an X-ray generator was used in the scanning.

The last document he picks up has the heading of "Incident Report." As he reads the report, Josh learns of an attack on the facility in Ashdod in which a rocket-propelled grenade was fired at the new building and a bomb exploded one of the team's vehicles near their hotel. From what Josh could gather, no one was hurt in either incident. It seems Roger's activities struck a nerve with someone. At the bottom of the first page, Roger wrote that he felt Hamas, or an Israeli crime family, was responsible for the attacks.

He flips to the second page, which looks to have screen captures of what the scanner found. The first shows a row of rifles in a crate, and the other shows something that is showing up white on the screen and is circled in red. What struck Josh the most about these images is that they were crisp. He concludes that he could see everything that is in the container, including things that are in their own container. Josh surmises that, apparently, nothing could get past this scanner.

He replaces all the documents into the envelope, careful not to bend or tear any of the pages. Grabbing the other newer envelope, Josh opens it in the same way he opened the first. He pulls out another stack of computer printed papers, except this stack is much smaller. On top is a letter from Roger to the defense minister of Kuwait. It outlines a proposal to place some type of scanner for vehicles that could be placed at a border entry location. It refers to a drawing that is attached. Josh flips over to it. The drawing shows some kind of scanner for trucks that, based on the drawing, is portable. Another drawing shows how the scanner could be deployed at a border crossing and how traffic would be routed. It looks like the vehicles would pass by the scanner. Josh places all the pages in a neat stack and puts them back in the envelope. He wonders if this proposal ever came to fruition or not.

Feeling very tired, Josh checks his watch. Almost three hours have gone by that he is down in the basement. He decides to call it a night, but the things he had seen bothered him. In fact, he feels a mixture of anger and sadness that Roger didn't think it is important enough to tell him at least a little bit. Roger did some dangerous work in not-so-fun places in the world. In the documents he looked at, there was no mention of the Navy. So this must have been work Roger did after the Navy but before Badger Power. Why didn't Roger mention any of this to him? There is most likely a very good reason he didn't make this part of his life known to close friends and even his wife.

He then takes the envelopes and places them in a lockable drawer in his tool chest and puts the key in his pocket. "Better keep these under lock and key, no telling who would want them," Josh muses to himself.

When Josh slides between the sheets, Marsha is sound asleep. He wants to fill her in on what he found in the envelopes tonight, but he doesn't want to disturb her. It will wait until tomorrow. Josh turns off the light on his nightstand, and as he lies back to sleep, he thinks, *What else don't I know about Roger?* He would soon find out exactly what little he knew of Roger.

CHAPTER 19

Stormfront

The two men in the black SUV observe that the Bishop house is now dark. Their weapons are at the ready next to them in their seats. They decide not to enter the house since they don't know for sure if the material from Incheon is in there, thinking Josh did not have that one. They don't bother to stow them away as they pull out onto the road from their hiding place and start driving north on Highway 22. They get on Highway 21 and drive west toward the interstate, which they will travel south to Portage where their hotel is located.

On the way to the interstate, neither man sees the county sheriff's deputy hidden behind some trees by the road. The black SUV catches the deputy's attention since there hasn't been many cars on this road tonight. Watching the SUV drive by him, he guesses it is a rental since people that live around here don't drive new cars. Once the SUV passes him, the deputy notices the license plate light is not on.

"Well, lookee, lookee," whispers the deputy. He shifts his gaze to the radar gun; they are going the limit.

Out of boredom, he turns on his headlights and pulls out to follow the SUV. When he gets close enough, he reads off the plate number to dispatch, and they run it to see if there are any warrants or if it's hot. The plates come back clean, and yes, it is a rental. He decides not to pull the vehicle over since the driver wouldn't be responsible for replacing it. "It's your lucky day, bud," says the deputy, talking to himself. Perhaps, tonight, the deputy is the lucky one.

CHAPTER 20

Tagger

The next morning, the Bishops go through their morning routine and head to work. Josh tells Marsha some of what he discovers the night before. Her reaction is disbelief, telling Josh that everything in the past few days has been unreal. They promise to talk more later when they get home.

Josh drives to the laydown yard, which Badger Power still cannot fully make use of. The line crew has been put on another construction job until this one can resume. The company is talking to the Waushara County authorities to see if they can take their material and equipment out, under police supervision, and move it to another laydown yard.

The weather is warmer today, about twenty-five degrees; however, overnight snow fell to the tune of six or seven inches. Tagger is already at the yard and is starting up one of the end loaders to start plowing snow around the trailers and the driveway into the yard. Josh notices that the sheriff's deputy is not here this morning.

Josh drives up to the trailer and climbs the steps inside, with the sound of aluminum clanging. Tagger already had the snow cleared on and around the stairs. Once inside, Josh pulls his laptop out of his backpack and gets it set up on his desk. His primary task today, based on the voice mail his boss left him, is to find another laydown yard since the company wants to complete construction on this project by the end of spring.

The plan will be to review satellite pictures from Google Earth to find any promising locations and then drive out to visit them. Josh pours himself a cup of coffee that Tagger already brewed when he got in. Sitting at the laptop, he launches the application and enters his current location. He starts the search of finding another suitable space radiating out from this location. Josh settles in since this usually takes a while.

Tagger finishes the snowplowing and heads inside to talk to Josh, who hears him clanging up the steps to the trailer. Once inside, the two men greet each other as Tagger gets a cup of coffee. Still in his jacket, he sits and drinks his coffee while Josh scans Google Earth for the next laydown yard. He breaks the silence, "Hey, Gif, I gotta idea. What if I make up da rest of dem framin' kits?"

Framing kits contain the hardware and insulators that get put on the pole before they set the pole in the hole or on top a foundation, and there is one kit per structure. Making the kits saves time because all the items that go into them are in two or three different pallets and in the parts trailer. All the parts are put into a big plastic bin and is placed with the pole pieces. This work was started a couple of days before the murder and was never finished.

Josh looks up from his computer. "Yeah, I guess that would be okay. If I find a promising lead on a new laydown yard, I'll want you to take a ride with me. Hey, do you know why we don't have a deputy parked here in the yard?"

"Not sure why da cops ain't here. Maybe dey gotta call? Well, I guess I'll git to it." Tagger drains his coffee cup, stands, and heads toward the door. He stops in his tracks and turns to Josh. "Hey, dem empty bins still in da parts trailer?"

"Yeah, as far as I know, they are still there."

Tagger leaves and walks to the parts trailer and climbs the portable stairs to get in. He drags several stacks of plastic bins to the top of the stairs. He looks up to see where the pallets of material he will need to fill the bins. As he looks around, he catches a glimpse of a vehicle parked in an access for the farm field across the road from his location, and it is pointing at the laydown yard.

Acting like it is no big deal, Tagger continues to work, bringing down the empty bins and over to where the rest of the material is located. He makes a mental note to keep an eye on the vehicle. The vehicle doesn't look like a cop car from around here; it's too new and they don't use black SUVs.

Before Josh jumps back into looking for a new yard, he grabs his cell phone and finds Ralph's number in his contact list and thumbs the phone number to activate the call. The number rings twice and then it goes to voice mail, indicating the mailbox is full. He presses the End button and stops to think. Trying to remember other engineers in the group Ralph works in, he begins to scroll through his contact list. He finds a name of another engineer he is working with and calls her. After a couple of rings, the engineer answers the phone.

"Hi, Whitney, it's Josh Bishop calling. How are you?"

"Hey, Josh, I'm doing fine. How about you?"

"I'm good. Hey, I have a question for you, Whitney."

"Okay, shoot."

"I've been trying to get ahold of Ralph Peterson with a question on a project he and I are on, but I haven't been able to find him. Do you know where he is?"

Whitney's exasperation comes through the phone. "Man, I wish I did. You and I are not the only ones who need to talk to him. Everyone is looking for him. It's like he fell off the face of the earth."

Josh tries one more question, "When was the last time you saw him?"

Whitney pauses a moment, thinking about the question. "I saw him last week on…Wednesday. I remember because it was the day before that project manager died. Wasn't that awful?"

"Yeah, it was really bad. Thanks for the information. You were very helpful. I need to get going. It was good talking to you. Bye."

"Sure thing, Josh. Bye."

Josh returns to his search on his computer but is thinking about what Whitney said. Thinking to himself, *He vanishes the day Roger is killed? That can't be a coincidence, can it? Did Ralph kill Roger? The big question is, why?* Shaking his head, he focuses on the task at hand.

After another thirty minutes of searching, he has come across a promising location although it is a little out of the way for the project. It looks good enough to go check it out, so he reaches for his cell phone to let Tagger know they are going on a road trip. But as he touches the phone, it rings. He picks it up and notices that it is Tagger calling. He presses the green button to connect the call.

"Tagger, I was just going to call you. I got a place for us to check out."

Tagger sounds agitated. "Never mine dat. We gotta problem!"

"What's up?"

"I'm bein' watched! Der's a black car across da road and it's watchin' me."

"Tagger, maybe it's an unmarked squad car."

"No way! It's no police car. Look at it fer yurself."

Interested now, Josh goes to the window in his office and looks out toward the gate and the road. He spots the black SUV and says in the phone, "Yeah, that's no police car."

"What ya think we should do, Gif? Walk over der and give 'em hell?"

"How do you know they're looking at you?"

"I can see 'em in there. Two of um. And dey lookin' at me."

Sensing that Tagger is getting overly excited, Josh decides to try a game on him, suppressing the urge to laugh. "You know what, Tagger? They're from the local strip club, and they're looking for new talent."

Tagger explodes, "Dis is serious and yer makin' jokes! My life might be in danger, Gif! And I don't got my gun, thanks ta you!"

"The only danger you're in is if they were blind and desperate. Now lock things up in the yard. We're going to check out another location. If they follow us, then I will do something about it. Emphasis on I."

"Okay, if ya say so." Tagger locks up the material trailers and meets Josh at the truck, all the while giving the black SUV the stink eye. Josh comes out of the trailer and locks it, then he comes down the steps and to the truck and hops in. Tagger jumps in on the passenger side.

"Gif, I know yer thinkin' I'm crazy, but der's somthin' really wrong with dat car. I just know it."

As Josh pulls up to the road, they are directly across from the black SUV. Josh looks at the occupants and then looks left and right for traffic. As they pull out onto the highway, Tagger flips off the occupants in the black SUV. Josh looks at him and shakes his head. He's got one more little surprise for ol' Tagger when they get back.

They are going north on Highway 22 toward Wautoma, looking for a gravel pit north of there by a few miles. Gravel pits are usually the preferred place for a laydown yard since they would be at the bottom of it—out of sight, out of mind. This one is smaller than what they have now, but they could make it work if they got creative.

The driver of the SUV starts the engine and is going to follow the truck. His partner puts out a hand toward him and shakes his head. "We have been made. We cannot follow them without the risk of an altercation. Let's go back the house and plant the listening devices."

The driver nods and pulls out in the opposite direction. They become alarmed when the big scruffy man working in the yard made them. Both men have their weapons ready in case the man decides to come toward their car. They sense he would do them harm. Their target, on the other hand, does not seem concerned, which was good news for now.

Tagger and Josh come back from their recon mission, which is very successful. The owner of the pit is open to loan them the entire thing since he isn't hauling anything out of there lately. Josh calls the company's real estate person on the project to set up a lease. When they get back toward the trailer, Tagger pronounces, "Dose varmints skedaddled. Good thing too, I was goin' to let 'em have it."

As Josh turns into the driveway of the yard, he stops abruptly, gets out, and walks over to the gate, acting like he is picking something off it. He comes back to the truck, and as he gets in, he holds up a business card to Tagger.

"See, Tagger, they were from the"—Josh pretends to read it—"Naughty Gal Gentlemen's Club, and they wrote 'Call me' on the back."

"Whatcha talkin' 'bout?" He snatches the card from Josh and looks at it. He then realizes that it is a card from a vendor they used and recognized the handwriting of Josh on the back. "Very funny!"

With that, Josh breaks down laughing at the joke he pulled on Tagger, who joins in.

CHAPTER 21

More Pulling

When Josh returns home, he usually goes through the garage to remove dirty work clothes although today they didn't get dirty. He could have come through the front door, but it is a force of habit to come through the garage. As he comes into the kitchen, he notices Marsha is rooting around in the walk-in pantry and he joins her.

She announces, "Hey, you're home! How did things go today? I was getting stuff together for you to make you famous chili for supper."

"It went okay. I'm trying to wrap my head around what happened, and I think there is a lot of things I don't know." He exits the pantry with a half a dozen cans of food to make his chili. He jokes, "My sous-chef is a can opener."

As he works his magic, she tells him, "Oh, hey, before I forget, would you take a look at the front doorknob? It doesn't seem to be working right today for some reason. It takes more effort now to turn the knob."

"Okay, I'll look at it once I get everything in the pot to simmer. Maybe it needs some oil in it to loosen it up."

After getting his ingredients in the pot and putting it on simmer, Josh goes out to the garage and gets a small toolbox and a spray can of WD-40. He makes his way to the front door. Opening the door, twisting the knob in one direction, it seems to be fine, but when he twists the knob in the other direction, it is indeed difficult to turn.

He disassembles the lockset from the door and inspects it. Spraying the WD-40 on the moving parts doesn't seem to help much. On closer inspection, he observes that something is preventing the knob from turning all the way and keeping the lock from locking as well. He fishes it out and looks at it. It appears to be a slender piece of metal, like part of a key or something. He tests the lockset again, and it works perfectly. Satisfied, Josh reassembles the doorknob onto the door and checks it out one more time, which works fine.

While Marsha and Josh eat dinner, he tells her he fixed the front doorknob and what he found. He asks her, "Did you break off a part of your key in the lock?"

"No, I would have remembered that. How do you think that piece of metal got into the lock?"

Josh shakes his head. "I'm not sure. It's almost like someone tried to pick the lock and left part of the pick in it. But who would do something like that?" He changes the subject and asks Marsha how her day at work was. She works as the office manager for a metal fabrication shop, owned by Michael Dunn, in Red Granite, which is a few miles east of Wautoma.

"After I left yesterday, a friend of Michael's came by with a couple of coworkers needing a rush job on some kind of vibrating caisson. Anyway, Michael puts everything else aside and works on their project all night long and into this morning to get the job done for them. I told him that he should charge at least double or triple what he normally charges. He said no since it was for a friend of his who was in a bind. What about you?"

Josh tells her about Tagger and the black SUV as well as the joke he played on him. "I think I got ol' Tagger pretty good that time."

Marsha shakes her head. "Boy, you're a regular HR nightmare." She furrows her brow. "Do you think that black car has anything to do with Roger's murder? I mean, when was the last time any car parked across from a laydown yard you worked in?"

"No, I can't remember a time that has happened, but I don't know if that car is tied to the murder. I don't remember seeing a black SUV anywhere that day."

Marsha points a finger at him. "No, but maybe one of your guys do. Have you talked to them about that day?"

"No, I haven't. Looks like I'll have to go visit them early in the morning tomorrow."

After cleaning up the dinner dishes, they head downstairs to look at the rest of the manila envelopes. Josh tells her about a job Roger had after the Navy but before Badger Power where he led installations of security equipment in foreign countries. He then walks over to the tool chest, unlocks the drawer, removes the envelopes, brings them over to the big table, and drags over a stool for Marsha.

As Marsha sits, she says, "Well, talk about hiding things. What made you want to lock them away?"

"Well, I thought if Roger felt it necessary to hide them, then somebody may be looking for them. So I locked them up there in the tool chest."

"What about the memory sticks? Did you look at what's on them?"

Josh is now sitting. "I tried, but they are password protected. I still have them here in the drawer."

He uses the same X-Acto knife he work with last night to open the flap of the envelope with the label Lightning Rod. Unlike the other two he opened, this contains a larger stack of papers. Sitting next to each other, Josh shows the top piece of paper to Marsha. The name of the project is Lightning Rod and is located in the central Asian country of Kazakhstan.

This stack of papers have the same type of documents and drawings the other two have, but just more of it. One by one they look at each page in the stack. When they get to the end of the stack, Marsha reads another incident report. "So from this, it looks like Roger had his hands full with the local organized crime that did not want whatever he was installing.

Josh adds, "What we have seen so far makes me believe what they did here was the largest installation Roger had done given the amount of equipment that is listed on the first page. It seems like all these installations created problems with the criminal element operating in Kazakhstan."

Josh carefully places the pages back into the envelope and closes it. He grabs the next envelope on the table and opens it. The envelope he is opening has the word *Javelin* on it and has similar stack of computer pages. At the top is the summary page which he makes a point to look at first.

They both look at the summary page and notice that this project was done in Incheon, South Korea. Based on the information on this summary sheet, it appears only a port system was installed there. There were a couple of drawings showing the location of the scanning building and how containers will move through the system. There also is a document that showed test results on the system. It indicated the X-ray system could penetrate seventeen feet of steel and has the resolution of fifteen millimeters, which meant it could detect a very thin wire after penetrating seventeen feet of steel.

After reading that, Josh whistles and points out to Marsha, "That is a very powerful system to be able to see everything in the container down to that minute size. Maybe that is what got the bad guys' interest. They wanted to steal the technology."

Marsha counters, "Or they wanted to destroy it!"

There is one document that is different. It outlines a test that is conducted on a random container in the yard that yielded an image of gold bricks, guns, and a lead-lined container. Apparently, it got a lot of attention, given the nature of this document. As a result, the head of the Korean Customs Service and a senior member of the Foreign Affairs Ministry visited the site. It turns out the container originated in Hong Kong and the Korean officials decided to confiscate all the containers in that shipment and run them through the scanner. According to the document, what is initially found is just the tip of the iceberg.

Marsha points at the document. "Man, that test sure paid for the system. I wouldn't be surprised if the Korean government bought another one to put somewhere else."

Josh adds, "And I'm sure it really pissed off the people in Hong Kong who sent the containers."

Josh puts the documents back into the envelope and grabs the last envelope. This envelope has the words *Blue Horizon* on it. As with the other envelopes, it has a stack of computer-printed paper. Predictably, it has a summary page on top that provides information about the project. *Blue Horizon* was built in Rabat, Morocco. Marsha learned that Rabat is an industrial port city east of touristy Casablanca. As with the other installations, there is a drawing of where the equipment was to be installed. There is an incident report for this one too.

Marsha holds the report up. "At this location, they must have had a lot of trouble with the locals. They had one person injured, having to bug out quick after they completed the installation."

Josh, holding up a printed e-mail from the stack, says, "Yeah, the government wanted another system somewhere else, but this e-mail to Roger, from someone else in the company, indicated that he was to finish the installation in Rabat and then come home."

Marsha continues to read the incident report, "It says here that a group of politicians in their parliament introduced a bill to make it illegal to install scanning devices in ports or on their borders, but it doesn't say what happened to that bill."

Josh taps on the report. "I bet they were in bed with organized crime." Putting the papers back into the envelope, he asks, "So what are your thoughts on all this?" gesturing to all the envelopes on the table.

Marsha stands up and walks around a little to unstiffen her legs. "So you're telling me that Roger was going around the world, pissing off gunrunners, drug smugglers, and human traffickers? Does that sound like Roger?"

Josh shakes his head. "No, that doesn't seem like him at all, but here we are. He never mentioned any of this, not even in passing. I'm almost mad at him that he didn't value our friendship enough to tell me about this."

"Or maybe he was protecting you. I'm surprised people weren't coming after him before now."

Josh shrugs his shoulder and points to the stacks of envelopes. "But what was the point of hiding this information? There is nothing here that jumps out at me that is worth going after. The drawings don't show how those systems operated."

Marsha, now pointing to the drawer where the memory sticks are still at, says, "Maybe the important information is in there. But you're right. Why bring all this home with you?"

Josh thinks about that, then, snapping his fingers and pointing to Marsha, says, "Unless there was someone at the security company that was trying to sell the information to the highest bidder and Roger found out about it. To protect the information, Roger brought it home and hid it and told no one that he had it. But somehow the word got out years later. Does that sound plausible?"

"Very. It explains a lot. Besides, if Roger wanted to sell off the information, he would have done it long ago."

Josh shakes his head. "What I can't figure out is if or how Ralph is involved with this. The very day Roger is murdered, he disappears. Today I talked to someone that sits across from him, and she said it was like he fell off the face of the earth. How does that happen? I think something like that has to be planned in advance, and if that's the case, then he knew when Roger was going to get murdered. Maybe he provided the needed information to the killer."

Very early the next morning, Josh drives out to the other project where his crew is currently working and gets them together so they could talk. Standing in the middle of the circle of men, Josh addresses them, "Hey, guys, thanks for taking the time this morning to meet before you head out to work. I'm sure you are all aware that Roger Simmons was killed back at the other laydown yard. I want to ask you some questions to gain any information that might be useful. I guess the first thing I want to ask is if any of the authorities have come and ask you questions."

Every one of the group shakes his head, which doesn't surprise Josh, given who is working this case. He then asks, "Did anyone see a gray GMC truck in the back of the yard, and when did you see it?"

There is some silence at first as people are thinking about the question. Then one guy says he saw the truck at lunchtime and then again when he was done for the day. Most of the others agree with that assessment. Then another pipes up. It is Chopper. He got his nickname since he is a lineman that is qualified to work from helicopters. Because of that, he seems serious all the time, not cracking jokes with the others.

"I saw the truck when I came back to the yard to get more shackles from the parts trailer. I also saw a black SUV parked across from the yard that seemed odd to me."

"Why was it odd, Chopper?"

"I don't know exactly. There were two serious-looking dudes in the SUV looking at the laydown yard. It's not something you see every day. They seemed suspicious."

Tagger interrupts, "See, I'm tellin' ya da people in dat black SUV are no good! Heck, even Chopper sez so!"

Josh looks at Tagger, taking in what he said, then asks Chopper, "What time did you see the truck and the SUV?"

"It was about ten or ten thirty in the morning, definitely before lunch."

"What did you see in the back of the yard?"

Chopper pauses while he thought about it. "I saw the truck and I saw Simmons."

Josh raises his eyebrows at this. "What was he doing?"

"Gif, he was looking east toward the woods, just standing there. It was like he spotted something in the woods and was trying to figure out what it was."

This news stuns Josh, and he doesn't know what to say, to think that Roger saw who was coming for him.

"There was one other thing that I just remembered, Gif. I know the two of you were friends and I wouldn't talk bad about the dead, but I saw what I saw. You know we have had problems with aggressive coyotes at that yard, and I thought there was one that was getting too close for Roger's comfort. I know you preach to us about not bringing guns to the jobsite or we'll get fired. But..." His voice trails off and he is looking apprehensive.

Josh gets the impression Chopper is trying to hold something back to protect Roger. The story about the aggressive coyotes is bull;

they haven't seen any out at that site at all. He walks up and looks him right in the eyes. "But what?" He is feeling uneasy about what Chopper is going to say.

Chopper sighs, then exclaims, "Gif, Roger had a gun in his hand, and he was pointing it at something in the woods. I saw the gun as clear as day."

Wall Cloud

The two Triad men sat in their SUV, listening to everything going on in the Bishop house that evening, thanks to the listening devices they installed after they left the laydown yard. They even had enough time to do a cursory search for the envelopes, without success. The hope was that they find out if the Bishops are keeping the information they are looking for. They do not want to attract unwanted attention by killing these people without getting what they came for. They could work it so they aren't discovered for a couple of days, but that might not be enough time to get out of the country or have enough time to track down what they came for.

When Josh told Sarah about the front door lock, the two men looked at each other and the one in the passenger seat shook his head. The piece of metal he installed earlier in the lock was supposed to let the Bishops think that the door was locked, but in reality, it was not, making it easy for the two men to reenter the house. The metal must have slipped out of where it was placed, probably because the lockset was old and worn. Next, they heard about what occurred at the laydown yard earlier and were wondering if they had been compromised. However, the more they listened, it seemed they were not in immediate danger of being discovered.

For those people from other countries that learn the English language, they are overwhelmed by the fact we may have several different meanings for the same word. They anguish over which meaning was intended in that conversation. To make matters worse, the use of American idioms, or slang, just complicates things even more. Such is the case when Josh and Marsha called the flash drives that Josh retrieved from the basement *memory sticks*. The two men from China do not know this phrase and assumed it had something to do with a stick of wood. They understand *flash drive* or *portable memory device*, but not *memory stick*. As a result, they totally missed the references of information that are stored on the flash drives in the possession of Bishops.

The two men listen intently as Josh and Marsha discuss what they found in the envelopes. They become very focused when the topic of the Incheon project came up. They both nodded when they heard that an entire shipment was confiscated. That had caused their organization a hundred million Hong Kong dollars, which precipitated their mission, finding the last copy of the scanner specifications. So where is it?

CHAPTER 23

Gathering

The medical examiner finally releases the body of Roger Simmons to the family after Sarah Simmons called the sheriff to find out why she could not bury her husband. She complains that it is almost two weeks and what more information could they get from Roger that they didn't already have. Sheriff Steve Cantor relents after talking to the medical examiner. The body is picked up by the employees of the Hathaway Funeral Home in Portage, Wisconsin.

The next day, Sarah and her two children go to the funeral home to make the arrangements for the wake and funeral. Sarah asks Marsha to set up the lunch reception after the graveside service, which she gladly accepted, and she reserves a banquet room at Dino's in town. Sarah calls Josh and asks him to say a few words at the service, perhaps a funny story about Roger.

Josh protests, "You want me to tell a funny story at a funeral? You're not supposed to tell jokes at a funeral! You want me to do a roast of Roger? I'm not comfortable with that."

Sarah smiles at the phone. "No, Josh, I'm not asking you to roast Roger. I'm asking you to tell a story that speaks to his character, and if it is a little funny, then that's okay."

"Oh well, if you put it that way, then I'm good with it."

Sarah's smile disappears. "I have one more request of you, Josh."

"What's that?"

"I know I've been relying on you a lot, but could you please be a pallbearer?"

Without hesitation, Josh says, "Sure. I would be honored to."

Sarah thanks him, and they hang up.

The day of the wake has come, and Sarah is a mixture of sadness and nervousness. The last time she saw Roger, he was alive and well. She remembers well that morning, unaware of what was about to happen. Their conversation was superficial, talking about what their days will bring. She didn't tell him she loved him when they parted that morning, something she regrets now. Sarah tells herself she needs to be strong for her kids and in front of others, but that might be easier said than done. Her daughter is already a mess and her son is strangely quiet; maybe he is trying to keep it together.

As is customary, the family gets to view the body alone. The funeral director lets Sarah know they can go and *view* Roger. Sarah and her children enter the chapel where Roger's body is laid, and they walk toward it. When the trio reach the front of the casket, any pretense of Sarah staying strong for the kids evaporates. Upon seeing her dear Roger, she begins to sob and her knees buckle and she drops to the floor. Her son kneels to help her up, but she is making no moves to get up, and so he just caresses her back and holds her close. Her daughter is at the casket sobbing, and she turns, talking to her mother, but notices her kneeling on the floor sobbing. She helps her brother get their mother up in the nearest chair. The three hold one another and cry.

The Bishops arrived early as well to provide any help that may be needed. Through the window of the closed chapel door, they see Sarah and the kids huddled together and crying. They both enter the chapel quietly and sit in the chairs directly behind them and gently rubbing shoulders and backs of the family. Josh looks up at Roger, the first time he has seen him since that frigid night, and becomes immensely sad by the sight. *Could I have done something to keep him alive?* Thinking back to what the ER doctor told him, most likely not. Even if he stayed with Roger the whole day, it may not have mattered. He would have been killed as well. *What did Roger do to make someone kill him?* Now more than ever, Josh feels compelled to find the answer to that question.

As Josh looks at Roger in the casket, he notices that he has a lot of makeup that changes his facial features. Josh stands and all sorts of memories come flooding into his mind. All the fun times they had, the trips they took together, and the talks they had are no more. They are just memories now, memories that he will need to keep and not forget. He finds himself covering his face and quietly sobbing.

By the time the wake is about to start, the family composed themselves enough to meet those that came to pay their respects. The first ones to arrive are the extended family of the Simmons and some of Sarah's immediate family, followed closely by some coworkers of Roger from Badger Power. It isn't long before the chapel and lobby are full of people. As the wake progresses, attendees spill into the empty chapel across the lobby. There is a lot of chatter of many different conversations. There is a line of people out on the sidewalk of coworkers, friends, and acquaintances of Roger. Even Tagger shows up wearing a suit and dress shirt, not to mention he trimmed his beard and got a haircut. Coworkers of Sarah, as well as close friends of hers, also arrive to pay their respects.

There is one guest at the wake who isn't there to pay his respects to Roger. He make his way on the periphery of the groups of people talking among themselves. They do not pay attention to this person, which is how he wanted it—to be the proverbial fly on the wall. He listens to the conversations to determine if any of them might give him some information he needed. He is at the wake for a good hour, and before leaving, he removes his cell phone from his jacket and takes pictures of each page of the guest register. As he is taking pictures, the funeral director, Wade Campbell, spots this person and comes up beside him and confronts him, putting himself between the man and the stand that held the guest book.

Campbell speaks in an angry whisper to the intruder so as not to cause undue attention to the situation, "Just what do think you are doing?" The funeral director is a large and formidable man. He played a linebacker in college and may have ended up in the pros if it wasn't for a career-ending knee injury he sustained before he graduated. Without waiting for a response, he takes the man by the front of his jacket and walks him straight back into his office off the lobby. The man reaches into his coat for something, but the director prevents him from removing his hand from the jacket.

Closing the door of his office with his foot, he tosses the man into a chair across from his desk. Still standing over the intruder, Campbell releases his grip on the man. The camera-happy intruder removes his hand from his jacket and reveals what he tried to remove earlier. He shows Campbell his credentials and announces to the director that he is Detective Eric Halvorsen of the Waushara County Sheriff's Department. Wade understands now what is going on. The detective is casing the wake for suspects and wants names and addresses to go with the faces and takes pictures of the guest book. The only problem with that is you don't have a way to exactly match the faces with the names and addresses. Campbell steps back away from the detective.

"You know, you could have just asked me for the names and I would have provided them, don't you?"

"I have a right to do what I did, and I got what I wanted."

"You're lucky a guest didn't notice. They might see it as someone trying to get personal information."

"No one was paying attention to me anyway."

"Well, not everybody." Wade winks at the detective. "Well, since you got what you wanted, I suggest you leave. I also suggest you leave these people alone unless you have good cause."

"Sure, I'll leave, but I will be back if I want to and you won't be able to do anything about it," comes the response from the detective. With that, the detective gets up from the chair and leaves the director's office and the funeral home.

At the end of the wake, Josh asks Sarah and Marsha if they want to stay behind and talk about what he has found in the materials recovered from the walls. Sarah begs off, saying that the day has been emotionally draining and she is exhausted. So they part ways, and as Josh and Marsha drive home, he tells her about what he learned when he talked to his guys.

Josh is driving and looks over at Marsha. "A lot of the guys remember seeing Roger's truck when they left the yard and when they returned and didn't see anything out of the ordinary. A couple of guys saw his truck at lunchtime too."

Marsha looks at Josh questioningly. "Did any of them see that black SUV you were telling me about?"

"Do you remember meeting a guy I called Chopper at the Christmas party last year?"

Marsha looks up as if the answer is written on the headliner of the truck. "Yes, I remember now. He seemed like a serious guy."

"He told me that he saw Roger's truck and the black SUV around 10:00 AM. He said the SUV was parked across the road from the yard, like it was the other day. He also said he thought the SUV was suspicious. I asked him why, and he said there were two very serious-looking dudes in it looking at the yard or more like through the yard to something at the far end."

Marsha's eyebrows shoot up at this. "So what you are saying is that they were looking at Roger? Maybe they are the ones who killed him."

Josh looks over at her again. "I don't think so. They were west of the yard. Whoever killed Roger came from the east."

Marsha turns and looks right at Josh. "You seem certain of that. Why?"

"Well, I saw foot and car tracks in the snow, in and to the east of the woods. That was my theory until Chopper told me what else he saw."

"So what else did Chopper see?"

Josh hesitates for a long moment. "He said he saw Roger point a gun at something in the woods to the east."

Marsha exclaims, "Wha-what! He was pointing a gun into the woods? At who? Did he shoot someone? Holy crap, Josh, that's a huge piece of information! How is it that he dies, and he has his gun pointed at someone? This is definitely something you need to tell Sarah about!"

"I don't know the answers to any of those questions, unfortunately. It indicates he had a gun in his truck, which is a no-no at Badger. We'll have to keep that on the QT. It does tell me that he may have heard or seen his killer just before he was shot."

CHAPTER 24

Final Parting

The next morning, the funeral service is scheduled to begin at 10:00 AM, but people start to arrive early. At Sarah's request, Wade made the calls ahead of the funeral to have full military honors at graveside, and he receives confirmation that the honor guard are on their way to the cemetery. They also finalize the order of events for the service, putting Josh's remarks at the end.

At about nine thirty, Detective Halvorsen parks his unmarked car across the street from the entrance to the funeral home and gets his digital camera ready. As people walk toward the door, he snaps pictures. He does this in case there is someone who comes to the funeral that did not go to the wake the night before. As he takes pictures of all the attendees of the funeral, he is blissfully unaware that he is not the only one watching the attendees, and in fact, they are watching him as well. If the detective looked in his side rearview mirror, he would see the black SUV four cars behind him.

A handful of the linemen that work for Josh come to the funeral, including Tagger and Chopper. No one else from Badger Power are in attendance, which Josh thinks odd.

The funeral service begins, and the chapel is full of attenders. The casket is now closed and a flag is draped over it. The funeral director begins the service, and the pastor from the local Lutheran church delivers the eulogy and a message about *walking well* in life since we don't realize how short life is. The messages are interspersed with older hymns and contemporary Christian tunes. As the last item in the service, Josh comes up to tell his story. He is a little nervous at first but then quickly gains his voice, telling the story of how he and Roger met and how he impressed Josh with his character. He shares how he learned that your word was everything and that Roger's contract with people was his handshake. He finishes the story with a funny anecdote, which draws some polite laughter from the group.

The full military burial includes sailors in dress uniforms that will conduct the service, which includes taps, gun salute, and the folded American flag given to the family. For this service, the military honors includes replacing the black hearse used by the funeral home with a Navy hearse, gleaming white with the Navy seal on each door and two small American flags on the two front corners.

The pallbearers move the casket into the waiting hearse. The motorcade travels to St. Mary's Cemetery with a police car providing escort. When they arrive at the cemetery, they come through the only entrance and turn right into the new section. They stop by the large white canopy that shelters the newly dug grave for Roger replete with a handful of chairs for the family and the obnoxious AstroTurf that hides the dirt.

The honor guards, made up of seven sailors, gather at the back of the hearse as the funeral director opens the door. The highest-ranking member of the guard, which, in this case, is a Navy master chief, walks up to the back of the hearse and pulls out the sled that holds the casket so that it is halfway out. The other members then fill in on either side, and the ones closest to the hearse begin to pass the casket forward to the other members of the guard until it is completely out. The honor guard then carries Roger to the grave and places him on top of the grave-lowering device. They back away, give a slow salute, and then file out from under the canopy. Through all this, the master chief gives orders in a whisper.

Most of the people that came to the graveside service have not seen a military funeral, and so they hang back and watch the honor guard at work. Once that is completed, people come forward and gather under the canopy.

Some of the linemen come to the cemetery, including Tagger and Chopper, and hang out at the back of the crowd. They talk among themselves and look around as they wait for the service to begin. As Tagger scans the cemetery, he spots something that makes him go rigid. Chopper notices the change in Tagger and looks at him. Tagger meets his eyes and slightly nods in the direction of what he saw. Chopper catches a look that way and notices it as well, causing his eyebrows to raise, but looks away. Both men just spot the black SUV in the rear of the cemetery.

Tagger leans in. "What da heck are dey doin' here?"

Chopper shrugs his shoulders. "Seems like they have some unfinished business with someone."

"Who ya thinkin' dat would be? I scared 'em the odder day when I was at da yard."

"Maybe, Tagger, but I think they always seem to come around when Josh is around. It could be that they are wanting him for some reason."

"Ya think der tryin' ta kill 'em?"

"I don't think so. They had ample time to do that. No, I think he has something they want and they're keeping track of him."

"Well, I can't jist let 'em sit der bidin' their time to swoop in and grab Josh. I'm goin' to tell 'em ta skedaddle." He takes a step and Chopper grabs his arm.

"Not yet. Wait until the service is over. Look, we need to let Josh know what's going on. We might tip them off if we walk up to him right now and tell him."

Tagger nods in agreement. "Okay, Chopper, but we need ta keep an eye on 'em."

Eric Halvorsen makes an appearance at the cemetery; his car is parked with the others. He is watching everyone and takes pictures of people he may have missed going into the funeral home earlier. He is so focused on watching those at the graveside, thinking the killer is among the group, he is oblivious to the black SUV.

Everyone turns their attention to the grave as the service starts. The pastor quotes the Twenty-third Psalm, the passage in Ecclesiastes about the seasons of life, and delivers the message about making sure we are right with God because someday it will be you here, pointing at the casket. Once he is done, he moves away so the honor guard can continue their duties.

Two of the members of the honor guard come under the canopy and stand at attention on either end of the casket. A third member starts playing taps on a bugle while the remaining four members are standing away from the group with rifles at the ready for the gun salute. Once taps are completed, the four members come to attention and raise their weapons. They fire three volleys, each time various people in the group flinch at the sound of the rifles.

After the gun salute, the two under the canopy begin to remove the flag from the casket. After they free the flag from the casket, they begin to fold it in the unique way they do. When they are done, the flag is folded into a triangle and is held by the master chief. He then makes his way in front of where Sarah is sitting, kneels, and extends the flag to her.

As he does this, he utters the words no family, anywhere, of active duty soldiers or veterans wants to hear, "On behalf of the president of the United States, the United States Navy, and a grateful nation, please accept this flag as a symbol of our appreciation for your loved one's honorable and faithful service."

With that, the master chief slowly rises to attention and gives Sarah a slow salute. He then turns on his heel and exits the canopy. The funeral director then moves to the front of the group and tells them the service is concluded and the family would like to invite you to lunch at Dino's.

While people start filing to their cars, Tagger and Chopper place themselves so that the canopy is between them and the black SUV. They get Josh's attention, and they motion him over to them. He walks up to them and shakes their hand. "Thanks guys for coming out. I hope you—"

Tagger interrupts, "Dey is here, Gif!"

Confused, Josh replies, "Who's here?"

Chopper responds this time, "The guys in the black SUV. Here at the cemetery, toward the back."

Josh's brows go up, and he starts to move so he can look at it, but Tagger stops him.

"Hey, don't look at 'em. We don't want 'em to know we see 'em."

"It's kind hard not to see them. They're out in the open, right?"

Chopper says, "We have a plan to see what they are up to." Both he and Tagger fill in Josh on what they plan to do.

Josh has been watching some activity behind his linemen. "So you plan to confront the black SUV that is now leaving?"

Tagger spins around in time to see the black SUV head for the entrance to the cemetery. He sprints to his car and then shoots off toward the SUV. It looks like Tagger will T-bone the SUV, but it accelerates and Tagger misses. Turning quickly and causing his car to slide, Tagger gets close behind the other vehicle. The passenger-side window to the SUV opens and a man leans out, holding a gun. There is a loud report, and the windshield on Tagger's car explodes, causing him to stop abruptly. The bullet lodges itself into the passenger-side headrest.

There is a line of cars waiting to get out of the cemetery, creating a bottleneck. The black SUV keeps going down a cemetery road parallel to the exit road and getting closer to the street entrance. There is about twenty feet of grass between the end of the cemetery road and the street. The SUV then drives over the grass area and makes the turn onto the street, then accelerates and races down the street. The police officer observes what happened as he was directing traffic and gets in his vehicle to give chase with lights and sirens.

CHAPTER 25

A Long Thread

Later in the afternoon of the funeral, Marsha calls Sarah to see how she is doing. She invites Sarah over to their house to talk about some of the things Josh has discovered. Sarah likes the idea of coming over to the Bishops' home for a change in scenery but is apprehensive about what Josh may have found. She tells Marsha, "I don't know if I'm ready to hear what Josh has found. I mean, whatever he found sounds serious."

"Sarah, I think it is important that you know about all this sooner than later. I don't know, but you might be in danger!"

"Okay, I'll come over later after I have dinner with the kids. They want to do their own thing tonight. You better have some wine ready!"

Around 7:00 PM, Sarah arrives at the Bishop house and they gather around the kitchen table. Josh opens a bottle of wine, pours two glasses, and sets them down in front of the women. He retrieves a beer out of the refrigerator and comes to the table and sits down. Sarah puts down her glass and looks at both of her friends. "Hey, guys, I want to thank you again for all that you have done for me. I couldn't have made it through without you."

Marsha responds, "Hey, Sarah, anytime. That is what friends are for, to help us through the tough times."

Josh weighs in, "We were glad to help. I don't think we are capable of watching a friend suffer and not do anything to lend a hand."

Keeping her attention to Josh, Sarah continues, "Josh, I really enjoyed the story you told about Roger today. It truly portrayed his character. I also liked how you ended it on a funny note. I purposely had you speak last so everyone heard something funny about Roger. Maybe they left not as sad as they came."

"I'm glad you liked it. I had to think a while to come up with a story to tell."

Marsha chimes in, "I was pleasantly surprised at the turnout last night and today. I knew Roger was popular, but I guess he was well-liked by more people than I thought."

"Yes," Sarah agrees, "there were many people from Badger Power that came out, which reminds me. Josh, tell your linemen thank you for coming to the wake and funeral, especially how they showed respect by getting all dressed up. I'm sure they would have preferred not to."

"I will certainly pass it along to them. You know, I was very impressed with the military ceremony at the graveside. I had never seen that before."

Sarah nods. "I hadn't seen one either. I thought I was going to faint when that man handed the flag to me. He was very sincere."

Marsha adds, "I think I jumped out of my skin every time they shot their guns. You could see them get ready to shoot, but I still jumped anyway."

Josh chuckles, "I think everyone jumped."

Sarah asks, "Josh, what was all the commotion at the cemetery earlier? At the end of the service?"

Josh glances at Marsha before he answers, "It kinda ties in with why we are together tonight. There are people that, I think, are here to get something that Roger had, and they were at the cemetery."

Sarah stares at Josh in disbelief. "I guess we should have that talk of yours."

Josh nods. "Okay, sounds good. Let me go get some stuff from the basement and I'll be right back. Marsha, you might want to refill the wine glasses." Josh then goes to the basement and retrieves all the items he has collected while doing his investigation. He comes back up the stairs with an armload of pictures, envelopes, his handwritten notes, and memory sticks and places them on the kitchen table. He goes to the fridge and pulls out another beer.

Sarah is eyeing the items brought from the basement. "Looks like you have been busy, Josh."

"Yeah, there is a lot here. Maybe we go at this a little at a time." Sarah nods in agreement.

Josh starts with the pictures and shell casings he found at the laydown yard the day after the murder. He walks her through the pictures he took of the trail leading to the east, the small clearing just inside the tree line, and the farm road along the eastern edge of the woods. He tells her what he thinks happened: that two men in a vehicle drove up that farm road the passenger got out, stood in the clearing until he thought he could move in, and attacked Roger.

Sarah questions, "What makes you think that person came out of the woods to shoot Roger?"

Josh grabs the small baggie that holds the three shell casings he found and holds them up for Sarah to see. "I found these with my metal detector in the pathway I showed you in those pictures." He takes one of the first photos he took in the bucket truck and points out the location where he found the casings. "Somehow that person got really close to Roger."

Sarah asks, "Do you think Roger saw the man?"

Josh hesitates. "Well, Sarah, I'm not exactly sure. I can tell you that one of my guys had to go back to the yard to get some material about midmorning and saw Josh just before he left. He told me that Roger appeared to be looking at something in the woods…with a gun in his hand!"

A wide-eyed Sarah exclaims, "What are you trying to say, Josh? That Roger was trying to defend himself? Is this guy pretty reliable?"

"Sarah, I'm not sure what his actions mean. Chopper is one of my most reliable guys, and he only observed what he told me for just a minute or so. He didn't hang around because he probably thought Roger had things under control. Plus, he had to get back to the job with the material. I am convinced that witnessing a murder was not on Chopper's radar that day." Josh hesitates a moment and then continues, "So was Roger pointing a gun at his killer? I don't know for sure, Sarah. I wish I did."

At this point, Sarah's eyes are welling up with tears and she is looking down at the table, shaking her head. Marsha gets up and moves in behind Sarah and hugs her. After a long moment, Marsha looks up at Josh and asks, "Maybe we should talk about what you found in the walls."

Josh nods. "Yeah, sure. I showed you everything that I had about what happened at the yard anyway. I wish I had more information to give you."

Regaining her composure, Sarah looks at Josh. "Well, that is a whole lot that I didn't know before. I assume the cops figured this out too."

Josh shakes his head. "No. When they came out to the yard to process the scene. They stayed close to the truck and did not venture out away from it, which is where I found the footsteps and the shell casings. They took pictures of the truck and around the truck, which they impounded as well. So no, they don't have any of this because they didn't think it was worthwhile to get!"

Sarah senses Josh's anger toward the police and talks calmly, "Josh, the police must have this information if we want Roger's killer caught. You can't just hang on to it. Right?"

Josh shows a flash of anger. "Oh, so I'm supposed to just hand it over to 'Defective' Halvorsen? What, so he can screw that up too? He probably came to the conclusion that I did it and arrest me and throw me in jail." He is now shaking his head. "He can't seem to find his butt with both hands, so why do you think he can solve this?"

Marsha, this time, tries to calm him, saying, "Josh, we need to get this information to them or maybe to the DCI. But we have to get all this to someone if we want justice for Roger."

Sarah, now looking at Marsha, asks, "What is a DCI?"

Josh explains, "It is the Department of Criminal Investigation. It's the state's version of the FBI, but only has jurisdiction in Wisconsin. I like that approach better, and I'll tell them exactly why I went to them and not the county sheriff!"

"So tell me about the envelopes," Sarah replies.

"Well, there isn't a lot to tell. They contain high-level drawings and some notes on equipment that scans cargo containers in different parts of the world. I don't know the name of the company that made this stuff, but I'm assuming Roger worked for them between the Navy and Badger Power. The installations were in Israel, South Korea, Kazakhstan, Kuwait, and Morocco."

Sarah exclaims, "I wasn't even aware Roger had been to any of those countries!"

"At each installation, other than Kuwait, there were problems with the local crime element interfering with the project since this equipment would put a crimp on their business. There were no details of what the problems were or what was done about the problems they faced. They had to leave Morocco prematurely due to the issues they ran into. Marsha and I concluded that there is nothing in these"—pointing to the envelopes—"that is worth stealing."

"That's why I think the juicy stuff is in those." Marsha points to the flash drives.

Sarah looks confused. "Wait a minute! Who is wanting to steal this information?"

Marsha says, "Most likely the guys in the black SUV. They have been following Josh around."

Sarah now turns her attention to Josh with her eyebrows raised. "You are being followed? Why?"

"I guess I've been followed. One of my men spotted the SUV parked across the laydown yard Roger was murdered in. It was spotted again today at the cemetery, which was the cause of the commotion you heard. The same lineman saw them, and when the SUV went to leave, he tried to intercept it and got his windshield shot up for his effort. The same guy who saw Roger in the yard that day also saw the black SUV parked along the county road."

Sarah is clearly disturbed by this. "Do you think they were involved in Roger's murder?"

"No, because they were parked on the west side of the yard and he was murdered on the east side. My guess is that there are two separate groups at work here."

"But you didn't answer my question of why. Why would they follow you and not Roger? Why do you think those in the black SUV are wanting something from us?"

"I think at first they were following Roger. After his murder, they hang around and probably saw me take the envelopes out of your house. Then they started following me and biding their time to snatch the information."

Sarah turns to Marsha. "Earlier you said I may be in danger, but I think it's you guys who are in danger. More the reason to get all this to the authorities, Josh."

Josh nods. "Well, I have to tell you, Sarah. Going through all this material and learning things about Roger that I never knew, I question if I really knew him. If you asked me if I knew him well a few weeks ago, I would have said yes, I did. But now? I don't think I can make that same claim."

Sarah nods. "I'm in the same boat, Josh. But it's worse for me. I was his wife! It's like he led a double life, keeping them separate. But why?"

"Perhaps he was protecting you and us. The less we knew, the better. You know, ignorance is bliss," Marsha ponders.

Sarah gets out of her chair and walks around the kitchen, trying to wrap her head around everything that has been said tonight. She stops walking, looks at the Bishops, and says, "Why did Roger even bring all this home and hide it like he did? I mean, if he didn't bring that stuff home, he might still be alive."

Marsha responds, "We have a theory about that. On the surface, it would seem that Roger stole the information to sell to the highest bidder. The thing is, no matter what he has done, that is not in his character. We think that he found out that a coworker was going to sell the information, and Roger stole it before the other guy sold it. That's why he hid the items like he did—in really out-of-the-way places most people wouldn't look."

Josh adds, "And it must have taken someone a long time to figure out where the information went."

113

Sarah announces, "Well, I guess it's now my turn to play show-and-tell." She walks over to where her purse is sitting and takes a couple of items out.

As she does this, Josh asks, "What do you mean that it is your turn for show-and-tell?"

Sarah returns to the table and sits down. She looks at Marsha and Josh and says, "When I was looking through Roger's suits to pick one out to be buried in, I went through the pockets. I found these in the suit I took to the funeral home." She puts the two items into Josh's hands.

Josh stares at what is now in his hands. The first was another old clunky-looking flash drive, and the other was a piece of paper. The paper read, *We know who you are and what you did, and it's time to die!*

CHAPTER 26

Storm Warning

The black SUV is at both the wake and the funeral, and the Triad men did not come to take pictures like the cop parked in front of them a few car lengths ahead of them. They are watching him too although they are not concerned about him. The detective does not notice them at all, which is fine, one last thing to worry about. Both Chinese operatives have been careful about not being noticed by the Bishops or getting ahead of themselves, so they made sure the correct items are taken from them. All this has taken time, and hopefully their employer won't be impatient with them.

They know there would be a conversation between Bishop and the Simmons woman about what he found out. This was intelligence they gathered from their listening devices in the Bishop house when Josh was talking to his wife. They bring along a collapsible hyperbolic dish that captures conversations from a distance, thinking Josh would have a conversation with the Simmons woman at some point. If so, they would learn more about what he found out from the documents in the envelopes they thought contain the information their employer wanted.

After the funeral service, they notice that everyone is getting in their cars. There would be no conversation between Bishop and Simmons at this point. They leave quickly to go to the cemetery to observe and listen there. They know where the cemetery is, thanks to the death notice on the local newspaper's website and Google Maps. They situate themselves toward the back of the cemetery, far enough away as not to raise suspicion and close enough to hear any conversations. They then wait for the rest of the people to show up. They are surprised to see armed soldiers at the cemetery. The driver thinks they may have been made, but the soldiers are not paying any attention to them. Nonetheless, they keep their weapons handy in case they need them to get away.

Once the graveside service is completed, the two Chinese operatives guess they witnessed an American military funeral. The operative in the passenger seat is using his binoculars to watch the crowd, specifically Josh and Sarah. Then he notices something that disturbed him. Through the binoculars, he sees two men looking at him, and one of them is the man from the laydown yard they encountered before. The man in the passenger side tells the driver, who then starts the car and asks if they have been made. The other operative, still using the binoculars, observes the two men are now talking to Bishop, who glances in the direction of the black SUV. He responds to the driver they've been made and it's time to leave.

The driver notices that the entrance and exit for the cemetery is congested with people leaving. There was a police officer directing traffic, but at the moment, he could not make a speedy getaway. So he scans along the cemetery that parallels the street, looking for somewhere to exit. As he does this, he notices a car moving very fast toward him from the left. He guns the accelerator to make sure the other car doesn't broadside him. The car misses but gets in right behind him and the driver pushes the SUV faster to put some space between him and Tagger while still looking for a way out. The driver exchanges glances with his passenger and shouts, "Do it!"

The man in the passenger seat knows exactly what he meant. In one motion, he grabs his handgun and turns his body to the right as he presses the button to roll down the window; he does his best to aim the gun at the passenger side of the pursuing car. He holds his breath and fires the gun; immediately the windshield explodes from the bullet slamming into it. Then Tagger's car immediately stops just as the driver finds a flat spot to exit onto the street. The passenger returns to a sitting position and puts the safety on his weapon just as the driver clears the cemetery and makes a hard right onto the street, squealing the tires in the process. At the next intersection, the operative driving turns left, and as he does so, he notices the police car from the cemetery beginning to chase them.

In order to shake off the cop, they turn right at the next intersection and then make a few serpentine turns before making for the entrance to the interstate. The driver thinks he has lost the police car. He gets onto the interstate heading north until the next exit five miles away. He exits the interstate and, using the overpass, crosses over to the other side and reenters going south. He does not see the police car or other police cars driving north and assumes that the chase is over. His plan now is to drive to the airport in Madison where he will exchange vehicles.

After transferring items from the back of the SUV to the trunk of their new white four-door sedan, and they return to their hotel room at the hotel in Portage, where they will check out and find another hotel, making sure to use a different set of names. After checking out, they make reservations at a hotel south of Portage where I-90/I-94 splits with I-39. The driver suggested this location since it gives them more flexibility to go in any direction they need to quickly.

As they get settled in, their employer calls them, wanting to know the status of their mission. They speak in Mandarin over a secure satellite phone. The operative who sits in the passenger seat reported that the target, Roger Simmons, was killed by others and that the suspected material is no longer in the Simmons home. He explains another party had removed it and is now at their home. They have bugged it and have listened in to conversations to determine whether they have the wanted material or not. He also relayed to the employer they had searched the home but could not find the material. Their plan was to verify they did indeed have the information requested and they would enter the home with the occupants inside, coerce them to give them the material, and then kill all of them.

The employer shows his impatience by telling them they need to complete their mission sooner than later. He adds that, above all, their activity needs to remain secret and if anyone knew they were operating in the United States, there would be severe consequences. He also suggests they not use their guns when dispatching those in the house for fear of others hearing the shots and calling the authorities.

CHAPTER 27

Handoff

Louise Anderson, the investigator from the Wisconsin attorney general monitoring Waushara County, contacted the Waushara County district attorney's office and made inquiries as to what progress has there been made on the Simmons case. They indicated that other than obtaining a few warrants, nothing more has been done. Louise called the Waushara County sheriff's office and spoke with Detective Halvorsen, who indicated there is little activity on the case until new information becomes available. She collects this information and has a feeling they are not spending much time on this or at least the case needs some additional horsepower. She adds this observation to her report to the AG, along with the information provided. As a result, the attorney general, feeling the same way Louise did, requested a teleconference with the district attorney, the sheriff, and the detective investigating the case the next day.

The teleconference begins with the attorney general clearly in control. He requests an update on the investigation from the detective, hoping there is some progress. If there isn't any, then he will find resources to kick-start the investigation.

"It appears the deceased was murdered in broad daylight. We are assuming he was surprised by his killer. Autopsy reports the victim was shot three times and then stabbed. There is nothing we found that tells us where the killer came from or where he went. We found a person of interest who vanished the day of the murder and executed a search warrant for the suspect's apartment. The search yielded nothing to help us, and the BOLO sent out has not yielded anything either. The name has not come up on any manifest or flight list, and no one with that name has rented a car either," reports Halvorsen.

The attorney general asks, "Were there any other potential suspects you investigated? Any witnesses?"

The detective responds, "Yes, I followed a lead about a beef someone had with him from one of the contractors his company works with, but that came up empty in that he had an alibi. I also interviewed the person who found the deceased and he had an alibi as well. I also did a deeper dive on the victim and couldn't come up with anything worthwhile other than he was an officer in the Navy."

The AG says in an exasperated tone, "So you basically have nothing at this point?"

Halvorsen responds, "I wouldn't say nothing. Just no solid leads right now."

Louise interrupts, "Detective Halvorsen, did you just say the victim was a naval officer?"

Everyone could hear him going through the pages of his notes. "Yes, he was a lieutenant for five years and served on a submarine."

Louise says to the AG, "Sir, the murder of a naval officer, wouldn't this be within the jurisdiction of the Naval Criminal Investigative Service?"

Sheriff Cantor protests, "We are leading the charge on this investigation!"

AG retorts, "No, you really are not leading anything with just one investigator. Louise, you make a good point. I will have to look into this. Let's reconvene at 4:00 PM." With that, everyone clicks off the call.

Everyone reconvenes at the appointed time, again with the AG in control of the meeting. Cantor has a bad feeling he is going to lose this one. The AG conveys his findings, "I talked with the US attorney's office and with the director of the Naval Criminal Investigative Service. They both tell me that this should be a federal case and the Navy should take over the investigation. I also agree with the assessment. The director of NCIS did not like how this one smells, his words not mine. The feeling is that someone targeted a Navy officer, from an attack submarine no less, and could be a result of some form of espionage. He is assigning this case to his Office of Special Projects, or OSP, out of DC."

NCIS's Office of Special Projects handles special cases involving espionage, counterintelligence, and terrorism involving the US Navy. They operate worldwide and utilize the resources from the NCIS field offices, the cyber unit, and the REACT (or Regional Enforcement Action Capability Team) tactical unit.

"Sheriff Cantor, expect two agents to show up on your doorstep tomorrow, and I expect one hundred percent cooperation from your office! Got it?" barks the AG.

Cantor responds quietly, "Got it, sir."

Within the hour of the director's decision to take over this case, the assistant director over the OSP, Adam Brandon, makes a call to the special agent in charge, or SAC, of the Washington, DC, OSP. The SAC is William Hawkins, or as everyone calls him, Hawk, who has been with the NCIS for over twenty-five years. He is a tall, thin man with a shock of red hair and tortoise shell glasses perpetually perched on the end of his nose. He picks up the ringing phone and, with his gravelly voice, answers, "Hawk here."

"Hawk, it's Brandon. How are things with you?"

Hawk responds, "Always living the dream, man. How may I help you today?" cutting off the chitchat.

"Hawk, the director has made me aware of a case we are picking up involving the death of a submariner officer. We are giving this one a high priority since it may involve espionage. The director even requested a couple of your agents to take the case."

Hawk leans forward in his chair. "Which ones?"

The assistant director responds, "He wants Tuganov and Dempsay. What are they currently working on?"

"They are currently between cases, so I have them working a cold case."

"Okay, put the cold case back into the refrigerator and get them going on this one. I'm sending you an e-mail with what we currently know and when they will need to be on a plane today to Madison, Wisconsin." Hawk hangs up after his conversation with the assistant director.

Hawk looks over the information in the e-mail sent to him, raising his eyebrows as he reads. Next, he calls in Tuganov and Dempsay into his office where they make their way from their small bullpen area. Sitting in the chairs across from Hawk's desk, they greet him.

Hawk, to the point, says, "Look, I took a call from the assistant director a few minutes ago, and you have been requested to take a new case. It is a murdered submariner, a former lieutenant, Roger Simmons."

"Requested by who?" questions Dempsay.

Hawk responds, "By the director himself!" Dempsay and Tuganov exchange looks while Hawk adds, "You two need to get on a plane today and start the case tomorrow morning."

Tuganov asks, "Where are we going, Hawk? For how long?"

"You're flying to Madison, Wisconsin, and then driving to some Podunk county sheriff's office. You will be there until you crack the case," responds Hawk. He then fills them in with what he knows.

Tuganov ponders and replies, "Sounds like a professional hit, especially with the assailant appearing out of nowhere and exiting without a trace." The other two nod in response.

Hawk orders, "Now get going and call me tomorrow night with what you find out."

As Dempsay stands, she replies, "Copy that, boss."

Olivia Dempsay is a NCIS OSP senior field agent. She was born in Taiwan and was abandoned by her birth mother at the hospital. She was adopted by an American couple when she was very young and lived most of her life in New York City. Before NCIS, she was a gold shield detective with the New York City police department. Once making the jump to NCIS, she worked in the Asia field office for a few years, then transferred to OSP five years ago, where her investigative skills flourished and caught the attention of the higher-ups.

Her partner, Alexander Tuganov, is a NCIS OSP special agent who was born in Azerbaijan. Five years later, his family, which includes his father, mother, and younger sister, emigrated to the United States. After receiving his degree in criminal justice, Tuganov joined the FBI and worked in the Middle East field office for four years. In a joint FBI-NCIS operation in Hong Kong, he got the attention of William Hawkins, who recruited him to join NCIS, and he worked in the Asia field office before moving over to OSP three years ago. Both agents worked in the Asia field office, but she left to go to the OSP two years before Tuganov and recruited him to come work in the OSP.

Both agents make it to Madison later in the evening, landing at Truax Filed on a government flight, and go straight to the Concourse Hotel in downtown Madison. They fly on general aviation since there were no commercial flights to Madison until the next day. They set up a time to meet with the county investigator prior to going to the sheriff's office.

The next morning, they meet at six, Dempsay has her stuff together and is ready to go. Tuganov, on the other hand, is not ready to go and looks tired. He greets her, "Hey, how did you sleep?"

"A whole lot better than you. Didn't sleep last night? You look like hell. How come you are not ready to go, Toog?"

Because they have worked together for a long time, they know each other pretty well. Their skills complement each other and their insights are usually spot-on, and together they are a force to be reckoned with. Because of their close working relationship, they have created nicknames only they know about. Both nicknames come from shortening their last names—she is Demps and he is Toog.

"Demps, I was thinking about this case last night. If someone wanted the victim dead, why wait all this time to kill him? Did it take that long to find him? Or is the timing coincidental?"

"For crying out loud, Toog, not even the first day on the case and you're losing sleep over it. I think we'll get the information we want today after our meeting with the local detective."

"From what I've seen of what he's done so far, I highly doubt we're going to get anything of substance."

When they get to the sheriff's office, the reception is very cool. No courtesies are extended to them; after all, the sheriff agreed to be cooperative, but he wasn't told to be hospitable. They are led to a conference room, and Halvorsen enters with a file in his hand. Both agents introduce themselves and ask Halvorsen for a rundown of what he has found so far on the case. Halvorsen launches into the same summary he did the day before for the attorney general.

Dempsay asks, "What physical evidence did you find at the crime scene?"

"Not much," replies Halvorsen. "There was a lot of snow on the ground. We processed the truck that was at the scene and only found the victim's prints on the outside and inside, along with his loaded handgun in the console. The technicians did not see any tracks in the snow or any other weapon lying around."

Tuganov asks, "Didn't you find it odd that the deceased had a loaded weapon in his truck and not have fired it, given the circumstances?"

"That is why I thought he was surprised by his killer. Otherwise, he would have made a move for it," replies Halvorsen.

Tuganov presses, "But wasn't the passenger door found to be open, maybe suggesting he was going for it? Were there any prints on the gun?"

Halvorsen shakes his head. "The technicians found no prints on the gun. It was found fully loaded."

Dempsay interjects, "So it was wiped clean?"

Halvorsen shrugs. "I'm not sure of that actually." Dempsay and Tuganov share a knowing look between them.

"Detective, did you personally go to the crime scene and get a look around for yourself?" Dempsay says flatly.

Halvorsen responds, "No. That's why we have crime scene investigators. I trust them, and so I go and do other things like interviewing people like at the deceased's employer. That is where I got the information about an angry contractor and the address along with the make and model car of the person who disappeared." This elicit another glance between the agents.

Dempsay continues, "Is the body still in the morgue? Can we look at it?"

Halvorsen replies, "The body was turned over to the family and was buried two days ago. There are photos attached to the autopsy report."

Tuganov interrupts, "Do you have a working theory on how the shooting went down?"

Halvorsen shakes his head again. "No. There isn't much there to make one. Based upon the wounds, I would say that the perp shot the victim at a distance, then stabbed him to make sure the deed was done."

Dempsay concludes the interview, "Detective, I think we have all the information you can give us. I think we will leave now and get out of your hair. Can we keep this file?"

"Yes, I copied everything I had and placed it in there." Halvorsen points to the file.

Tuganov asks, "Can we take the weapon found in the victim's truck?"

"Yes, you can have the weapon, but you'll need to sign for it. Just give me a call if you need anything." He stands and shakes the agent's hands.

Dempsay replies, "Yes, we certainly will, and thank you for your time."

While Tuganov drives back to Madison, Dempsay looks through the rather thin file cataloging all that it contains. She notes to him that they aren't too welcome at the sheriff's office.

"What I don't get is that Halvorsen guy, how did he become a detective? He sure missed a lot of things."

"I agree. We don't have much to get started on, but we have had less."

"Demps, what bothers me right now is that we have a victim who had a gun in his truck, fully loaded and was wiped clean. Why would that gun be wiped clean?"

"Unless the killer handled it, But why would the killer handle it if he had his own gun?"

"Maybe the victim got off a shot or two, and for some reason, the killer wanted people to think that the gun was never fired, and he put in bullets to make it look like there was a full clip. He cleaned it and returned it to the center console of the truck."

"Toog, why would the killer go through the trouble of doing that?"

Tuganov turns his head away from the road and briefly makes eye contact with Dempsay. "That is what is bothering me. We should have forensics look at the bullets in the gun and see if there are any mismatched ones."

"Wouldn't they all be the same if he put in 9 mm bullets?"

"Unless the killer is from another part of the world where there are other bullet manufacturers!"

"Toogs, you're a genius!"

CHAPTER 28

Digest

Back at the hotel, they set up shop in Dempsay's room, splitting up the contents of the file and sit in the chairs in the room. He has the detective's notes and the crime scene investigator's report, and she takes the autopsy report. Both are quiet for a while as they absorb the material. She breaks the silence, "Toog, are there any notes there about how the body was found? The autopsy reports eludes to the detective telling the coroner that the body was found facedown."

Tuganov flips pages on the report and finally says, "Yes, it says here that according to the person who found the body, the victim was facedown when it was discovered. The person, a Josh Bishop, turned the body over to administer first aid."

"So if the stab wounds are delivered to the front of the body, as the coroner's report indicates, then how did he end up facedown?"

"Demps, what if he was standing when he was stabbed, then shot after he falls to the ground? Maybe the killer didn't want to make noise and used a knife, perhaps to get close to the victim and wanted to make sure the victim dies. He fires three shots into the victim who could still be alive to finish him off."

Tuganov abruptly stands up with his eyes wide-open. "Demps, what if the killer used the victim's gun to finish him because he didn't have one? What if the victim struggled and the killer didn't want to risk getting close to continue the stabbing and used the victim's gun?

But he would have to know where it is and how would he know that."

"Maybe he didn't have to. Maybe the victim was holding the gun or had it close to him."

The agents let that soak in for a long moment. Tuganov raises his eyebrows. "Demps, that is a very plausible theory."

She grabs a legal pad and begins to write and says, "We need to have our pathologist go over the autopsy report and pictures to see what they have to say about how the victim was killed. We also need to have the gun totally checked out. We need to go somewhere and have copies made of all this material and send it to the lab right away."

They got on the phone with the forensic supervisor to fill her in on what is coming her way and if she can spare the manpower to jump on it right away. The supervisor tells them she can have a pathologist look at the autopsy report right away, but the analysis of the gun can't happen for a few days since they are backed up right now. It's now 6:00 PM, and they give Hawk a call to let them know what they have.

After listening to what they found out, he says to them, "Well, it didn't take you two long to put a dent in this case. I can help on this end to push getting all the analysis done."

Dempsay explains, "Hawk, at this point, it is just a theory. We have nothing substantial yet to back it up."

"Yes, I know that, but I also know that your theories tend to pan out," agrees Hawk.

Tuganov asks, "Hawk, why is this case such a priority? Is there something we need to know?" Dempsay shoots him a look when he said that.

"To be honest, I don't know why the director is putting this case in the express lane. Let me look into that one. Oh, and, Tuganov, I wouldn't hold out on you two, so rest assured that you know what I know."

"Copy that, boss."

"Keep digging and keep me posted on progress," Hawk orders.

They hang up and Dempsay bores two holes into Tuganov with her stare. "What the heck was that? Hawk has always had our back."

"Demps, think about it. The director himself calls on us amid a large pool of agents to handle this case. So why us? I think there is more to this whole thing than meets the eye, and if that is the case, I want to know about it."

Dempsay squares off with her partner with her hands on her hips. "So you think you see a gunman on the grassy knoll now? Sometimes things can be taken at face value. Maybe they think we're good and want the best on the case. Or since we were working a cold case at the time, they chose us because we were available. Not everything done at our office has an ulterior motive."

Tuganov says, "Well, let's hope you're right, Miss Rose-Colored Glasses."

A little later, they decide to go out for dinner. The hotel's concierge suggests a local landmark, the Old Fashion, where anyone who comes to Madison has to go. So they walk to the restaurant and are seated in a booth. The waitress suggests they try the cheese curds, a specialty, since they are new in town and they never had them. They order those and their dinner. While they wait, Tuganov asks, "So who do we want to talk to first?"

"I think we should talk to the man that found him. He was the victim's friend and maybe detective first-class Halvorsen didn't ask the right questions." The part about detective first class was said sarcastically.

"I would like to know who made the trip all the way to Wisconsin to do this guy and why. Maybe we look for known felons traveling to the US."

"Well, right now that suspect pool is pretty big unless we can somehow narrow it down."

Their waitress brings food they selected. Dempsay went with a salad with salmon and beets while Tuganov went native, ordering a burger with cheddar cheese, bacon, and onion strings, a virtual mountain of a burger. She sits back and eyes the monster burger. "Really! Alex, you're going to kill yourself eating stuff like that!"

He smiles at her. "Ah, when in Rome…" He then attacks the plate of fried cheese curds. "Hey, these are spectacular! Try some." He looks up to Dempsay with a content smile on his face.

Dempsay reaches over and takes just one and puts it in her mouth like it was a spider or some gross bug. "This might be good if it wasn't fried!"

"Oh, come on, they're wonderful! They would be even better if they had bacon wrapped around them!"

She crosses her arms. "Men. I swear. If someone took a dog turd and deep-fried it and then wrapped bacon around it, you would consider it a delicacy."

At that, Tuganov looks upward as if he is contemplating this and says, "Well, maybe."

"Oh, you're disgusting!"

He laughs out loud at that comment. "Better lower your voice. I don't think the place would like you comparing the fried cheese curds to dog crap."

They spend the rest of the meal talking about their respective families. Tuganov asks, "So how is your mom doing?"

"Oh, she is doing okay for her age, complaining about getting old. Mostly she bugs me about hooking her up with some grandchildren, telling me my window is closing and you can't wait for the perfect man. I think she would be happy if I got knocked up by whoever just as long as I pop out a kid for her."

Tuganov chuckles. "Well, you could take out an ad in social media. I'm sure you would get some takers."

Dempsay shakes her head. "Oh yeah, that would be just great. Every weirdo and pervert would be calling me."

"Weirdos and perverts, sounds like a good start." At that, Tuganov starts laughing.

"Toog, you're not helping one bit and do not, I repeat, do not, call my mother about it. You'll give her ideas."

CHAPTER 29

Collaboration

Early the next morning, Dempsay is ready to hit the ground running and decides to call Josh Bishop to arrange a time for an interview. It's early in the morning, but she thinks he may be at work already. She dials the number that was in the case file and hopes it is correct. She gets the impression that she does not have the right number since no one picks up right away, but on the fifth ring, she hears the click that someone is answering the call.

"Bishop here," comes the greeting from Josh.

"Is this Josh Bishop?"

"Yes, it is. Who are you?"

"I'm Special Agent Dempsay with the Naval Criminal Investigative Service. We are taking over the investigation of the death of Roger Simmons. I apologize for calling so early, but I want to arrange a time that we can talk."

"It's not too early. When did you want to talk?"

"I would like to talk as soon as possible, if that is all right by you."

"Well, right now I'm a couple of miles from any road. Where are you calling from?"

"I and my partner are currently in Madison."

"Okay, well, let's meet at our trailer in the laydown yard. It will take you a good ninety minutes to get there from Madison. When we hang up, I will send you the coordinates for the meeting place."

"Coordinates? Isn't there an address?"

"No, where we are, there are no addresses. See you at nine o'clock."

He clicks off the call and finds one of the foremen working for him and informs him he needs to get back to the trailer for a meeting. He then gets into his work truck and makes his way back to the laydown yard.

Dempsay calls Tuganov and tells them they need to leave right away to talk to Bishop. They leave a few minutes later as she brings him up to speed and shows him the coordinates for the meeting in which he inquires, "Coordinates? What, are we meeting him in the middle of nowhere?"

"Yes, I guess we are. He did mention a trailer, so we have that going for us. How do you want to handle the questioning?"

"Since he talked to you on the phone, you should be the one asking him questions and I'll do my thing."

"Do your thing? You're not going to pace around and look agitated, are you?"

"Oh yeah, I'll try to rattle him. Hopefully he is more forthcoming than the detective was."

"You know, I hate it when you try and rattle someone. First of all, he's not a suspect, and secondly, you rattle me doing that."

"You sure he isn't a suspect? I don't want him to relax."

She responds exasperatedly, "Whatever!"

They arrive at the trailer and climb the stairs to the door. Josh opens the door. He introduces himself and she introduces herself, and Tuganov, who just looks at him without saying anything, show Josh both their credentials.

Josh offers, "Hey, you guys want some coffee?"

Dempsay replies, "No, we're good."

Josh then directs them to chairs in his office area, which only Dempsay sits down. Alex begins his pacing about, periodically looking out the window.

Tuganov breaks his silence in a snarky way as he is looking out the window. "So what is this place? It's in the middle of nowhere."

Josh responds flatly, "It's called a laydown yard, and it serves as a place to keep material and for linemen to park their vehicles and prep for work."

Tuganov turns away from the window and looks at Josh. "What kind of work do you and your linemen do?"

Josh responds, "We build high-voltage electrical lines."

Dempsay interrupts, "Is this were the murder occurred?" Tuganov resumes his pacing and looks out the window.

"Yes, it happened in the back of the yard."

Tuganov spins around. "So why are you still working here?"

Bishop responds with some annoyance in his voice, "We have been told we can use the front half of the yard, according to the sheriff. Soon, we will be moving out to a new yard."

Dempsay asks, "How are you going to remove your material and equipment from the rear of the yard?"

Bishop says, "I was told we would remove everything in the back half under the supervision of the sheriff's department."

Tuganov stops his pacing. "Well, that's not going to happen! The sheriff's department is no longer involved in this investigation," now pointing to Dempsay and himself. "We will be supervising anything you will be doing around the crime scene."

Josh responds to this new turn of events, "Okay, works for me. I will let you know the day before we get into that area."

She next asks Josh to walk through the day of the murder. Josh starts with the construction meeting in the trailer and the conversation he had with Roger before he left the yard in the morning. He then talks about what he saw when he came back to the yard, what drew him back to the back of the yard, and what he did to render first aid. Josh takes a good twenty to thirty minutes to describe everything without leaving out any details.

Tuganov interrupts, "Did you see a gun or knife when you were trying to give first aid?"

"No. It was dark, and I was concentrating on helping Roger, so I didn't purposely search for weapons."

"And you are sure Mr. Simmons was lying on his stomach when you found him, with his arms and legs outstretched?" asks Dempsay.

"Yes, I'm sure of it. I had to turn him over to render aid."

Tuganov inquires, "So there was nothing you found to indicate how Mr. Simmons died?"

"No, not that night, but I did the next day, in the daylight."

The agents look somewhat surprised and then Dempsay asks, "What exactly did you find the next day in the daylight?"

Josh shows them several blown-up photos, starting with the aerial shots he took while up on the bucket truck and the pictures he took on the farm road adjacent to the woods, pointing out the depression in the snow from the heat of the vehicle and the footprints from what would be the passenger side of that vehicle. He also points out that the vehicle is most likely a smaller SUV given the spacing and size of the tires.

Tuganov is looking intently over his partner's shoulder at the photos Josh provided. Then he asks Josh, "The one showing the small clearing in the woods, it looks like the killer was waiting for Simmons to show up."

Dempsay nods, "I agree," then asks Josh, "So you may not have noticed that spot without the aerial picture?"

"Yes. Once I saw a trail going off into the woods, I wanted to find out where it led, but I didn't want to obliterate the path with my own footprints, so I took pictures from above instead."

"You mentioned the county forensics people were out here that morning. Didn't they see the path?" asks Tuganov.

"They stayed close to the truck and only took pictures of the truck and right around it. They did not search beyond that point. So no, they wouldn't have seen the path in the snow or they didn't care about the path," Josh responds.

Agent Dempsay points to Josh's hand that holds the baggie. "What else did you find?"

"I found these with a metal detector." Josh holds up the plastic bag with the three shell casings. The two agents again show surprise.

Tuganov says, "Can I see those more closely?" He then takes the bag and looks at each casing individually without taking them out. "Dempsay, these are 9 mm and they are American made."

Dempsay turns to Josh and asks, "Where did you find these?"

Josh points to the first photo, "Right here," noting that it was in the path and a place between two steel pole sections.

"You still have the metal detector in your truck?" Tuganov asks.

Bishop, "Yes, I do."

Tuganov looks at Dempsay, then back to Josh. "Take us there."

They pile into Josh's work truck, and he drives them to where Roger's truck was located. Josh points out where the truck was and leads them to the path, which is currently covered in a few inches of snow, but the edges of it could be made out.

Tuganov asks Josh, "Show us where you found the shell casings."

Josh gets up on one the pole sections like he did that day and moves along it to where he believes he found them. "I make it a good ten feet from where Roger's truck was."

"Did you check around where the truck was?" asks Dempsay.

"Yes, but I didn't find anything."

Tuganov orders, "Check around where the truck was again. Now."

Josh goes to the truck and sets up his metal detector. He sweeps it around where the Simmons truck was located and then moves to where the body was located. After a few minutes of nothing, he gets a hit. The detector makes the double warbling noise Josh heard the day he found the other shell casings. He pinpoints the location, and Tuganov gets on his knees and starts to carefully move snow, digging down as he goes. Using his Pin Pointer, he indicates whatever made the noise is down farther. Then he says, "Don't forget we had a few more inches of snow since this happened."

Removing snow carefully, Tuganov continues to dig down farther. Using the Pin Pointer, Josh checks and it seems that whatever it is, is now out of the hole. After checking the last pile that Tuganov removed and Josh gets a hit on that pile. Tuganov produces a pair of latex gloves and puts them on his freezing fingers, and he takes out a small evidence bag out of another pocket. After carefully feeling for it, the first thing he pulls up is one shell casing, exactly like the others Josh found. He moves his hand around and grabs two more just like the first one. He puts all three in the evidence bag and triumphantly shows them to agent Dempsay.

"Wait a minute, that makes six 9 mm shell casings. Roger was shot only three times. So where did the other three end up?" Josh wonders aloud.

Tuganov is now looking toward the woods. "Good question. Were the trees checked for any slugs?"

"No, not that I know of. What are you saying? That Roger fired a gun at his assailant? Wait a minute..." Josh abruptly stops in his tracks and looks wide-eyed down at the snow.

Dempsay notices the change in Josh and instinctively moves her hand to the handle of her weapon. Tuganov, seeing what his partner just did, does the same and starts scanning his eyes around, looking for danger. Dempsay says, "Mr. Bishop, what's the matter?"

Still wide-eyed, he looks up at both agents. "Something one of my men said to me makes sense all of a sudden."

Both agents relax. Tuganov fixes his gaze on Josh and asks, "What did he say?"

"That Roger was pointing a gun at something in the woods."

Dempsay says, "All right, let's look at the trees and brush near the footprints. Mr. Bishop, could you scan the trees along the path with your small metal detector?"

They start making their way along the path, Josh on one side and the two agents on the other. Josh gets to the trees first and starts scanning the closer ones. The agents inspect the trees for anything that is embedded in them. At the fourth tree Josh scanned, he gets a hit and calls them over. He uses his knife and cuts away at the frozen bark. He cuts away enough to expose a bullet lodged in the west side of the tree. Tuganov produces another small evidence bag, and Josh frees the slug and puts into the bag. Josh and Agent Tuganov continue inspecting trees while agent Dempsay moves farther down the path, looking at those trees.

About halfway through the trees, Dempsay sees something that makes her stop. She calls out to Tuganov, "Get over here. I've got something."

While Josh continues to scan trees for bullets, Tuganov hustles over to her. "What do you have?"

Agent Dempsay points to a lower branch of a tree. "I found dried blood."

Tuganov confirms her find and calls out to Josh, "We need to use your knife a minute. Do you happen to have any large plastic bags in your truck?"

"I think so. Let me check." Josh heads back to his truck and starts going through the side compartments on the bed of the truck. He finds a pair of loppers but still hasn't found any big bags. He just remembers there is a whole roll of big plastic bags in the parts trailer. He yells to the agents that he has what they want but needs to go get them. As he gets into his truck to retrieve the bags, the two agents continue their search along the path.

Josh returns with the bags and takes three, grabs the loppers, and meets the agents farther into the trees. Agent Tuganov tells Josh that they found two branches with dried blood on them, and they think they found another slug in another tree. Dempsay grabs the loppers from Josh and goes to the first tree, cutting the branch off just above where the blood is, while Tuganov holds the bag open. They repeat the same process at the other bloodied branch. Josh uses his knife to extract the slug they found in another tree and gives it to Tuganov.

After they collected the evidence, Agent Dempsay says, "Well, we just accounted for two of the shell casings we found." Looking at Tuganov, she continues, "And you know what that means."

Tuganov responds, "Yeah, we have a wounded murderer out there somewhere."

CHAPTER 30

More Questions Than Answers

The trio return to Josh's office. Tuganov calls the forensics supervisor to tell her to have the technician carefully inspect the magazine first before test-firing the gun. She asks why, and he tells her he thinks there are mismatch bullets in the magazine. Also, that he will be sending her two slugs they dug out of a tree and blood evidence to be processed.

Dempsay asks Josh if he knew Roger owned a Sig Sauer. Josh nods and tells her that he has seen the gun before.

She asks, "Did he know how to use a gun after you two met?"

"No, he had guns prior to us meeting, and after the things I've learned lately, I'm not surprised."

Dempsay looks at Josh. "And what things would that be?"

Josh pulls out all the envelopes, the group picture, and the flash drives from his backpack and sets them on his desk. Josh looks at both agents and says, "I think these items go toward the why instead of the how." He walks them through how he found all the items.

The first thing he hands them is the photograph of Roger and the other men. Josh points out Roger and tells them he does not recognize anyone else. "I put the age of the picture at fifteen to twenty years." The agents study the picture closely and conclude the men in the picture are part of a paramilitary group.

"I think at some point after the Navy but before Badger Power, Roger worked for a company that supplied security equipment to other countries," says Josh. "I'm not sure exactly when or for how long."

He then tells them each envelope represents an installation in a different country. He shows them the contents of one or two since there are similar papers in in each envelope. The agents look at each document together but say nothing. Agent Tuganov closely inspects the red tape on the envelopes and raises an eyebrow but, again, says nothing.

Agent Dempsay asks, "You mentioned a gun hidden in the basement. What kind was it, and where is it now?"

"It was a Smith and Wesson snub nose .38, fully loaded. It hadn't been touched in a long time, and I doubt it would fire given the thick layer of dust on it. Sarah Simmons asked to keep it, so I cleaned it for her, and she has it in the house somewhere," comes Josh's response.

Now turning her attention to the flash drives, she asks, "What can you tell me about these?"

Josh tells the agents he thinks they are older based on their clunky look and small memory capacity. He also tells them he tried to see what was on them, but they are password protected.

Dempsay asks, "What kind of passwords did you try?"

"I tried Roger's birthday, his wife's and children's birthdays, and variations of his first and last names. Nothing worked. I think there is something on these that others want, and because of these, I'm being followed."

Tuganov holds out his hand to stop Josh. "You say you're being followed? By who?"

"That's a good question. I'm not sure who they are, but they've shown up where I'm at a couple of times that I know of. Both times they were in a black SUV, just like the one you're driving now."

"Do you know when they started following you?" asks Dempsay.

Josh shakes his head. "I'm not sure about that either. There were two occasions that one of my guys pointed it out to me. Both occasions were after I took these things out of Roger's house. He could give better answers than I can since he has seen them, and they shot at him."

"Shot at him!" Tuganov repeats. "Why did they shoot at him?"

"He was chasing them at the cemetery after the service. I think he would have caught them if they didn't shoot at him."

"Was he injured at all?" Dempsay asks.

"No, they just shot out his windshield. That really pissed him off, especially when the insurance company wouldn't pay for a new one. I can bring him in along with another guy who may have seen Roger out back before he was killed."

Both agents are amazed this interview is yielding so much information. Tuganov speaks up, "Bring them both in. We would really like to talk to them."

Josh grabs his walkie and gets ahold of one of the foremen, telling him to send Tagger and Chopper to the trailer. When he gets off the radio, he tells the agents, "It's going to be about half an hour before they show up."

Tuganov asks, "Why did you use a radio? Why didn't you just call them on your cell phone?"

Josh chuckles. "The cell service around here is spotty at best and downright nonexistent most of the time. Two-way radios are more reliable out here."

Agent Tuganov gets up and starts pacing around, and Dempsay sees that Josh is annoyed by this. She tells him that he does his best thinking standing or walking. Tuganov walks around some more in the larger room and then comes back to Josh and leans down. "So why didn't you take all this"—he points to the items Josh showed them—"to the sheriff's office?"

Josh leans back in his chair and says, "The detective on the case is a complete moron and wouldn't have a clue in what to make of all this. It would be a waste of time."

Dempsay notices that Josh is getting agitated but asks, "So why is it in a backpack?"

"After work today, I was going to take it to the DCI office in Madison. I figure they would know how to make good use of it all. Since you two are here, I'm giving it to you instead."

Tuganov starts pacing again and stops by the window. He has a clear view of the driveway into the yard. He also notices a white car parked across the way from the entrance. Still looking at the car, he asks, "So when the black SUV was here, where were they at?"

Josh turns around to look at him. "They were parked across the way from the entrance to the yard."

Tuganov turns to the other two and motions with his head. "Like this white car out there?" Both meet him at the window, and they could see a white four-door sedan parked across the road facing the yard.

"Yeah, that would be the spot," Josh responds. "I just wonder if my friends got themselves a different vehicle after the incident in the cemetery. Would make sense to me."

Tuganov says to Dempsay, "We should check them out when we leave. They would be less apt to bolt instead of storming out of here and rushing them. They would be down the road in a hurry." Dempsay agrees with him.

As they sit back down, Dempsay asks, "Josh, is there anything else you can tell us that you haven't told us already?"

"Yes, actually there is. Since the morning of Roger's murder up until now, there is someone that has just vanished. His name is Ralph Peterson, and he is an engineer that works with Roger and me. I tried calling him and calling him without out any response. I even talked to someone who sits next to him in the office, and she said it was as if he dropped off the planet."

Tuganov asks, "What do you think of that? Did he have a habit of going off the grid?"

"It's not normal for him. I could reach him whenever I called him, even after hours." After pausing to think about the first question, Josh replies, "I don't think it's a coincidence that he left the day Roger was murdered. As much as I hate to admit it, I think he had something to do with Roger's killing. He may or may not be the killer, but he's involved somehow."

Tuganov asks, "Why do you say he might not be the killer? Is there something else you know that rules him out?"

Josh thinks on this, trying to frame his words. "It's just a feeling I have. I never saw him display aggression or even anger, so I'm thinking he didn't have it in him to kill someone in cold blood."

Tuganov asks, "You have taken the time to collect all this evidence. Do you have a theory of what happened?"

Josh thinks a moment. "I think that two people in a small SUV drove up on that farm lane. Now they had to have intel from someone that Roger was going to be in that part of the yard that morning. Maybe that intel came from Ralph Peterson. The person on the passenger side gets out, walks into the wood, gets close enough to see where Roger is, and they wait for their opportunity. At some point, Roger sees or hears the person in the woods. Then the person in the woods comes out and maybe they struggle. I dunno. But in the end, the person in the woods kills Roger, and he escapes the way they came in."

Josh looks down, and the conversation stops at this point.

During the quiet that ensued, Josh's phone chirps and he looks at the caller ID. It's Tagger. He gets up and tells the agents he must take this call. Walking into the other part of the trailer, he answers the phone, "Hey, Tagger, what's up? Are you here yet?"

"Yes'n, I am, but is you okay? Dat dang black SUV is parked right outside the trailer! Do we need ta go in guns ablazin'?"

"Tagger, no. Everything is fine. There are two federal agents here and we have been talking about Roger's murder. They want to talk to you about the guys that you had a run in with. So come on in."

"You know they're back! Makes me want ta shoot out thar windshield and see how dey like it. They must be thinkin' we're stupid. Oh we'll get a white car and dey won't know it's us who are tryin' to kill 'em. It's insulting!"

"Tagger, we saw them. The agents are going to do something about it when they leave so your buddies don't bolt. Is Chopper with you?"

"Yeah. Gif, ya sure it's safe to go in thar?"

"Yes, it is and, Tagger, try to relax."

Tagger and Chopper enter the office area of the trailer, and Josh greets them. "Guys, there are two people I need you to meet. This is Special Agent Dempsay and Special Agent Tuganov." To the agents, he says, "This is Earl Watson," gesturing to Tagger, "and this is Jim Jacobson," gesturing to Chopper. Turning to his men, he announces, "These agents are investigating Roger's death, so tell them all that you know." The crewmen take two of the chairs, Dempsay takes the third, Josh sits on the edge of his desk, and Tuganov resumes his pacing.

Both agents show their credentials to Tagger and Chopper. Tagger scrutinizes both credentials for several seconds and announces that they look legitimate. Then he asks, "So why's y'all all a sudden got yer fingers in dis? It's been a month since dis happened."

Agent Dempsay answers, "We are involved because the victim was a naval officer and were made aware of this two days ago."

Tagger is astonished. "Two days ago. Jesus, Mary, and Joseph, y'all are takin' yer sweet time on dis! Especially somethin' dis big. I wooda figured y'all been involved a lot sooner, especially with dose idiots out dere, who by the way, shot at me." The last is said while he emphatically points to himself.

Dempsay ignores the comment and asks, "Have you seen the people in the white car?"

"Yep. I saw 'em twice before and just now when we pulled up."

Dempsay asks, "What do they look like?"

"They look like you." Leaning in a little closer, he asks, "Why is he"—pointing his thumb toward Agent Tuganov who has been pacing around since they got in the trailer—"actin' like a long-tailed cat in a room full of rockin' chairs?" responds Tagger.

Ignoring his question, Dempsay asks, "What do you mean they look like me?"

"Dey look Asian. Dey look more like you den yer partner. So I'm thinkin' they're East Asian, probably Chinese. Real serious-lookin' dudes ifin' you ask me."

The two agents share a look and the look on Tuganov's face tells Dempsay that this case has just gotten more complicated.

Tagger turns to Josh now. "Hey, Gif, der's somethin' I wanted ta tell you about dem guys."

Josh says, "Yeah, what is it?"

"When dat one dude leaned out ta shoot me, I saw 'em and da gun. Saw both clear as day. The gun got me confused, never seen anythin' like it before." Now looking at Agent Dempsay, he continues, "I've seen plenty of diff'rent guns but not like dat."

Josh asks, "Can you describe it, maybe compare it to a Glock?"

Tagger pauses a moment to think. "It was shorter den a Glock, from end of da barrel to da edge of da stock. Da grip was longer too, maybe ta hold a bigger clip. Da trigger was bigger, which is good if you were wearin' gloves. Da barrel wasn't as long, kinda reminds me of an old German Luger."

Agent Tuganov stops his pacing, knowing Tagger just described a Chinese-made QSB handgun. This confirms their unstated assumption that the Chinese government is involved since they are the only known entity that carries that weapon.

Dempsay looks at Tagger. "You said you got a good look at the man who shot at you. Could you pick him out in a photo array?"

"Oh yeah. I can do dat. Jist let me know when yer ready."

Tuganov resumes his pacing and Agent Dempsay then turns her attention to Chopper. "Mr. Jacobson, Mr. Bishop told us that you saw the victim pointing a weapon into the woods the morning of the murder. Is that true?"

Chopper looks at Agent Dempsay. "Yes, but I could not see what he was pointing the gun at."

Dempsay questions, "Did you see the weapon he was holding? Did you hear shots? Did he say anything?"

"From what I saw, it looked like a Sig Sauer, but I could be wrong since I was quite a way away from him. I didn't hear any shots or any conversation."

Tuganov stops and asks a question to Chopper, "What time did you see all this?"

"Well, it was midmorning, maybe ten or ten thirty. I needed to come back and get some materials we needed that we forgot to take with us to the work area."

Tuganov adds, "Why didn't you hang around?"

"Well, I needed to get back to the work area. Otherwise, people would be waiting on material. I really didn't think Roger was in danger since he drew his weapon. Besides, I just thought he was shooting at an animal."

The interview concludes with Josh gathering up the items that he had and puts them back into the backpack and hands it over to agent Tuganov. He helps the agents collect items they found this morning and get them into their car. The agents say goodbye and tell Josh to call them if there is anything else he remembers or finds. With that, Josh, Tagger, and Chopper get into Josh's truck and head back to work.

CHAPTER 31

Chase

The agents get into their car and wait for Bishop to leave to see what the guys in the white car will do. When Bishop pulls out and heads north, the white car does not follow them. So much for following them as they follow Bishop's truck. Tuganov thinks it's time for a little offense. He says to Dempsay, "When we get to the road, stop while we get a good look at them. I'll take a couple of pictures with my phone. Then just go straight across and let's see what they do." At this, he unholsters his weapon.

Dempsay nods her head and puts the car in reverse to turn around to leave. When she gets to the road, they are directly across from the white car. Initially, Dempsay looks both ways as if she is going to turn. Meanwhile, Tuganov is looking straight at them and raises his phone and snaps off a few pictures of the men in the car. This alarms the two men in the white car to the point the driver starts the car and puts it in gear. Before the driver can move the car, Dempsay shoots across the road right at them. Tuganov raises his weapon and readies it while rolling down his window.

Before the black SUV reaches their side of the road, the man in the passenger seat leans out of the white car and fires a shot at the SUV's windshield, shattering it into a mass of spiderwebs. The shot then strikes the rear window, shattering it as well, as it exits the SUV. At the same time, the driver of the white car makes a quick right turn onto the county highway, heading south, and avoids colliding with the agents. Tuganov returns fire, his shot entering the white car through the driver's side rear window and exiting through the windshield on the passenger's side, nearly hitting the man in the passenger seat. It also makes it nearly impossible to see out the right half of the windshield. Once on the road, the driver punches the accelerator and gets onto the interstate to put some distance between them and the agents in the black SUV.

The agents are unable to see out the windshield, so they work together and use their legs to kick out the windshield. After a few minutes of kicking, they manage to fold the windshield down so Dempsay can see the road. She accelerates and works her way to the interstate, thinking it would be the easiest way to escape at high speed. They see the back end of a speeding white car as it tops a hill to the south. Dempsay gets on the interstate and heads south in pursuit of the white car going in excess of a hundred miles an hour. It isn't long at all until the agents see the white car in front of them.

As both vehicles speed past a rest area, they do not notice a state trooper on the ramp. As the white car passes him, his radar clocks them at 93 and then, shortly after that, a black SUV clocking in at 102. As they pass, he notices the windshield is damaged on the black SUV and begins to pursue them, with full lights and sirens. He calls it in and requests backup. The dispatcher comes back to him, indicating county sheriff's officers from Waushara, Columbia, and Dane counties are responding to the situation south of his position.

It isn't long for the trooper to catch up to the two agents in the black SUV. Through his PA, he is telling them to pull over. Dempsay ignores this and gooses the gas pedal. In the meantime, county sheriff's deputies are clearing traffic off the interstate in front of the speeding cars. Seeing this, the driver of the white car looks for an opportunity to get off the interstate with other cars; he slows down and gets himself between three semitrucks—one behind, one in front, and the third alongside him. By doing this, they can exit the interstate with traffic without being noticed. They head west at the posted speed and escape being captured.

The trooper, seeing the black SUV is speeding up, radios that he going to attempt a PIT, or pursuit intervention technique, maneuver to stop this vehicle. The trooper knows at these speeds this is a risky proposition, causing injury to the people in the black SUV or himself. He rationalizes that this is the only way to stop them before they cause a major accident. He lines up his passenger-side front end with the black SUV's driver's side rear end and punches the gas pedal to the floor while bracing for impact. He surges ahead and slams into the left rear corner of the black SUV, causing it to immediately turn sideways, almost flipping it. It slides sideways down the left shoulder. Once it hits the dirt in the median, the black SUV spins completely around and now faces forward. Dempsay tries to gun the engine but finds that it quit. Before she can try to restart the vehicle, they are surrounded by deputies with their guns drawn, barking commands at them.

CHAPTER 32

Assumptions Unravel

Both agents are back at the hotel, bent over their respective laptops, filling out paperwork. There is no conversation between the two other than the occasional curse words as they progress through their reports. They are humbled by the fact that they, for a short time, are on the other side of the gun, being treated like criminals. Being the senior field agent and driver of the vehicle, Dempsay is filing a report detailing what precipitated the chase and why it ended the way it did with a totaled rental car, including what led to Tuganov's actions. He is filling out a form regarding the discharge of a weapon in public, even if he did not fire first. They were instructed by Hawk, in no uncertain terms, to get these filled out right away.

Upon receiving the reports, Hawk looks them over. Satisfied, he calls the agents. He admonishes them again for not requesting backup before trying to engage the Chinese. "What the hell were you thinking, going up against Chinese operatives by yourselves?" Not giving them time to answer, he continues, "You two really stepped in it this time. On the other hand, it sounds like you had a productive day with the case. You got yourselves a regular unicorn with this Bishop guy. I want a call later today on progress, understood?" Without allowing them to answer, he adds, "By the way I am sending up another OSP team. This case seems to be expanding in unexpected ways. Dempsay, you're in charge of the investigation." Hawk terminates the call abruptly.

Tuganov crosses his arms and, using a sarcastic tone, says, "Well, that went swimmingly."

Olivia counters with a gloomy face, not catching his sarcasm. "No. It didn't. We're in the friggin' doghouse. We were basically told that we can't handle this investigation on our own."

"Well, why don't we send off the latest evidence and then go through what we know at this point? There may not be anything new to learn, but we will be ready to brief the other two agents on their way."

Dempsay responds, "That makes sense." Brightening somewhat, she continues, "We can get some lunch too. I get hungry after being yelled at. Just ask my mother."

They gather all the additional evidence they received from Josh, along with the items they found the previous day, and send it to the forensic lab. They send the flash drives separately to the cyber operations unit in hopes they can find out what is on them. Lastly, Tuganov e-mails the pictures of the two men in the white car to the leader of the forensic team, Hanna Greer, to determine their identities. Next, they call her to let her know more items are coming and ask if they looked at items they already sent. Greer indicates someone will be contacting them later in the day with results.

Tuganov starts calling the rental car companies that serve the Madison airport and ask if any of them recently received a vehicle with windshield damage. The guy at the Hertz counter claimed he has a white sedan with left rear window and right-side windshield damage. They said the renter gave him the insurance information and left.

Tuganov asks, "Did they rent another vehicle?"

"No. Not that I would rent anything to them at this point."

"So where did they go?"

"They said they had a flight to catch. I didn't ask where."

"Do you have a copy of a driver's license for the guy who rented the car?" he asks, knowing that the name on the driver's license is most likely fake, but he is hoping the picture is the same as the one he took of the two guys in the car. He would also have a name of one of his aliases.

"Yes, I just had it out to do insurance paperwork. Do you want a copy of it?" Tuganov tells him that he will be there within the hour to pick it up.

Later, the agents make their way back to the airport and retrieve a copy of the driver's license one of the Chinese agents used. They compare the picture to the one on Tuganov's phone, and it is a match. Next, they look at the name he used on the license; it is for a Steve Norbert.

Tuganov shakes his head. "Yeah, he's Steve Norbert and I'm the queen of England!"

Afterward, they head back to Dempsay's room to review what they know. Before they get started, they call around to law enforcement agencies and hospitals to see if they know of someone with a gunshot wound seeking medical treatment the day of the murder. They come up empty-handed, at least for now.

"So, Demps, where do you think the other team is coming from? DC or New York?"

"I don't know. Everybody seems to be up to their eyeballs in work. I guess they will get ahold of me when they have their plans set."

Changing topics, Alex asks, "What do you think of the three guys we interviewed today? Do you think they were telling the truth?"

Dempsay thinks about this, then responds, "I believe Bishop and Jacobson are telling the truth, but I'm not sure about Earl Watson. He seems reckless and very opinionated. I don't know if I believe him."

"Now, Demps, that's where I disagree with you. Watson doesn't take crap from anybody. Why else would he go after two Chinese operatives? He's fiercely loyal to Bishop and has no problem telling it like it is. He is very observant. He described the Chinese handgun to the tee. I think he is very believable."

"It seems like what they have told us and what we found yesterday lines up with our theory that the victim struggled with his assailant."

"Yes, that's true. What I want to know is how the Chinese operatives are involved. Were they part of the murder, or are they here for something else? My thought is that if they were here for the murder, then they would be gone already. No, I think they are here for the stuff Bishop found."

"What I'm struggling with is why the victim hid all that information. There doesn't seem to be anything worth killing for in those envelopes. But why hang on to it all this time?"

"Maybe the jackpot can be found in the flash drives. Maybe Simmons hid it from someone who was going to sell the information. If he was going to sell it himself, he would have done it a long time ago."

Dempsay is about to say something when her phone rings. She picks it up and sees the caller ID shows NCIS. Swiping to answer the call and putting it on speaker, she answers, "Dempsay here."

"Dempsay, it's Himmel and Johnston from New York. We've been told to lend an assist on a case you are running. Hawk says the case is getting bigger and bigger by the day." Himmel chuckles. "We also heard that you were channeling your inner NASCAR driver."

Dempsay ignores the dig. "Yes, the case is turning into a real peach. When you guys coming out?"

"Funny you ask that question. We were told to meet you and Tuganov out there in Wisconsin and started to make plans to get there. In fact, we had a ride on a C-130 from Kennedy all the way to Truax in Madison. But before we could pull the trigger on that, my SAC waves us off, saying that we would better help you from here or in DC. I think they did it so we can help you and keep working a hot case we have been working on."

"That's news to me. But okay, whatever. Will you be able to bird-dog all the evidence that we sent down to DC today?"

"Yeah, we can work from DC since we're following through on leads. We'll keep your desks warm."

"Thanks for the assist, Himmel. I guess I owe you."

"You betcha. Before I forget, we were to bring you tactical gear, but since we are not meeting up, your SAC is arranging to have the

Great Lakes field office bring some to you and Tuganov, probably tomorrow."

They click off, and she turns her attention to Tuganov, who is on his phone for most of the conversation. "Looks like Himmel and Johnston from New York won't be coming up here, Toog. Brass has them helping us from DC. Once they get there, they will run point on all the evidence we sent down. Hawk has the Great Lakes office bringing us tactical gear tomorrow."

Tuganov responds with raised eyebrows, "Himmel and Johnston? I know those guys. They're good. It will be good to have another set of eyes looking at things."

Dempsay receives a text notification and picks up her phone to read it. "Okay, I got a text from the forensic pathologist. He wants a Skype meeting with us." She then texts him back, asking to give them a minute.

They are sitting at the hotel room's desk in front of Dempsay's laptop. She activates the Skype application and connects with the pathologist, Dr. Charles Schweigel. Everyone in the Washington NCIS office calls him Chuck. He has been a forensic pathologist for over twenty years. Before that, he was a medical examiner in Chicago for ten years. He is a short, thin man with almost white hair, wearing a dark green suit and multicolored bow tie. He is known for his wild-looking bow ties.

Dempsay speaks first, "Hi, Chuck, how are you?"

Tuganov follows, "Hey, Chuck."

Chuck responds, "Agents Dempsay and Tuganov, good to see you again. How is life in the land of milk and cheese?"

Tuganov responds sarcastically, "We're having a blast here. It's colder than a mother here. We've been shot at by Chinese operatives, and we got to meet the state troopers here, along with county deputies from four counties, while Dempsay tried to break the land speed record with a six-cylinder engine. Other than that, the cheese curds are to die for."

Dr. Schweigel decides not to respond to Tuganov's sarcasm by adding his own. Instead, he launches into his findings, "Well, I went over the autopsy reports and photos, along with the statements from the witnesses that found the victim, and I came to the conclusion that the medical examiner and the initial detective got it all wrong. At least with the manner of death and the order of events. My guess is the lack of experience and exposure to different weapons led to their misguided conclusions."

Dempsay interjects, "You're saying the manner of death is wrong? What did you see?"

Chuck further explains, "It's a tale of two stab wounds and boils down to the shape of the wounds. I believe that there were two knives involved. There is a small wound at the top of the chest that indicates it was a smaller throwing knife that could have been thrown a fair distance. It appears to have penetrated just enough to cause the body distress. The knife in question is rather ubiquitous and can be found anywhere.

"The other wounds are a different story altogether. If you had a straight blade knife and made these wounds, you could conclude that the assailant was standing over a victim who is lying on his back. But the wounds are not of the correct shape for that conclusion. The shape of the wounds are more supported by a curved blade delivered while face-to-face with the victim."

"So you mean a knife like a scimitar?" Tuganov asks.

"No, a scimitar has a gradual curve to it and broadens more toward the tip. It is considered by most aficionados as a short sword. It would be too long to make the wounds in these pictures. What I'm suggesting is not a scimitar but a Gurkha, which has a forty-five-degree downward bend in the middle of the blade. It is the only weapon that fits with the wound shapes on the body."

Dempsay asks, "Where do Gurkhas come from? Who would be experts at using them?"

Chuck continues, "The scimitars got their origins in the Middle East and had their heyday during the Ottoman Empire, but Gurkhas have their origins from the nomadic tribes of Northern Africa and have been around a lot longer. I would suspect you would find them prevalent in countries like Algeria, Morocco, or Tunisia. Maybe even Libya."

"So there is no chance they are used in China?" asks Tuganov.

"No. Chinese fighting knives are straight, and the blade widens as they get closer to the hilt. Plus, there are no indications from historical texts that the Chinese adopted Gurkhas at any point. Agents, your killer hails from North Africa."

"You said they had the timing of events wrong too. What do you think they are?"

"Based on what I know, the victim received his first wound in the chest from the throwing knife, ostensibly to incapacitate him. Then the assailant gets close to the victim and stabs him with the Gurkha. Now it should be noted that the wounds from the Gurkha did not kill the victim. Maybe because the victim is fighting for his life and struggles, or possibly the four layers of clothing the victim wore. I am of the opinion the assailant resorts to shooting the victim. The gunshots prove to be fatal."

The two agents say nothing as they absorb what they have heard. Dempsay says, "Thanks, Doc! You have given us a lot to think about now."

"Well, by the looks on your faces, I've just sent your investigation into a tailspin. Sorry. I will let you know if I find anything else. I'm glad to be of service. Goodbye."

After the call ends, the two agents are quiet. Dempsay breaks the silence, "So which country do you think Gurkha man came from? And who brings a knife to a gunfight?"

Alex mulls it over. "Maybe it was supposed to be a knife fight. It seems clear to me the murder was to occur using knives. But the victim goes for a gun and turns the knife fight into a gunfight. I'm thinking the killer came from Morocco since one of the envelopes talked about trouble there. As far as we know, Simmons was not in any other northern African country."

Dempsay stands and puts her hands on her hips. "Well, you know what else?"

Alex nods. "Yeah, we have two distinct groups involved in this case."

"We better get Hawk on the phone."

CHAPTER 33

Moving On

Since there is no timeline from the authorities when they can use the laydown yard, Badger Power decides to move to a new location. Today, the crew will begin the loading and transport of the pole sections, starting from the north end of the yard to the south end. They have moved in a large crane and several semis with flatbed trailers.

Josh has called Dempsay and Tuganov to witness and supervise the removal of the steel poles. They arrive and instruct the crew to look inside the pole sections for anything that doesn't belong, and if the crew finds something, they are to have them look at it. The agents request that if something is found, try not to touch the item since it will be evidence.

The work crew removes the pole sections with the crane and load them onto the flatbed trucks. The removal process continues without incident, and the agents begin to wonder if nothing is left there. They even ask Josh to use his metal detector on the ground that has recently been uncovered, without success.

After lunch, the agents are thoroughly bored with the whole thing, and to pass the time, they talk about the case. "So, Demps, you think our Chinese friends have really left, like the rental car guys said?"

"No. If our Chinese operatives didn't kill Simmons, as Dr. Schweigel suggests, they came to get something from him, and they don't have it yet. So I think they are still around but are lying low. They do not want another incident like the other day. I think they want to get what they came for without anyone noticing."

"Now that we have their pictures, we could go to the motels in the area to see if the managers have seen them."

"So we would start local and then work our way outward?"

"Makes sense, but we'll need to be careful since they know we're on to them. We should run this by Hawk so he doesn't flip out over it."

They give Hawk a call, and he stresses they need to be very careful. He tells them to go into this with their assault rifles at the ready and under no circumstances do they separate. The agents tell Hawk they will start it when the crew knocks off for the day. Their boss inquires about the progress of the removal of poles and if they found anything. Dempsay tells him that nothing has been found as yet.

About the middle of the afternoon, the crew is now working close to where the path in the snow is located. A pole section just to the side of the path is being lifted when one of the crew members looks intently inside it. He immediately signals the crane operator to stop and motions for Josh to come over. Josh tucks his head inside the hollow pole and removes it. He jogs over to the agent's vehicle, and Tuganov lowers his window.

"Agent Tuganov, I think we found something. A small knife and a larger one with a bend in the middle. I've never seen anything like it before."

The agents exit the vehicle with a couple of evidence bags and wearing latex gloves. They walk quickly to the pole in question, and Dempsay sticks her head in the pole, holding a flashlight. She sees the Gurkha with its wood handle and bloodied bent blade, just like Dr. Schweigel said it would be. She pans the flashlight over to something else that is inside the pole—a smaller knife with a straight blade. It has some blood on it, but certainly not as much as the Gurkha has. She tries unsuccessfully to reach the items, backs out of the inside of the pole and asks Josh if they can tilt the pole so the knives can slide out.

Josh gives the crane operator hand signals to slowly raise up one end of the pole. Crew members are helping as well to encourage the knives to slide out. Eventually, they slide out onto the ground. Before picking them up, Tuganov takes pictures of them with his phone to send off later to Dr. Schweigel. Dempsay holds the bag while Tuganov carefully grasps each knife and places it in their respective bags. Once in its bag, Josh and the crew get to see the strange-looking knife. Tagger makes the comment that it would be good for field dressing deer and inquires how he could get his hands on what he calls a "Girkey."

Tuganov texts the pictures to Dr. Schweigel with a note, "Are these what you thought were the knives in question?" A couple of minutes later, he receives a return text from the pathologist indicating they are exactly what he expected.

To hurry things along, Dempsay asks Josh to have his men look in the remaining pole section while they are on the ground with a flashlight. After looking at all the pole sections, they find nothing else. The agents tell Josh to continue with his work and to let them know if they happen to find anything else. With that, Tuganov and Dempsay get into their warm car and start back to Madison to ship off their latest finds.

C H A P T E R   3 4

Hide-and-Seek

Before they go to Madison, Dempsay and Tuganov make a stop in Portage where there are three motels. The agents thought this would be a good place to start. They first stop at the Best Western and show the front desk clerks the picture of both men in the white sedan. No one has seen them. They talk to the manager and some of the housekeeping staff but come away empty-handed. Next, they try the Super 8, again showing the picture to the people behind the front desk, manager, and housekeeping. No luck there either. The agents are beginning to think this was a waste of time as they pull into the Ridge Motor Inn. The motel manager was working the front desk at the time. When Tuganov shows him the picture of the men, the manager studies it and then announces that they have stayed there at the hotel. Dempsay asks the man if he is sure, and he convincingly tells the agents the two men stayed there awhile.

Tuganov asks, "Are they here now?" Both agents are now looking around the lobby.

"No, they checked out last week."

"Do you remember anything unusual about them? Did they tell you where they were going next?" Dempsay asks.

The manager replies, "No, they didn't tell me where they were going. They kept to themselves and kept strange hours. They would stay in their rooms most of the day and leave at night, almost thought they were vampires. For their whole stay, they left the Do Not Disturb sign out. They would come to the desk and get more towels. Let me tell you that room was utter mess when we could get in there to clean it. Food and drink containers everywhere. There was a mound of old wet towels that stunk up the place. We had to spend a whole day cleaning that place up. I hope you find them so I can sue them for damages."

After leaving the Ridge Motor Inn, Dempsay and Tuganov look to see where other similar hotels are located, thinking the Chinese guys would go to the same type of hotel. Their mapping application showed them two hotels just to the south and west of Portage, where I-94/I-90 split from I-39. Dempsay points to the map on her smartphone. "I remember passing these on our way from our hotel in Madison up to the crime scene."

Tuganov asks, "You want to try them? There isn't much in the way of motels or hotels until you get closer to Madison."

They drive to where the hotels are located and go first to the Comfort Suites and repeat everything they did at the last three hotels. This time, the front desk clerk hesitates and says, "They were here, but we didn't have rooms to give them. They stood out because they were acting so different."

Tuganov asks the clerk, "Why do you say they were acting differently? Why would you not have rooms available?"

"They acted almost secretively. While the one was trying to get a room, the other was watching out the window. The one in the driver's seat in your picture seemed like he was going to explode when I told him we had no rooms. I got really uneasy, and I was feeling for the panic button. Before I could press it, they just walked out without saying a word. As far as not having rooms, we have a ski hill just west of here, and they were having an event or race. Anyway, between them and the usual business travelers, we filled up."

The agents thank the clerk and leave there and go across the road to the Days Inn. The manager is the front desk clerk today, and when he is shown the pictures, he gets very upset. "Yes, they stayed here for a few days. The morons left the room a complete mess. I want to get my hands on them!"

Tuganov says, "Well, you'll have to get in line."

"Yeah, who's in front of me in line?"

"We are!" Then he asks, "Did they tell you where they were going? Did you get a look at the car they drove?"

"No to both questions."

The agents thank him for his time and return to the parking lot. Dempsay looks around. "Look at this place, Toog. You can jump onto the highway and go in any direction you want to. I'm thinking they are still in the general area, but they are spooked and probably aren't very close now."

"Well, we could see if Great Lakes field office could call around and make inquiries. We would just need to e-mail them this picture."

On their way back to Madison, Dempsay calls Hawk to give him an update. She fills him in on what they found and what they learned from the rental car employee. She also tells him they have checked all the local hospitals and police departments for anyone who sought medical treatment for a gunshot wound any time after the murder and came up empty. She also tells Hawk they tracked down the last known location of the operatives and found they had checked out the same day they turned in the white sedan and not mentioning to anybody where they were going.

Hawk tells them, "Okay, kids, it's time to come home. I think you need to work the case from here. I don't think there is a point in staying there any longer. I have a flight for you out of Truax in the late morning. You'll be on an FBI G-5 back to DC, so behave yourselves. You will be their guests."

Dempsay replies, "I'm not comfortable leaving Bishop to twist in the wind. We think the Chinese operatives are still in the area. Can we get some protection for him and his wife?"

"Okay, fair enough. I'll contact the Wisconsin DCI and arrange to have a car sit on them."

"Could we ask Great Lakes to call around to a wider net of hotels to see where the Chinese operatives are holed up?"

"Yeah, I think we can do that."

"Okay, Hawk, we'll see you tomorrow."

"No, I'll see you the day after tomorrow. Get a good night's rest before coming in. That's an order! Oh, before I forget, bring a jump bag." He is referring to a packed bag to take at a moment's notice to go anywhere in the world.

Dempsay says, "Copy that, boss."

The agents don't think to look north of where they are, which is fine with the operatives. They get a room at a rundown Super 8 in Wautoma and are waiting there, biding their time to strike!

CHAPTER 35

Ralphie Boy

Tuganov and Dempsay landed at Joint Base Andrews, and an agency car took them back to their homes. Both are looking forward to a relaxing rest of the day and evening.

Alex talks with his family, his parents in Fairfax, and his younger sister, Rayana, or Ray, as he likes to call her. That evening, he absent-mindedly watches TV while thinking about the case. *Is there a connection between the Chinese and the Moroccans?* He ends up falling asleep on the couch.

After settling in, Dempsay Skypes her mother who lives in New York. Since Dad passed a couple of years ago, and being the only child, she feels it is her sworn duty to keep tabs on her mother. After the pleasantries, her mom goes right to the point by asking Dempsay when she is going to find a man to marry. Of course, Mom has to remind her that she's not getting any younger and can't understand what she's waiting for. After hearing her mother complain awhile more, they end the call. That evening, she checks her work e-mail for anything new she needs to know before tomorrow.

In the morning, both agents make their way to the OSP office near Foggy Bottom. The two agents go and check in with Hawk, who is waiting for them with one eyebrow raised. "You two look vaguely familiar, or are you the new probationary agents HQ sent me?"

Tuganov smiles. "I'll go with the probationary agent thing. Ah, to be new and blissfully ignorant."

The three have a good laugh over that. Hawk tells them they have a meeting with the forensic folks at nine. "They have been very busy and have lots to tell you. I've seen what they found, and I have a few comments that I'll hold until you two have the chance to go over it first. I will say this, the case is no longer just a murder of a naval officer. It is something a whole lot bigger."

They walk back to their bullpen area. Tuganov is ahead of Dempsay, who stops and says to him, "Hey, Toog. After having you as a dinner partner all week, I learned that eating alone really sucks. The next time we have a break like that, what do you say to giving a girl a call?"

He jokes, "Okay, as long as I don't have the entire Washington Redskin cheerleader squad over for a rousing game of scrabble."

Shaking her head, she chuckles at that, "Fair enough."

The agents make their way to one of the conference rooms in the office to meet with Hanna Greer and her team to talk about some of the evidence from Wisconsin. Hanna and two of her technicians are already in the room and have a laptop connected to the large screen at one end of the room. Greer is considered a well-known expert in the field of forensics, and she is asked to speak at national symposiums. With a thick Southern accent, she is brash and always ready with an opinion and sometimes no filter. Standing just over five feet, her personality puts her at seven feet five.

As the agents enter the room, Greer, with a big smile on her face, greets them as only she can, "Hey, y'all, how's my favorite NCIS power couple doing?"

Both agents just smile as they sit down, knowing full well if they protest the comment Greer made, they will be digging a bigger hole.

Turning to her two technicians, she says, "These are the two best agents and the biggest badasses NCIS has." She makes the introductions all around. "Now before we get started, Olivia sweetheart, I understand you were chasing a bad guy at very high speeds and trading paint with state troopers. I did not peg you as a speed junkie. How long have you been harboring this NASCAR habit?"

Dempsay rolls her eyes and smiles. "I guess it's been there all along. I pull it out when I need it. You know, because I'm such a badass, I go in the middle of the night and steal Tuganov's Mustang and thrash it while he's asleep." This last part gets a surprised look to Tuganov's face.

Greer responds, "Ah, we're in smarty-pants mode this morning. Well, let's get to the evidence in your case, shall we? This morning, we're going to discuss the handgun you sent along, as well as information on your friend Mr. Peterson. Mathew, fill in the agents about what you found about the gun they sent us."

Mathew is a young thin man that Tuganov puts him in his late twenties or very early thirties. He has a full beard and long hair tied up in a bun. He decides to refer to him as Bun Boy.

Bun Boy begins, "The Sig Sauer you sent us is a registered weapon belonging to the victim. As you asked us, we check the clip before we did anything else to it and found six .38 caliber bullets on top of the 9 mm bullets in the magazine. The bullets were clean, and the gun showed evidence of being wiped down, which begs the question, why would someone wipe down a gun? It wouldn't make sense unless, of course, it was used to murder the victim."

Tuganov asks, "Did you happen to find out where those .38s were manufactured?"

"Yes, the manufacturer's mark is one from the outskirts of Cairo, Egypt."

The agents trade a look, which Hanna picks up on. "Yes, it looks like our murderer is most likely from a country in northern Africa, especially if you factor in the Gurkha y'all found. We're in the middle of processing it."

Dempsay asks, "Is there evidence in the barrel that the gun had been fired recently?"

"Yes, there was residue in the barrel consistent with it being fired. Usually, the residue is burned off, but with the extremely cold temperatures, it stayed intact." Looking at his phone, he checks the time and continues, "I have to run to another meeting. If you have any other questions, don't hesitate to call me."

The agents turn their attention to Hanna, and Tuganov queries, "Hanna, you said you have information on Ralph Peterson."

Greer replies, "Oh yes, darlin', we have a lot to talk about Mr. Peterson." Hanna now turns to the young lady sitting next to her and across from the agents. "This is Chloe Walsh. Dear, would you be so kind as to fill them in on what you have found about Mr. Peterson?"

Tuganov has sized her up as well. From his perspective, she is a computer nerd, pale skinned and introvert. Walsh is a thin redheaded girl with shoulder-length hair pulled back into a ponytail. When she opens her mouth, her Boston accent betrays her origins.

Walsh has her laptop plugged into the conference room display showing a picture of Ralph Peterson from his ID badge from Badger Power. She addresses the agents, "This is the picture of Ralph Peterson from his work ID. I ran the name in all our various databases, even at NSA, and found that Ralph Peterson did not exist two years ago. It seems the information he gave to the company prior to his hire was a created identity. Nothing in the information I saw suggested this was a bona fide, created by a particular country's intelligence gathering group. So it is very possible that the new identity was created by an independent cobbler." A cobbler is a name for someone who creates false identities or bona fides.

She continues, "Next, I ran his picture through our facial recognition program and did not get a hit. So with a little help from our friends at TSA"—showing a video of Ralph going through security and later boarding a plane—"we were able to establish he boarded an early-morning flight from Milwaukee to Chicago the day of the murder. Then at O'Hare airport, he boarded another flight in the international terminal to Riyadh, Saudi Arabia. As you probably know, Saudi Arabia does not have an extradition treaty with the US. The interesting thing here is that he has used up three sets of bona fides, most likely backstopped to make sure no one knows where he went."

Dempsay interrupts, "Excuse me, Walsh, but you mention getting information from NSA and TSA. Did we obtain this information aboveboard? In other words, can we use this in court?"

Hanna fields this question. "Yes, dear, we obtained this information through warrants we issued to obtain them. So y'all can use this chain of evidence in court, unlike some people I know who run afoul of the law." Her voice trails off on the last part, putting in a dig, which elicits a smile out of Tuganov.

Dempsay, ignoring the dig, says, "Okay, that's good. Thanks. Walsh, please continue."

Walsh resumes, "We ran Mr. Peterson's picture through the facial recognition database that Interpol uses that contains pictures of known criminal foreign nationals and got a hit. Ralph Peterson is actually Rashid Houtan, born in Tajikistan, but in recent years—wait for it—lives in Marrakesh, Morocco!"

The eyebrows go up on both agents. Tuganov speaks up, "Walsh, is this for real?"

"I assure you that it is. Kind of solidifies the northern Africa thing, doesn't it?"

"What do we know about this Rashid Houtan guy?"

"Well, here is the bad part. Rashid Houtan is an independent contractor and acts as a go-between or, in some circles, they would call him a fixer to gunrunners and human traffickers and terrorists based in northern Africa. Interpol reports that he is very ruthless and does not value human life. In fact, there are reports that he killed innocent people just to cover his tracks. He is a known, and very bad, criminal wanted by several countries, as well as the FBI and NCIS. Apparently, he was instrumental in a terror attack at a military base in Bahrain."

Dempsay leans forward in her chair. "So what is a guy like that doing in the middle of Wisconsin of all places?"

CHAPTER 36

Shared Interest

Late in the day, Dempsay gets a phone call from Bun Boy with news regarding the slugs they took out of the trees at the laydown yard in Wisconsin. She puts it on speaker phone so Tuganov can hear the conversation.

After pleasantries, Mathew says, "Agent Dempsay, I have compared the slugs you and Agent Tuganov pulled out of the trees at the crime scene. They come up as a match to the victim's Sig Sauer, which means he fired his weapon twice in that direction."

"That's good news, Mathew. It confirms that weapon as one of the murder weapons. The thing is, there were six shots fired from that gun. Three into the victim, two into the trees, so that leaves one unaccounted for."

"Yes, that's right. I forgot that six bullets were put back into the magazine. Do you think that slug is still at the crime scene?"

Tuganov states, "Mathew, I believe the slug is in the killer since we have blood on branches away from where the victim was found. So I'm thinking if we find our killer, we'll find our sixth slug."

"If he got hit with a 9 mm bullet, he may not have gotten very far, depending on where he was hit. Right?"

Dempsay says, "Once we have a name and a face, we can circulate it to local law enforcement, hotels, and car rental places."

"Makes sense. Let me know if there is anything else you need."

"Mathew, thanks for your help, and we'll let you know if we need any more assistance." She clicks off the call and speaks to Tuganov, "Looks like our theory is panning out." Tuganov nods in agreement.

As Dempsay and Tuganov are engrossed in a conversation about the case, they hear a small knock on metal, standing in the doorway of the agent's bullpen is Walsh, holding her laptop to her chest.

Alex greets her, "Hi, Walsh! Judging from your body language, I think you have something big for us."

Walsh answers, "Yes, I do. I have the names of your maybe Chinese operatives."

"Maybe? Let's see what you have." He beckons her into the bullpen and she sits down and plugs her laptop into the LED display on the wall.

After tapping on the computer keyboard, the faces of two Asian men appear on the display. "The one on the left is Zhang Wei and the other one is Li Jun. I got their names from our facial recognition database, which means we have had dealings with them in the past."

Dempsay sits up straight after hearing the names and seeing the faces. Turning to Tuganov, she says, "Do you remember these guys?" Then she turns to Walsh. "They are in our system because Tuganov and I put them in." She turns back to her partner. "Remember we busted them in Hong Kong back when we worked in the Far East office?"

Tuganov moves closer to the faces on the display and scrutinizes the pictures. He turns to both women. "It has been a few years ago, but yes, I do remember them. As I recall, I thought they got long prison sentences, so what they are doing out of prison?"

Dempsay jokes, "Apparently vacationing in Wisconsin. There is something not making sense to me." Her eyebrows are scrunched up and she is frowning. "These guys are Triad, so what are they doing with Chinese intelligence issue weapons?"

Tuganov replies, "Well, they could have stolen the weapons or, more likely, they were hired by Chinese intelligence to come here."

Walsh got caught up in the conversation and surprised the agents by asking, "Why would they come halfway around the world for? It would have to be very important, right?"

Dempsay responds, "That's a very good question, but we really don't know why."

Tuganov chimes in, "I think they came to retrieve something. You heard Bishop. They were tailing him and watching his movements."

Dempsay looks at him. "If they came to get something and they think Bishop has it, then why don't they just grab it and go?"

Walsh interjects, "Unless..." She hesitates, thinking she has already overstepped her bounds, but both agents are looking at her expectantly. "Unless they are waiting for instructions."

There is silence as both agents think through this piece of information. Finally, Dempsay breaks the silence, "Crap! Why didn't I think of that! Of course, it makes sense. Walsh, thanks for that insight!"

The forensic scientist looks at her smart watch and announces she needs to leave. She unplugs her laptop from the display and stands to leave, "Thanks guys for letting me be part of that." She then leaves quickly.

Tuganov now says, "We should drag her up here more often. I think in our pursuit of the less obvious, we miss the obvious."

"Toog, I don't think we need to drag her up here. I think she enjoyed herself."

He shifts the conversation, "Is there a connection between the Moroccans and the Chinese? There has to be one, right? They had to at least be aware of each other in Wisconsin. It's not like they just bumped into each other at the Souks, the largest open-air market in Marrakesh, and planned a trip to bucolic Wisconsin."

"Is it Roger Simmons that is the common denominator? Or Rashid Houtan? If it's Simmons, then how?" Dempsay wonders.

"There is no information NCIS has to indicate Houtan worked for the Chinese although it is not outside the realm of possibilities. My money is on Simmons, but like you, I don't know how they are connected."

As they continue to discuss the Chinese-Houtan connection, the pictures of the Wei and Jun are still up on the screen in their bullpen. A couple of other agents in a nearby bullpen walk over and stand in their doorway. Dempsay and Tuganov don't notice the visitors until they interrupt, "Hey, guys, hate to interrupt but we noticed the two pictures on your screen there. Are they part of the Wisconsin case you're working on?"

Tuganov responds, "Yes. These are two Chinese intelligence suspects still in the area, or so we think. We'll be sending these photos to Great Lakes to start canvassing the area around Portage."

He is about to continue about why they are pursuing these men when the agent interrupts again, "Whoa, you are saying that they are here in the States, in Wisconsin? How long ago was this?"

Dempsay tells him, "A couple of days. We chased them while we were there, but they got away." She continues in a sarcastic tone, "So these guys are friends of yours?""

"Yeah, you could say that. We've been after these guys since we caught wind of the human trafficking operation going through our naval base in Hong Kong. These two are the worst of the worst. Do you mind if we go up there and pick them up?"

"No, not at all. Just so you know, they are shadowing a civilian whom they think has something they want, and we have a couple of Wisconsin DCI agents who are sitting on a man by the name of Josh Bishop."

The two agents leave Dempsay and Tuganov to make plans to go to Portage. Dempsay looks at Tuganov and says in an exaggerated British accent, "Well, Dr. Watson, the plot thickens."

He chuckles and effects his own British accent, "Indeed, the game is afoot!"

CHAPTER 37

More Dots to Connect

Dempsay receives a call the night before from Hanna Greer about progress her team has made in the case and wanted to get together with Dempsay and Tuganov in the morning to go over the findings. Dempsay called Tuganov, after hanging up with Hawk, to fill him in. As the time of the meeting drew near, they return to the same conference room they were in yesterday.

Just prior to 9:00 AM, Hanna Greer, Dr. Chuck Schweigel, and Chloe Walsh enter the room and quickly sit down. Tuganov tells Hanna that Walsh was very helpful yesterday afternoon and that she brought a fresh brain to the discussion. He even suggests that her people be involved in more investigative discussions.

Hanna replies to the notion by putting up her hand in a stopping motion toward him. "Alex darling, it's a nice thought, and there may be some validity in it too, but my people are up to their eyeballs in work, and I don't see how we could accommodate that kind of effort and still get through our workload. Shall we get to it then?"

Both agents nods, but Tuganov senses disappointment on Walsh's face when Greer summarily dismissed the idea. Having another perspective, even if they are not agents, could be healthy in a complex investigation. He's not letting this go and plans on talking to Dempsay and Hawk about it.

Greer plunges forward, "We first looked at the smaller knife you two found at the scene and conducted an analysis of the blood found on it. First off, the blood was only found on the first inch or so from the tip of the blade. Secondly, the blood on it is a match to our victim."

"The fact that blood is only evident on the first inch of the blade is consistent with it being thrown and the blade only penetrating an inch or so is due to the layers of clothing," Dr. Schweigel adds.

As Dempsay was about to say something, Hawk enters the conference room and takes a seat. "Sorry, folks, for being late. Please continue."

Dempsay says to Hawk, "We were just getting into the blood analysis of murder weapons."

"Thanks, Dempsay. By the way, who is the new face in the room?"

"Excuse me, sir, this is Chloe Walsh. She is one of my newer forensic scientists," Hanna explains.

Hawk reaches across the table and shakes Walsh's hand. "Welcome aboard, kid."

Dempsay now turns to Dr. Schweigel and asks, "Would that wound incapacitate the victim? Or make him drop what he has in his hands?"

"I can see where you're going with this. The wound itself may not have injured him to the point of stopping whatever he was doing, and I doubt that it would incapacitate him or make him drop a weapon. It is very hard to make any certain claims without the benefit of having the victim's body here to conduct further analysis."

Tuganov asks, "Is it possible that the victim shot the assailant before the attacker threw the knife?"

Dr. Schweigel counters, "Well, that is certainly a viable theory, but I have nothing scientific to back that up with."

Greer moves on. "Let's look at what we found on the Gurkha."

Walsh clears her throat. "I found two types of blood on the Gurkha, one belongs to our murder victim and the other to someone else. They had a different blood type all together. There was a lot of blood on the blade from our victim, but there were large droplets on it from the unknown source. I ran a DNA analysis on the unknown blood sample and found it had markers for someone that came from Northern Africa. So this indicates to me that both the victim and the assailant were wounded when this knife was used."

Tuganov asks, "Could the assailant used the knife on someone else prior to attacking our victim and not cleaning off the blade?"

"Yes, that is possible. However the next piece of information refutes that. The blood on the branches found on the scene was of the same blood type as the large droplets on the blade. So this would indicate the assailant was injured and bleeding as he left the scene."

"Any chance of getting an identity of the assailant off the DNA?" asks Dempsay.

"Yes, it is. I further ran the DNA profile against our database and got a hit. The name of our assailant is Nabil Mubarak, a lieutenant in the Moroccan syndicate. It appears he has a rap sheet longer than Route 66."

Hawk interjects, looking at Walsh, "Are you sure that is who killed our naval officer?"

Nodding, she responds, "Yes, absolutely with a 95 percent confidence from the data." This comment yields a very concerned look on Hawk's face.

Dempsay asks, "Hawk, what's going on?"

"Your two friends from New York, Himmel and Johnston, are working on the Bahrain Naval Base terror attack and they have three guys in their sights. Two of them are involved in this case. Nabil Mubarak is one and Rashid Houtan is the other." He looks at Greer. "Hanna, you got anything else to share with us?"

Greer responds, "No, that's all we have for now."

"Can I have the room?" With that, the forensic people stand and begin to leave the room. Hawk stops them. "Very nice work, folks! Thanks for turning it around so quickly." Hanna thanks Hawk and leaves, closing the door behind her.

Hawk addresses the two agents, "This case is getting bigger and bigger. Now what I suspected has been proven true, and now we have a murder of a naval officer potentially tied, somehow, to a terror attack in the Middle East."

Tuganov interrupts, "Not to mention it may also be tied to a human trafficking case in Hong Kong. Hernandez and Loach saw the pictures of the guys we chased and said they were prime suspects in that case. Walsh found the names in our database and now we have those. The interesting thing is that Dempsay and I busted these guys back when we were in the Far East field office."

"I wasn't aware of that. So now we have three cases with suspects in common. I want to set up a task force to put these three cases to bed. I want you two and the other four agents to work together." Hawk turns to Dempsay. "I want you to lead the group."

"Hawk, I have an idea. The other day, Walsh was showing us new information she came up with and she was very helpful in analyzing that data and lent an insight. I would like her to join the six of us to provide analysis in real time, and she may even have an unbiased insight that will help the case. What do you think? I floated the idea with Hanna, but she would have none of it."

Turning to Dempsay, Hawk asks, "You okay with that?"

She responds enthusiastically, "Oh yes, she pointed out something to me that I didn't even think of. Quite frankly, Hawk, if we merge these three cases, it will be one of the biggest cases we have worked on. We need as many good hands on deck as possible."

He stops to think for a moment and then continues, "Okay we're all going to work together and share everything. Himmel and Johnston are on their way back here, and I'm going to tell the other two to stay here. I need the six of you to figure out how all three are tied together. If you really think Walsh can contribute, then you have her. If I see that she is not, then I'm going to pull her. Got it!"

Both agents nod their heads and thank Hawk.

"I'll make nice with Greer."

Tuganov responds, "I'll go get Hernandez and Loach and call the other two to see where they are at. Maybe they can call in if they're tied up." Tuganov gets up and leaves the room.

Fifteen minutes later, four of the six agents were sitting in the conference room while the other two Skyped in; their faces are projected onto the screen in the room. Himmel asks, "Hey, Dempsay,

Tuganov, what's going on with your case? We're hearing that we all are after the same people."

Dempsay responds, "We found out this morning not only is Rashid Houtan involved in our case but also Nabil Mubarak, whom we think is the triggerman in the murder of the Navy lieutenant. So apparently, Himmel, these two guys are high on your suspect list for the Bahrain terror attack. We also found out that two Triad foot soldiers, or two Chinese intelligence agents, are also involved in our case somehow. These two are Hernandez and Loach's prime suspects in a human trafficking case in Hong Kong. Given this news, Hawkins has instructed me to run point on a joint investigation of all three cases. So we will need to share information and work together to see if we can kill three birds with one stone. Anybody got issues or questions right off the bat?"

Hernandez chimes in, "So how are these people connected to one another and the victims in all three cases? At first glance they don't seem like they are connected."

Tuganov says, "That's the key question, and I think if we figure out the answer to that, then the pieces may fall into place."

Dempsay adds, "And that's where we will start in the morning. Hawkins says this will be our war room. Himmel, when do you think you and Johnston will be in?"

"We should be in the office by 9:00 AM unless we run into more flight delays."

"Okay, let's reconvene then. Bye all." She then terminates the connection.

CHAPTER 38

Convergence

The next morning finds Tuganov and Dempsay in early and setting things up in the war room. They set up one end, with the large display, with a table and chairs around it. At the other end, they set up two separate tables with chairs to do work separately if needed.

As they complete the arrangement of the room, Walsh comes into the conference room with a backpack and a traveler's mug. She looks around and notices the changes to the room. She walks up to Dempsay, who is sitting and looking at e-mails on her phone, "Hey, Dempsay, you want me in a particular spot?"

Dempsay stands. "Hi, Walsh, thanks for helping us with this. I really appreciate it!"

"No, thank you for giving me the opportunity! I never thought I would get to do something like this until I was here a lot longer. I promise not to let you down."

"Nonsense, you'll be fine. Actually, it was Tuganov's idea to bring you on board. I'm going to my desk to get something for you to chew on." She leaves the room as she takes a phone call.

Tuganov walks up. "Hey, Walsh, welcome aboard. I'm looking forward to working with you. You bring a lot to the table, and we need all the help we can get."

"Dempsay says I have you to thank for this. I promise I won't let you down. I have to admit I'm a little intimidated working alongside six agents."

"Don't worry about it. Once they see how helpful you will be to this investigation, they'll be treating you like their kid sister."

"Are you sure?"

"Walsh, you will be fine. So tell me, how wrapped around the axle is Greer at me?"

"I would steer clear of her for long while. She's pretty pissed."

"Well, thanks for the warning."

"So where do you want me to put my stuff?"

Tuganov looks around. "You know, I'm not sure what Dempsay got up her sleeve yet. So just hang tight."

Loesch, Hernandez, Himmel, and Johnston roll into the conference room. They greet Tuganov, and he, in turn, introduces the foursome of agents to Walsh. They are standing in the middle of the war room, talking as Dempsay enters the room with a stack of the manila folders that Josh Bishop had given her. She sets them down on a table and walks over and greets the other agents. She tells the group how they are going to work and the agenda for today. But before she could get started, Hawk and Greer enter. He is wearing a smile and she is clearly not on board with this arrangement.

Dempsay addresses Hawk and Greer, "Hawk. Greer. We were just about to get started."

Hawk speaks first, "Okay, folks, it's really simple. The seven of you are going to work together to close the Bahrain, Hong Kong, and Simmons cases. There has been work done on all three by each of the teams, but it will take a collective effort to get these bad guys. This is why I put together this task force to show you how serious I am about getting all the suspects involved in these cases. I have added Walsh to the group at the behest of Agent Tuganov. Don't make me regret that decision. I also put Dempsay in as lead agent on this and expect cooperation from all. I am going to request a daily update on progress."

Greer, seeing that Hawk is done speaking, chimes in, "This"—pointing a circle around the group—"is an experiment. How successful this turns out and if we do this more in the future will depend on you and how Walsh is utilized. If I hear that you have squirreled her away to a corner and don't let her contribute or if she turns into your personal gopher, then she's out of here faster than you can say forensic scientist. Got it?" With the last words, she is looking right at Tuganov. All members of the task force nod their heads, including Walsh. With that, Hawk and Greer leave the room.

Tuganov makes a smart comment about not being on Greer's Christmas card list this year, which draw laughs from the rest of the agents. Walsh seems to be of the opinion that Agent Tuganov tends to think outside the box and takes the heat for it when it comes.

Dempsay picks up where she left off. "So what I would like to do first is to have the other two team to go through their respective cases to see if there is something that ties all these people together. Walsh, I want you to capture anything that we see as relevant so we can review it again later. Then I want to go through the information in those"—now pointing to the stack of manila envelopes—"and look for anything that might point to the other two cases."

They gather around the big screen as Hernandez walks through the Hong Kong case using his laptop. He explains to the group that sailors were loading empty containers onto a supply ship to return to the States to get refilled. The supply ship was late getting into Hong Kong due to weather. The crew working the transfer noticed a foul smell and investigated. When they opened the doors of the container, they found the bodies of ten women. We don't know how long this has been going on at this base. Usually, they utilize normal shipping vessels to move people and contraband.

Tuganov asks, "So what changed to make them use military shipping?"

Hernandez answers, "We're not sure, but whatever it was occurred several years ago. As I said, we don't know when they got so brazen as to use military shipments. After doing some investigation, we found evidence that the Hong Kong Triad was behind this, and that is what led us to Wei and Jun. We believe they are the primary actors in that ring. What I'm confused about is what they are doing in Wisconsin."

Dempsay asks, "Is it possible that Madison, Wisconsin, is one of their outlets for trafficking women?"

"Not that we could find. It seems like their outlets are on the West Coast. Maybe there is a distribution network that send their captives eastward, but we haven't found it."

Walsh asks, "Have you found any connection between the Triad and Houtan?"

Loesch responds, "There is nothing that we have come across that looks like a link between our two suspects or the Triad and Rashid Houtan. He operates in a whole different part of the world. That said, this Wisconsin case leads one to think there is one."

Himmel chimes in, "Houtan would want a piece of the action for whatever he did for them. I just don't see the Triad needing his services."

Walsh ponders, "Hmmm. So we have not found a connection, but there could be one that we haven't come across yet. What if the Triad decided to expand their operation to conduct business on the African continent, or the supply of women is dwindling in the Far East and want to find new areas to obtain them? If so, they could have reached out to Houtan to help them."

Himmel adds, "If the Triad wanted to do that, yes, they would eventually have to talk to Houtan. He is a fixer. He can put them in touch with anyone else in that part of the world to get whatever they want."

Dempsay asks, "So we have a potential connection between Houtan and the Triad. What about the Moroccans?"

Johnston replies, "We have established the group, Al Shabaab, was the brains behind the attack at the naval base in Bahrain. They mainly operate within the confines of the African continent, so I think they farmed out the muscle on this to the Moroccan syndicate to attack the base."

Tuganov asks, "Why would Al Shabaab be concerned about a naval base in Bahrain?"

Himmel replies, "Normally they wouldn't, but we think that Al-Qaeda is somehow involved in getting Al Shabaab to do it. Al-Qaeda would definitely be interested in terrorizing that naval base, and with all the attention they are getting, maybe they decided to farm it out."

"So," asks Walsh, "Houtan would be the go-between in that deal as well?"

Himmel nods. "Oh yes, he would have made the introductions all up and down the whole thing."

Tuganov asks, "But how does that get the Moroccans in Wisconsin? Same thing with the Triad guys, what brought them there? And with Houtan in the middle of it?" He then pauses a moment. "Maybe the question to ask is, what did our murder victim do to attract everybody's attention?"

Dempsay adds, "Perhaps the contents of those envelopes will help us answer those questions." They all go to the table at the other end of the room where the envelopes are sitting. She then proceeds to dole out the envelops to the two sets of agents and Walsh, explaining, "Tuganov and I already looked at these, but maybe we missed something. I want some fresh eyes on these."

They study the pages from their stack in silence until Johnston asks while still looking at a piece of paper, "What are we looking at? I see drawings and other papers but not sure what it is."

Dempsay explains what the envelopes contain and asks they pay special attention to the locations where the equipment was installed and the incident reports. She further explains, "These are locations where our murder victim led an installation of port and border security equipment."

Hernandez sits straight up in his chair. "The one I'm looking at is a system that was installed in Rabat, Morocco. According to this report, they got plenty of pushback from the locals to the point they scrapped plans to install equipment in Casablanca. Maybe this accounts for the Moroccans going after Simmons."

Walsh leans forward in her chair and puts her elbows on the table, pointing at the paper she is holding, "This one is an installation in Incheon, Korea, where, get this, they found contraband from Hong Kong and all cargo from there was frozen for a while. I'm sure this pissed off the Triads!"

"So it looks like Roger Simmons is the common denominator, or at least what he did. That puts them both in Wisconsin, but why? It seems to me they had different objectives," Himmel says.

Dempsay questions, "How does that get Houtan in Wisconsin?"

Tuganov says, "We know that Houtan is a fixer. Maybe he contacts both and sets up a deal where he locates Simmons for them for a fee. After all, he was in Wisconsin long before either the Moroccans or Chinese show up. If that is the case, then Simmons is the reason he shows up in the land of milk and cheese."

Walsh adds, "That makes sense with the other evidence we have. We know that Houtan left the day of the murder, which means he knew when it was going down. He locates Simmons, gets a job at the same company to keep close to him, and then lets the Chinese and the Moroccans know where he is."

"So the Moroccans wanted to kill him, but what about the Chinese? They wanted…what, the tech? To steal the technology of the system they installed in Incheon? Which could explain why they are waiting around to do something," Loach chimes in.

Dempsay turns to Walsh and asks, "Speaking of waiting around, have the computer people found out what is on the flash drives?"

Walsh responds, "The geek dudes have them. I'm not sure where they are with them." Dempsay makes a mental note to see if it can get sped up.

Dempsay's phone chirps, and she looks at the caller ID; it's the Great Lakes office. She answers and listens to the caller. In the process, she grabs a pen and notepad and starts jotting information down. When the call is over, she looks at the group. "We asked the Great Lakes office to try and locate the Moroccans by contacting hotels starting in Portage. They got a hit and it turns out both checked into the Best Western in Portage two days prior to the murder and checked out early the day of the murder. Great Lakes says they are waiting on a photo from the surveillance camera in the lobby to get a picture of the men as they checked in. And get this, the parking lot footage shows the pair getting out of a small white SUV."

Tuganov says, "The timing is right, and the vehicle was right, according to the evidence we got from Bishop. Did they get an ID on the other guy?"

Dempsay responds, "No, at least not yet. Maybe we'll get lucky and can ID the guy from the lobby photo." She then has the group going through the timing of all three crimes to see if that lines up. She continues, "I'm expecting that the murder in Wisconsin occurred after the other two."

Himmel and Hernandez walk through the timing of their cases. They seem to have been committed concurrently, but before the murder of Simmons. All three crimes were committed after the installations of security equipment at both locations of interest. In fact, they established that the Incheon installation was completed prior to the one in Morocco.

Tuganov announces, "Things are starting to fall into place. Now all we need to do is get the name of the second Moroccan guy and see what's on those flash drives."

CHAPTER 39

Confab

Later that afternoon, Dempsay receives a phone call from the police in Madison, Wisconsin. The officer tells Dempsay that he is calling at the suggestion of the NCIS Great Lakes office. They found a body stuffed in the back of a small dark blue SUV parked in an out-lot of the Dane County Regional Airport. He further tells Dempsay that the body has a 9 mm slug in the abdomen as well as a .38 gunshot to the head. They also found a .38-caliber handgun with the dead man. She asks the officer if they happen to know when the car was parked in the lot. They had checked surveillance cameras and told her the date, which was the day after the murder. The officer indicates that the police and autopsy reports should be arriving same-day delivery to her attention. She thanks him and hang up the phone.

Dempsay gets the group together and tells them about the phone call and that they should be receiving reports later this afternoon. When they arrive, she brings it into the war room and opens it up. There is the police report, which she gives to Tuganov and Himmel to go through and gives the autopsy report to Hernandez and Loach. There is an eight-by-ten photo of the dead man in the SUV and she gives that to Johnston and Walsh.

Johnston takes out a photo of Mubarak from his file and confirms they are the same. Walsh, to remove any doubt, runs the image on the picture against facial rec and the name Nabil Mubarak comes up. So there is no doubt that the man killed in the SUV is, in fact, Mubarak.

Tuganov announces, "They also included a ballistics report with the main police report. It is consistent with what they told you over the phone. They also recovered a .38-caliber handgun next to the victim, which was wiped clean of prints. Are they sending the gun and slugs to us?"

Dempsay responds, "Yes, they should be here tomorrow via private courier. Looks like we will have all the murder weapons and all the slugs from Simmons's 9 mm."

Himmel chimes in, "The SUV was a rental that has been reported missing. In fact, that is what caught the attention of the police initially. They could not find any prints on the car. Must have taken the time to wipe down everything. It says here the police did not find anything else in the car or evidence of something that was placed in the car."

Hernandez and Loach look over the autopsy report. "No surprises here either. Coroner indicates the gunshot to the abdomen did not kill the victim, but the shot to the head did."

Tuganov looks at Dempsay. "Dempsay, do you want me to make the call or do you want to?"

Dempsay responds, "I'll make it." She then leaves the war room and goes to her desk, which is quiet at the moment. She dials Josh Bishop and waits for him to pick up.

Josh answers the phone, "Bishop!" He barks it out and seems clearly annoyed.

Dempsay hesitates, then says, "Josh, it's Special Agent Dempsay calling. Sorry, did I catch you at a bad time?"

"Hi, Agent Dempsay. No, it's okay. I'm not having the greatest day here. How can I help you?"

"Josh, the reason for my call is to let you know we found Roger's killer."

"Really! Was he wounded as you thought? Is he alive?"

"Well, Josh, I can't get into the details with you, but suffice it to say we have him in our custody."

"Okay. Have you found out why Roger was killed? What about the data on the memory sticks? What did you find there?"

"We are making progress as to the why, but I can't get into details with you. With the information you provided we are beginning to close in on suspects. I will fill you in on more details when I can give them to you. Josh, one more thing, have you seen the two men who were following you?"

"No, but they may have a different car now. Nothing has been standing out right now."

"And you still have the officers watching over you?"

"Yeah, they have been sticking close. How much longer do I still need protection?"

"For a while yet. I will let you know when it is all over, and we can pull the security detail. Listen, Josh, I have to go. Thank you for all your help. Goodbye."

"Goodbye, Agent Dempsay."

While at her desk, Dempsay looks for any recent e-mails with the hotel picture on it. She scans down the list of unread e-mails, and there it is. She opens the e-mail and the attached JPEG file to look at the photo. There they are at the front desk of the hotel, and you can clear see both faces. She quickly closes the image and forwards the e-mail to Walsh's computer, then steps back into the war room.

"Hey, Walsh, we just got the photo from the hotel, and I forwarded it to your e-mail."

Walsh opens the e-mail with the JPEG image and magnifies it so the faces of the two men take up most of the screen on her laptop. The others gather around to view the photo. Himmel is the first to speak, looking at Johnston, "That's definitely Mubarak on the right, but I'm not sure of the guy on the left."

Johnston moves in for a closer look. "Not sure. Looks to be Moroccan. He's not ringing a bell with me."

Walsh says, "Let me run his face through facial rec and see who he is." With that, she engages the facial rec database, then sits back to let it do its thing. As faces fly by to the right of the photo on the left on her screen, they wait. After about twenty minutes, the facial rec software stops on a face that is a dead ringer for the one in the picture. Walsh looks at the name and announces, "Our grand prize winner is…Habib Bakkali. Ring any bells with anyone?"

Himmel and Johnston are in shock. Himmel replies, "We have heard the name and is tied to all things the Moroccan syndicate is involved in. We just never had a picture of him. Holy crap, Walsh, you just put a face to a name we have been trying to find for a long time. Good job!" He claps her on the shoulder; she only took twenty minutes to find someone they have been after for years.

Tuganov says, "So a very important part of the Moroccan syndicate travels to Wisconsin to kill Simmons. I would say it was a very important mission for them." He gets nods all around.

The other teams leave the war room to update their files with this new information. Tuganov goes back to his desk to check e-mails, which leaves Dempsay and Walsh in the war room alone. Dempsay notices that Walsh looks troubled.

Dempsay asks, "Hey, Walsh, for someone who put a major crack in the case, you look a little down. What's up?"

"I'm sickened by all this," Walsh replies. "The human traffickers, the terrorists, and the murderers. How do you handle it?"

"That's a hard one. It wears on you to the point it numbs you. The key is to keep it from making you numb. I have learned to block out the emotion and focus on building a case to lock up the bad guys. It's easier said than done, but give it a try. I'll be here to help you, if you are interested."

Walsh meets Dempsay's gaze and nods in agreement. Both women look up as a commotion enters the war room, namely the five other agents. Tuganov announces, "It's beer time. Come on, you two."

Walsh tries to beg off, feeling like she wouldn't fit in. She has never been asked to go out with any team, even in the forensics department.

But then Dempsay intercedes, "Nonsense, Walsh, you're coming. After all, I need a wing woman to balance out all this testosterone."

With that, Walsh acquiesces by throwing up her arms, stating, "Oh, what the hell!"

Tuganov announces, "I heard Walsh say she is buying."
Walsh protests, "Hey! What! Wait a minute here!"

Dempsay jokes, "Well, yeah, you're the newbie and the new-bies always pay for the first round. It's the price of cracking the case. Besides, you're getting the new-agent treatment!"

Walsh, smiling, says, "Well, okay, I guess."

A mid-investigation night out is out of the ordinary, but the team feels they made substantial progress. Unbeknownst to all is that in the coming days, they would never be together again.

Harbinger

The next day, the team reconvenes with the goal to find out more about the Rabat security installation since it seems to have precipitated the murder of Roger Simmons. Walsh was blown away by the acceptance by the other agents when they went to the bar the night before. Energized by that, she spent some time prior to the group getting together to look further into the Rabat installation. She finds out it was the last project before Simmons left for Badger Power.

Walsh thinks to herself, *So what happened that he left? Was he fired because he cost the company an additional installation in Casablanca? Was he fed up with all the problems with installing these systems?* She may not know for sure, but she looks for reports from the Department of State regarding this and finds one report directly attributed to it.

It indicates that the company Simmons worked for was running into issues with the installation in Rabat that affected the deal in Casablanca. But more importantly, it was causing issues with the completion of the Rabat installation. According to the report, the team in country was being threatened, and in fact, one of the software engineers was attacked and injured. This was unusual in that she did not see any other installation where someone was attacked. The injured engineer was sent home, but the company did not send a replacement. This required Simmons to complete the job with the resources he had in country. This would have put stress on the team, especially if they ran into other software problems.

As the group gets together in the war room, she shares her findings with them. Walsh brings them up to speed on what she has been doing. Himmel, thinking out loud, says, "So I wonder what happened to provoke the attack. Whatever it was, it must have struck a nerve with the syndicate."

Johnston interjects, "They usually leave Americans alone since the Moroccan government is such a tight ally. They would come down hard on the syndicate. Walsh, was there anything in the file indicating what made the Moroccans go off like that?"

"No. There isn't even a hint of it in the incident report or any other notes that were in that envelope."

Tuganov asks, "Was there a name on that Department of State report? That could be a place to start, assuming they are still around."

"Yes, there was a name on the report. A Blake Roswell wrote it." She then checks the Federal Employee Database and finds what she is looking for. "According to the FED, Blake Roswell still works at the State Department."

Dempsay tells them, "Okay, let me make a call over there and see if we can meet with Mr. Roswell. When I get a time set up, Walsh, you and I are going to Foggy Bottom. Himmel and Johnston, I want you to go to your Moroccan informants to see what they can tell you about what happened in Rabat with Simmons. Hernandez and Loach, I want you to dive into what Simmons did from the time he returned from Morocco until he started working at Badger Power."

"And what task am I to do, Dempsay?" asks Tuganov.

"You have the assignment of giving Hawk a situation report. After that call the North Africa office in Cairo and see if they can locate Habib Bakkali and Rashid Houtan. Oh, before we part ways, I need a word with you."

The others go off to take care of their assignments, and Walsh excuses herself to the bathroom, leaving Dempsay and Tuganov by themselves. Standing in front of her with his hands on his hips, he asks, "What's up, Demps?"

"Toog, I need you to get Hawk to apply some pressure on the computer people to give us the contents of those flash drives. They have been here a week, and we've heard nothing except they are working on it."

"Yeah, sure, Demps. You going to see Amy while you two are at State?"

"Yes, she's my navigator over there. The place is so compartmentalized that is would take me forever to figure out who the right person to talk to." Both agents could not figure out what exactly Amy Cho did at the State Department, but Dempsay and Cho developed a good friendship.

CHAPTER 41

State Department

Dempsay and Walsh take the Metro to Foggy Bottom, and they meet Amy in the first-floor lobby of the building. Dempsay and Cho greet each other warmly, and Dempsay introduces Walsh to Amy.

Cho gets down to business, "Olivia, I'm a little pressed for time right now. Otherwise, I would catch up with you. Let go see Blake." The trio starts walking through the labyrinth of hallways.

"Thanks for taking the time to meet with us on short notice. So what does Blake Roswell do for the State Department?" asks Dempsay.

"He is the assistant secretary of African Affairs. He has been with us quite a while and knows a lot about the politics on that continent."

"I just hope he can help with an incident that occurred in Morocco."

"He most likely can."

When they reach his office, they enter and come face-to-face with the assistant secretary's aide. Amy introduces the agents to him, and he says they have been expecting them. He goes over to another office door and opens it just wide enough for him to enter. They can hear the two men have a conversation, and the aide reappears, ushering them into the assistant secretary's office. Cho makes the introductions to Roswell and then leaves. The two agents are invited to sit at Roswell's desk opposite him.

Roswell, an older man with white hair and wearing an older blue suit, smiles and extends his arms from his sides. "How can I help the Naval Criminal Investigative Service today?"

Dempsay responds, "Well, Mr. Roswell, I was hoping you could shed some light on an incident that occurred in Rabat, Morocco, several years ago in which you were involved. It concerned a company that installed a port security system there, and one of the company's workers was injured and sent home. There was a State Department write-up on it with your name on it."

"Why are you interested in something that happened a long time ago?"

"Well, the man you helped was murdered recently, and we think it has to do with something that happened back then."

Roswell, now looking at Walsh as if he just noticed her, asks, "What was the name of the man?"

Walsh responds, "Roger Simmons."

"Hmm, let me look in my files and see what I have." He shuffles over to a tall file cabinet, opens a drawer, and produces a file folder with the word *Rabat* on it. He returns to his desk and opens it in front of Walsh, facing her. Apparently, Roswell is more interested in talking to Walsh than Dempsay. Is it that she is younger or her red hair or both? Both women catch on, and Dempsay nods to Walsh to conduct the interview.

Roswell reads his notes in the file folder. "Well, it seems that Mr. Simmons had a run-in with the syndicate and one of his team members was shot. Our consulate there, along with my people, got the injured party out of the country after he was treated there of course."

Walsh asks, "So the injury was not life-threatening?"

"I don't recall, but it must have been serious enough to have surgery. We made sure he was escorted to his flight leaving Rabat and he got around under his own steam."

"So what caused the syndicate to shoot this man?"

Roswell thumbs through his report, reading sections of it using his finger to guide him. He then stops abruptly and looks up at Walsh with a troubled look on his face. "It doesn't look like that information was captured in this report."

Walsh feels he is clearly lying to her and the look she is getting from Dempsay confirms it. Walsh then shifts gears and asks if she could look at the report herself. He declines, but she persists and leans forward. "Oh, come on, Blake. It's just me here, and it won't leave this room." She flips her red hair for added effect.

Roswell, taken in by her flirting, says, "Well, as long as you don't take it out of this room, then yes, I will let you see the report." He removes the report from the file folder and hands it to her.

Walsh takes the paper from him as he begins to look at another paper in the file folder, not paying attention to Walsh. She looks at the page he was reading. Her eyebrows shoot up and turns to give Dempsay an "I found something big" look. The agents then lean in together so that Dempsay can read what was in the report. They resume their normal position, and Walsh fiddles with her smartphone.

Walsh looks at the wall of pictures behind Roswell, then asks, "Hey, Blake, who is that with you in the picture over there?" She points with her free hand at a picture on the far right on the wall opposite where she is sitting.

Roswell looks up and then turns around to see where Walsh is pointing, putting his back to her, then says, "Oh, that. That is a picture of me with the prime minister of Tanzania."

As he turns around to look at the picture, Walsh brings up the smartphone and snaps two pictures of the page they are looking at. She then quickly lowers the phone onto her lap with Roswell none the wiser.

Roswell continues, "Why do you ask?"

Walsh, now with an enamored look on her face, responds, "It is a very nice picture of you, and the other man looks interesting."

Roswell smiles. "Well, thank you, Agent Walsh."

Walsh flashes a big smile and cocks her head to one side. "Oh, Blake, you can call me Chloe."

Dempsay, who is watching this, is not sure what Walsh is up to at first but is impressed how smooth she is. When Walsh looks over at Dempsay, she gives Walsh a wink.

Walsh, still smiling, continues, "Blake, could I see the rest of the file, if you don't mind?"

Roswell's smile vanishes. "Well, I'm not sure about that."

Walsh turns up the flirting to include twirling her hair with index finger. "Oh, come on, Blake. Nothing happened when I looked at that other report. Right?"

Roswell nods. "You're right, Chloe. It's hard to say no to such a beautiful young lady interested in my work. Here." He hands over the entire folder to Walsh, and she begins to scan through the documents, knowing that Roswell will get bored and stop her if she takes too long. As she quickly scans through documents, she abruptly stops and looks up at the wall again.

"Blake, when I was looking at that picture a minute ago, I noticed there was a plaque next to it with your name on it. What did you get that one for?"

Predictably, Roswell turns his back on her to look at the plaque. As he does so, she photographs the page she is looking at. Then quickly she lowers the smart phone onto to her lap.

Roswell responds, "I received that as an award for all the humanitarian aid that I brought to Tanzania." Then he adds proudly with a smile, "I helped a lot of people there."

Walsh is feigning interest. "Blake, that is very impressive! You must be very proud of that one."

"Oh, I have received many awards." He stands and begins to show off all his many awards.

Walsh cuts him off, "Oh my gosh, Blake, I lost track of time. I need to get back to my office for a meeting with my boss. If I leave now, I will be able to get back in time. Can you please excuse us, Blake?"

"Yes, Chloe, of course! I'll have my assistant escort you and Agent Dempsay to the lobby. Thank you for coming today, and if there is anything I can help you with, please call me."

Back in the main lobby and free of Roswell's assistant, Dempsay turns to Walsh with one eyebrow cocked up. "So, Walsh, you're sandbagging me. I thought you never handled a law enforcement interview before. You didn't hesitate to jump in when he showed interest in you and went with your instincts, not to mention you played him like a fiddle and got some intel we wouldn't have gotten without a lot of fuss. Nicely done."

"Well, that was my first ever interview, Dempsay, I swear. I just played him like any other guy who has a thing for redheads. I think we make a good team! Right, Dempsay? We're like Cagney and Lacey."

Dempsay chuckles. "Cagney and Lacey? Isn't that a little before your time?"

"My mom watched it in syndication when I was younger."

"Okay, Cagney, let's get back to the office. After all, you have a meeting with your boss."

They both have a good laugh over that.

CHAPTER 42

Downburst

Since the altercation with the federal agents, the two Chinese Triad operatives, Zhang Wei and Li Jun, sat in their motel room in Wautoma. They kept to themselves and did not go out during the day. They also wanted to give the impression that they left so they would not be pursued further. Both men knew they were in trouble with their employer with the car chase and shooting at the federal agents. Yes, there employer would know about this; they have been keeping tabs on them.

Late on the third night after the incident, their satellite phone rings, and both men look at each other with dread. They are expecting this call but are not looking forward to it. Wei answers and listens to his boss on the other end, berating them for their clumsy actions with the federal police. The voice on the other end reminds Wei that they are to stake out where the plans are and take them without anyone knowing the wiser. Now based on their actions, they can just post it on the internet that two Chinese operatives are in Wisconsin, up to no good. The boss tells them to abort the mission and start making their way back to Hong Kong tomorrow. Wei hangs up and relays the conversation to Jun, both men relieved they will be returning home but uncertain of what will be waiting for them. They pack their bags, make travel arrangements, and call the front desk to tell them they are leaving early the next morning.

At 3:00 AM, when both Wei and Jun are sound asleep, the door to their room opens noiselessly, and two figures dressed in black enter the room. They have neglected to throw the deadbolt and put the chain across, so all the intruders needed is to use the skeleton key card to gain entry. Once in the room, the two uninvited guests locate the two men in bed quickly. They quietly draw weapons with silencers from the back of their uniforms and go to the foot of each bed, where Wei and Jun snore blissfully. The two intruders look at each other, one nods, and they fire simultaneously, shooting both sleeping men twice in the head. They retrieve the satellite phone, burner phones, and a laptop and quietly leave the room.

Later, the two black-clad assassins decide to hit Josh Bishop before the end of the next day, assuming that the two they shot kept their stakeout notes on the laptop. However, Wei and Jun never did. All that information is now splattered all over the headboards in the Wautoma motel room. The new operatives assume that Bishop still has the information they want and are unaware it is in NCIS custody. They need to locate Bishop and retrieve the information. They have also been instructed to kill him.

Pandora's Box

The next day, the team reconvenes in the war room earlier than usual. There is a lot of ground that needs covering. Dempsay notices that Tuganov is not in the room yet, so she engages in chitchat with the other agents, along with Walsh. Twenty minutes later, Tuganov arrives. Dempsay gives him a wondering look and taps her watch at him but doesn't say a word. He takes a seat with the rest at the one end of the room with the big screen.

Dempsay turns to Himmel and Johnston. "Okay, did your informants tell you anything that happened in Rabat?"

Himmel responds, "From what we were able to gather, the security equipment found three or four cargo containers of weapons of various sizes that were confiscated by the Moroccan authorities. These arms were heading off to several places where there are terrorist strongholds. Seems as though the syndicate was supplying arms to terror groups on a large scale. We're not sure exactly where these arms are coming from. I am assuming that the Moroccans were acting as the distributors and not the suppliers."

Walsh interjects, "We were able to corroborate the arms shipments via the file the State Department had on the incident. But we also found evidence that there was a shipment of women in a cargo container heading to these same areas that was intercepted.

Apparently, the terrorists were running out of vestal virgins to violate." This last she said with anger in her voice.

Tuganov asks, "Himmel, what is the dollar value of the weapons seized?"

"According to the government report on the weapons confiscated, they put it at between seven and ten million dollars. They had some sophisticated technology in those containers. Add to that whatever they were to get from the sale of the women, and it is big money."

Johnston adds, "It is big enough that the Moroccans would lose future sales if they could not guarantee delivery, not to mention they were counting on the proceeds of the sales of the arms. The pressure was on to get rid of that system and perhaps get control back on the containers that were seized. So it looks like they went after Simmons and his people to interrupt the completion of the system in Rabat and thwart the one being planned for Casablanca."

Dempsay states, "I'm surprised they didn't come at Simmons a lot harder than they did. Maybe the police got involved after they put two and two together on the seized women, contraband, and the attacks on the installation team."

Tuganov asks, "Hernandez, did you find anything about Simmons after Rabat?"

"Yes, we found after he returned home from Rabat, it was his last project for that company. Seems like he had a falling out with management over the way Rabat went down. Three months later, he quits the company, and after a few weeks of time off, he moves to Wisconsin and goes to work for Badger Power. A few months after he leaves, the company is bought out by a bigger company and it basically dissolves. We were able to track down a coworker of his who also didn't survive the sale of the company. He confirmed that Simmons was blamed for losing a sale for the Casablanca deal. The coworker also thought the company felt what happened in Rabat may have affected the sale of the company, giving it a bad mark. He stated the sale of the company was kept from the employees and only the CEO knew about it."

Tuganov quips, "Just another example of corporate America caring more about profits than their employees. Simmons thought he was doing the right thing by his coworkers by getting out of Rabat only to be labeled a scapegoat if the sale of the company didn't get as much as the fat cats wanted."

Dempsay asks Hernandez, "Did you broach the topic of the envelopes of information we have?"

"Actually, he brought it up, asking if we found the information Simmons has been hiding. Just to be clear, we did not discuss the case as it is but did tell him that we are investigating the events in Rabat. According to this person, their immediate boss, who was privy to the sale of the company and was not happy about it, was going to sell all the information we collected, including what is on the flash drives to the highest bidder. Simmons caught wind of it and stole the information and took it home. He then quit soon after he stole the items."

Dempsay turns to Tuganov and asks, "Tuganov, did you talk to Hawk yesterday?"

"Yes, we should have a visitor this morning with all the information about those flash drives. I also talked to the North Africa office in Cairo to have them start looking for Bakkali and Houtan. Earlier this morning, they called me back to tell me there has been some chatter about Houtan being on the run but is certainly not anywhere on the continent of Africa."

Just as Tuganov finishes his update, a young man steps into the war room. He is atypically dressed in his buttoned-at-the-top shirt, khakis, and sneakers, not to mention the longer hair and the full beard. He is also carrying a laptop in his hands. No one in the room notices he is in the doorway, so he says hello in a cheerful voice. All turn toward him as he greets the room.

Walsh was the first to speak, "Hi, Bensen, come on in." As he crosses the room to the group, she continues facing the group. "I want to introduce you to Miles Bensen from the Cyber Operations Unit. I imagine he has something to tell us about the flash drives."

"Welcome, Benson. Please have a seat. What do you have for us today?" asks Dempsay.

"Thanks. First, I have to apologize for taking so long to look at the contents of the flash drives. They presented quite a challenge in getting past the encryption. It was one I had not encountered before and wasn't until yesterday morning that I actually overcame it and was able to view what was on them."

Tuganov asks, "So what was it about these flash drives that made it hard to break the encryption?"

"First of all, these are old flash drives and they are not a type that were purchased in America. They were manufactured and sold in Russia probably fifteen to twenty years ago. As a result, I expected to find Russian encryption, but I did not."

Himmel interrupts, "Wait, did you say Russia? They haven't been on the radar on any of these cases. That's a new twist."

Walsh asks, "So the encryption was an old Russian type not in use?"

"That is what I expected, but it was not. It was an older Chinese encryption that is not in use."

"So we have old Russian hardware with old Chinese software?" Now looking at both Bensen and Walsh, Tuganov muses, "Isn't that kind of odd?"

"Yes, it is very odd. I'm not sure why anyone would do that."

Hernandez says, "You wouldn't unless you're playing both sides against each other. I think whoever put the information on the flash drives wanted an insurance policy of some sort."

"So, Bensen, what was on the flash drives?" asks Dempsay.

Bensen explains, "Well, all three flash drives had the identical files on them. So whoever created them made three copies. As far as what is on them, let me show you." He connects his laptop to the screen in front of them and a list of files can be seen on it. "As you can see, each flash drive has three files on it. These files represent the complete plans for the X-ray scanner, explosive detection system, and the radioactivity detector used in the company's security product. These plans contain not only all the hardware specifications but also source code for each one."

Tuganov asks, "Was there anything on them that would be considered classified?"

"No, not by US Government standards. However, these plans are very detailed and represents, in my opinion, an attempt at industrial espionage. Whoever was going to end up with the flash drives would have everything they need to recreate the entire system, including the special sauce that makes it all work together. Something more troubling is the fact a complete set of plans for a twenty-megawatt X-ray generator was included in the scanner plans. I think if this got into the wrong hands, it could be turned into a large-scale weapon."

"Like an X-ray gun?" questions Tuganov.

"Without a doubt and potentially other weapons."

Dempsay interjects, "So this is what the Chinese are after. They lost their chance to buy it, so now they are trying to steal it. Do we know if there are other copies of this flash drive around?"

"We have no way of knowing how many were made. It is possible that whoever kept these hidden thought they were the only ones in existence, but others could have been made."

The group looks at one another as they absorb what Bensen just told them. Dempsay speaks up, "Bensen, thanks for the report out. It has been very helpful." She is about to say something to Tuganov, but then her phone buzzes and she looks at the caller ID, decides to take it, and walks to the other end of the conference room.

Tuganov knows what Dempsay was going to say to him. He heads off to find Hawk to fill him in on what they have learned about the flash drives. The other agents start discussing the potential of what these flash drives could mean.

Walsh stands up. "Come on, Bensen, I'll walk you out." Once they are out, she turns to him and says, "Hey, Miles, you did a good job in there. You kept it short and to the point, which they really appreciated. Catch you later." They part company, and she heads back into the war room.

Dempsay is talking to the Great Lakes field office. They inform her the local police found the bodies of Wei and Jun in their hotel room in Wautoma earlier this morning. The manager found them when they didn't check out early as they said they would and called the police when he discovered their bodies. According to police, they were executed in their beds sometime during the night. Dempsay thanks them for the call and hangs up. She passes the information to the rest of the team, adding, "It looks like we now have two unknowns operating in Wisconsin."

The other agents look at each other, and Hernandez says, "That can't be good. It means they failed their mission and they sent more to finish the job. I think your witness is in real danger. If they have no problem killing their own, they won't have any problem killing a stranger."

Dempsay turns around, heads out the door of the war room, sits at her desk, and calls Josh Bishop. "Hi, Josh, it's Agent Dempsay again. Hey, I just wanted you to know that the two Asian men following you around were found dead earlier this morning."

"Please tell me that's good news."

"Sorry, Josh, not really. It means that one or two others have replaced them and are most likely to up the ante against you. Please be very careful and do not try to shake your security detail."

"That doesn't sound like good news, Agent Dempsay. When is this going to be over with? I'd like to get my life back."

Dempsay says goodbye and hangs up, and she calls the Wisconsin Department of Criminal Investigation to talk to the agent in charge of the security detail for Bishop and his wife. She explains to him what has happened and requests addition resources to back up those already committed. The DCI agent tells her they will do their best.

CHAPTER 44

Escape

Three o'clock in the morning, Rashid Houtan (a.k.a. Ralph Peterson) lands in Riyadh, Saudi Arabia. On the morning Roger was killed, he drove to General Mitchell Airport and took a flight from Milwaukee to Chicago; from there, he boarded a flight to Riyadh. He did not stick around for the assassination, not because he felt bad that it was going to happen, but he was tired of staying in one place for so long, especially in America. Besides, he didn't want to stay for the aftermath, the questions that may come his way from the police or the company, so he left as soon as he could.

Rashid likes to call himself a provider of services, one who knows people and can provide all kinds of shadiness for the right price. Just think of him as a criminal concierge, whether it is fixing someone up with a fence for stolen goods, stealing antiquities, laundering money, or supplying people with *special* skills. As a result, he built and maintains a network of informants and go-to people throughout northern Africa, the Middle East, and Europe.

One of his trusted confidants in Saudi Arabia meets him at King Khalid Airport in Riyadh. Rashid had texted him prior to leaving Chicago to meet him at this airport. The plan was to hole up here for a while and then go on to another location yet to be determined. The man told Rashid that both the Moroccan and Chinese employers are aware that he is now in Saudi Arabia; they are angry and looking for him. This creates a new wrinkle in his plans, and he decides that he cannot stay in Riyadh despite being exhausted from travel.

The bad blood started when the Moroccan Customs Ministry decided to install a cargo scanner at their port in Rabat. Rashid told his Moroccan clients who employed him that the installation of a cargo scanner would not affect their business. However, it did affect their business in a big way, and he ended up being the scapegoat for the crime families involved. He was given a choice to either die or go to America to find Roger and get as much information about the equipment in Rabat and provide them information on Roger's whereabouts. They expected him to finish his search in six months or less. However, once he found Roger Simmons, he waited another year before letting his employers know. They weren't happy about the delay since they continued to racking up losses by spending more money rerouting their contraband to avoid Rabat. The Moroccan crime families decided to terminate their relationship with Mr. Houtan.

Houtan had a side deal with the Chinese government. He would tell them where they could find the plans for the Incheon scanner in order to copy it. Growing impatient, they sent two men to find out the whereabouts of the plans. Now they want him or their money back from him, which he already squirrelled away to use as operating funds for his "business."

Rashid hates the West and makes a point not to do business in or travel to any of the Americas. He made this one exception because the target made him look bad and the alternative was not pleasant. By waiting, he would make more money. To get close to Roger Simmons, he obtained a job with Badger Power as a transmission line engineer. Another reason he waited is that he saw an opportunity to make even more money from the evil imperialist. He would cash his paychecks and then wire the cash to a bank in Casablanca, where he could then wire it anywhere in the world. Besides, the target wasn't going anywhere. Badger Power was so clueless they didn't pry into his fabricated past. They did not reprimand him for poor performance; he showed enthusiasm but was doing just enough to show he was working. He even had time to take care of other clients while he was keeping tabs on Roger.

Wasting no time, he goes back into the Riyadh airport. As he turns to leave, his confidant asks him where he is going, and Rashid suggests that it would be better for him not to know. He pays his man for his time, arranges his flight, and turns off his cell phone so no one can track him. He books a flight to Dushanbe, Tajikistan, hopefully to avoid his employers.

CHAPTER 45

The Hunt Begins

From what the North Africa office could determine, Habib Bakkali has been staying in a home in Casablanca which is well guarded and fortified. The local office tells the OSP that they do not have the resources to launch an assault on the residence. SAC Hawkinson makes the short trip to the NCIS director's office to discuss how they will prosecute the takedown. By the end of the meeting, a plan is in place to launch *Operation Havoc* to be led by the NCIS Regional Enforcement Action Team or REACT, specifically their Echo team. The purpose of REACT is to support high-risk enforcement operations and operate much like special forces units. Along with the REACT squad, two NCIS OSP special agents of Hawk's choosing will join in.

Walsh was sent back to her Forensic unit with high marks for her contributions and a full recommendation by Hawk to have her enter in the Special Agent Basic Training Program, based on recommendations from all six of the agents. He assembles the special agents into the war room to discuss the operation and announce his picks for which special agents will participate. It is a hard decision, and there will be some hurt feelings since all of them have skin in the game. He then lays out the operation to go after Bakkali with a REACT team under the operation with the codeword *Havoc*. He fully expects everyone to ask if they can go but asks, "Any questions?"

Tuganov goes first, as Hawk thought he would, "Are you allowing any special agents to go along?"

Himmel says, "You can't shut us out, Hawk. We have too much invested in this."

Dempsay weighs in, "Are you planning to use agents in the North Africa office?"

Hawk is enjoying this only because he fully anticipated their reactions. He is disappointed that Hernandez and Loach didn't pipe up, but they are probably thinking this isn't their fight. He responds, "Yes, we are planning to use the local agents for on-the-fly intel and provide ground transport." He pauses a couple of beats, then continues, "I am also been given leeway by the director to add two and only two special agents from this group."

That got everyone's attention, including Hernandez and Loach, and all eyes are on Hawk to hear what decision he has made. Everybody is itching to get their hands dirty. Dempsay responds, "Okay, Hawk, spill it. Who's going?"

The REACT team, with all their tactical gear, are in a C-130 aircraft on their way to Naval Station Rota in Spain. The REACT Echo team of eight men is led by Commander Adam Nelson. They are dressed in navy blue coveralls, with no insignias or indication of what agency they work for. They have full-body armor and matte black helmets that have large ear openings to accommodate communication devices of any kind. They carry assault rifles, automatic handguns, and the two snipers in the group carry an M14 rifle and a longer-range carbine. The OSP agents, Himmel and Johnston, are chosen to be on the team for their familiarity with the area and who they are up against. They are dressed similarly but are provided smaller assault rifles since those are the weapons they are used to handling. The agents also carry their standard-issue semiautomatic handguns in drop holsters secured to their thighs. Commander Nelson made it crystal clear to the OSP agents that he is in charge and there will be no going rogue actions.

The entire team flies to Rota's naval base, changing planes to a smaller Osprey aircraft and land at the Mohammed V International Airport south of the city of Casablanca after dark. That airport cannot accommodate a C-130, but it offers anonymity since many US military aircraft use it due, in part, to the friendly relations the US has with Morocco.

As Operation Havoc is set up, the group will meet up with NCIS agents from the North Africa field office and take two vans to travel to the objective in the Sidi Maarouf district of the city. They are to arrive at an abandoned building next the Café Riyad Soumia and across from the house containing Habib Bakkali, according to intel they received. They will approach and park behind the building so they cannot be seen. Under the attentive eye of their overwatch, codename *Zebra 1*, they will then wait until sometime after midnight to enter that building to remove Habib Bakkali and take him prisoner.

Their exit, or exfil, will be to retrace their path back to the airport where the Osprey will wait for them and return them to Rota. If, for whatever reason, they cannot make it to the airport or the Osprey is compromised, their secondary exfil will be from the main seaport, known as Acienne Medina International Port. The *USS Stark* is moored there, which, again, is a common practice given the relationship between the two countries. If the skipper of the vessel receives a message that the group is heading toward the port, they will prepare to leave as soon as they arrive. The *Stark* will then set out north along the Moroccan coast, cross the Strait of Gibraltar, and make way to the port of Rota.

If the team cannot make it across town to the *USS Stark*, then the tertiary exfil plan is to have the *USS Boxer*, a helicopter carrier that is currently participating in drills off the coast of Portugal, dispatch Seahawk helicopters to conduct a search and rescue operation of the entire team. If this plan is used, the team is instructed to make their way west out of Casablanca to a set of coordinates and the pilots will use their GPS units to meet them. If anyone fires upon the team or the helos, the Seahawks will have orders to engage the opposition. They are fully capable surface warfare aircraft with two fifty-caliber machine guns at each side door and four hellfire missiles slung underneath.

CHAPTER 46

Home

Tajikistan is Rashid's home country, born and raised in a small village of Rohati up in the mountains, which is west of the capital city of Dushanbe. He spent his younger years playing in the mountains and exploring the capital city. His boyhood dream was to attend the Tajik National University and be the first one in his family to get a college education.

That dream is shattered one night when Rashid came home late from playing with friends and he finds that his family has been killed in a fire that destroyed their home. Suddenly, at the age of fifteen, he finds himself alone and homeless. He spends the next four years living in the streets of Dushanbe, stealing and hustling to get by.

At nineteen, he attaches himself to a crime family in the area, primarily selling and transporting drugs. During one of his transactions, he got caught up in a sting operation. In the ensuing seven years he spends in prison, he meets a man from whom he learns the fine art of being a criminal fixer. Upon release from prison, he begins his new vocation locally. He builds up a good business, and within three years he has an opportunity to expand, which caused him to move to Morocco.

Arriving in Dushanbe, Rashid takes a cab to the Vakhsh Hotel south of the downtown area. The Vakhsh was built in the early 1950s during the Soviet years. It was quite the place to be, but now it is rundown and not as popular as it once was. This is why Rashid chose this hotel so that he would potentially not be exposed and less chance of being recognized. He requests a room on the top floor facing the street so that he can have good sight lines and can easily escape if need to. He stays in his room and is constantly surveilling around the hotel. Refraining from making contact with people he knew here, he leaves his phone turned off. He has food brought from a restaurant he frequented in the past and left them instruction to leave it outside his door and would pick it up after they left.

This goes on for a couple of days until a knock comes on Rashid's door. He is torn between answering it or not. The knock comes again, this time louder. He goes to the door and feigns a gruff old man's voice speaking Russian, "What do you want?"

"It is Antebe. I come with news," the man on the other side of the door says flatly in the Tajik language.

Rashid knows Antebe very well but is still uncertain. The man on the other side of the door clearly understands Russian. Rashid decides to give him a test. "Where does my sister go to school?" Again, in Russian.

The other man sighs and says, again in Tajik, "My dear friend, your sister does not go to school for she has been dead many years."

With that, Rashid unlocks the door and opens it slowly, looking out in the hallway in both directions before motioning Antebe into the room. Once inside, Rashid closes and locks the door. The men embrace since they had not seen each other in a long time. They disengage and Rashid claps Antebe on the shoulder, and he says to his friend in Tajik, "It is good to see you, dear friend. How have you been?"

"I am well, but you have trouble, my friend! I came to tell you there are men from Morocco who are looking to kill you. They have come to Dushanbe, asking if anyone knows Rashid Houtan. I do not tell them I know you, but I think they smell a lie. The Moroccans are beating information out of people to find out where you are. They are convinced you are here, but no one knows you are in Dushanbe. I came here on a hunch that if you were in town and you knew people were after you, you would lay low in a seedy hotel far away from the busyness of the city. Rashid, you are in danger. You need to leave immediately."

"Thank you for the warning. Let me pack my bag and I will get a car to the airport."

"There is one other thing. I am hearing that a friend of yours in Riyadh was found in the Empty Quarter of the desert with a bullet in his head."

Rashid shakes his head in disgust and then looks at Antebe. "You are a true friend!"

"Rashid, now come. I have my car parked in the rear of the hotel. I will take you to the airport, but you need to promise me something."

"What is that, Antebe?"

"Wherever you go, take me with you, for I am a dead man if I stay."

Rashid nods and motions his friend out the door, taking the back stairs to the car. They take the back streets to the airport, parking near it. When they get into the terminal, they scan the departure board to see where they can go.

Rashid points. "Look, Antebe, there is a flight to Almaty within the hour. Shall we take that one?"

Antebe, still looking at the departure board, replies, "That would be good, but let's see what else is available." After further scrutinization, he announces, "Well, it looks like the flight to Almaty is the one to take."

Before they get to the Air Astana ticket counter, Rashid asks, "Antebe, do you need new papers and money to get on the plane?"

"Yes, I left my papers at home, so I would not use them. I am afraid I do not have enough money on me to pay for the ticket."

"Very good. I have a set of papers that you will not have any problems with. The picture on the passport matches the driver's license and is a good likeness of you." Rashid roots around in his backpack and pulls out a set of documents and hands them to Antebe. Reaching back into the backpack, he takes out a small stack of five hundred Tajikistani somonis, the local paper currency, and hands that to Antebe, saying, "This should be more than enough to buy your ticket and take care of any other expenses when we get to Almaty."

Antebe protests, "This is too much. I cannot possibly repay you!"

Rashid wags his finger at him. "Nonsense! Consider it payment for getting me out of danger."

"Well, we are not out of here yet. I will call ahead to a friend of mine that lives in Almaty so he can pick us up."

Rashid's eyes narrow. "Can he be trusted?"

Antebe smiles. "Yes, my friend, he can be trusted."

Both men walk up to the Air Astana ticket counter and buy a one-way ticket to Almaty, Kazakhstan. They pass through what Tajikistan considers airport security, which is a customs person checking to see if you have a boarding pass and a passport. As they wait to board, they are unaware of a young Asian man who has been following them since the ticket counter. He sits in a chair in another nearby gate, reading a magazine and periodically glancing their way.

Hearing the boarding announcement, both Rashid and Antebe rise and get in line to enter the plane. They are chatting between themselves and are oblivious to anyone watching them. As the two men disappear into the jetway, the Asian man takes out his cell phone and makes a phone call lasting only a few seconds. He then gets up and leaves the airport.

CHAPTER 47

New Start

The evening is cold and rainy when Antebe and Rashid land in Almaty. After breezing through customs, they meet up with a man in an old blue Russian Lada. Antebe makes the introductions, "Rashid, this is my friend, Nurlan Usenov. Nurlan, this is Rashid Houtan." Both men bow and nod slightly toward each other in greeting.

Nurlan offers, "Come, I have reserved rooms for the both of you at the Hotel Kazakhstan." With that, he opens the doors for the two men to get in and takes what bags they carried and puts them in the trunk of the old car.

As they ride the thirty minutes to the hotel, Antebe directs Nurlan, "Please do not take us to the front entrance of the hotel. Take us to the rear entrance."

Nurlan nods. "Yes, of course." As they near the hotel, Nurlan turns down a narrow alley which runs along the back of the hotel where there is a single service door. They exit the Lada, and Nurlan opens the trunk and removes their bags and hands them to his passengers.

Antebe asks Nurlan, "What name is on the hotel reservations?"

Nurlan replies, "I reserved two rooms, one under the name of Sattar Omarov and the other under the name Amil Kratova." Then taking cards from his shirt pocket, he adds, "Here is a driver's license and credit card for that name to use." He hands them over to Antebe.

Antebe thanks him and has one more request. "Can you please arrange for us to obtain some new papers tomorrow?"

"Yes, that will not be a problem. I will text you when I will come and pick you up. I assume you will be eating in the hotel tonight?"

Antebe nods and thanks him again. Nurlan gets back into the car and drives off. The two travelers gather their things and head into the hotel's back door. The hotel's restaurant is located in one of the back corners of the first floor with a combination hookah bar and strip club occupying the other rear corner. The hallway they are walking in separates the two.

The Hotel Kazakhstan was built in the early 1970s and was considered very posh and regarded as the premier hotel in Almaty. It boasts twenty-six floors, and the top of the hotel looks like a crown. In fact, when the hotel opened its doors, the media dubbed it the *crown jewel of Kazakhstan*. To make the lobby dramatic and opulent, it has gold foil wallpaper, gold leaf columns, gold-colored carpets, along with the fifty-foot-long front desk with its gold top and gold foil sides. The stair railings are gold, and the vases that hold the gold-colored flowers are gold colored as well. There are two things that are not gold in the lobby. The first is the milk white marble floor and the other is the seating. The chairs and couches are contemporary in style and are all made of black leather with gold metal frames. The decor of the lobby was so over the top that a couple of American rap stars tried to use it for a backdrop for a music video.

The two men check in under their assumed names. Rashid tells Antebe he wants to stop at the concierge desk and will meet him at the restaurant in an hour. Antebe takes the elevator to his room. Rashid walks across the lobby to the concierge desk and can see the concierge, Oleg Barkesinov, who is on the telephone, engrossed in a conversation.

This concierge has the unique talent of providing his guest anything they want, with the emphasis on the word *anything*. Rashid was hoping he could deliver on his request. Once he gets off the phone, he greets his guest, "Good evening. I am Oleg, your concierge. How may I be of service to you?"

"I am Sattar Omarov, and I just checked in this evening. I was wondering if you could obtain a pistol for me."

"Why, of course, Mr. Omarov. There are many different types at my disposal. Any particular make or model?"

"I would prefer a recent vintage Walther PPK."

"Very good choice, Mr. Omarov. Is there a price you are looking to pay?"

"Yes, I would like to spend no more than five thousand tenge for it." Tenge is the name of the currency in Kazakhstan.

"I can certainly buy one at that price. Now for seven thousand five hundred tenge, I can get you one with what the Americans say... has all the bells and whistles, and I will throw in a box of ammunition."

Rashid considers this, then responds, "That would be fine, Mr. Barkesinov. When can I pick it up?"

"Please stop by my desk tomorrow morning, and I will give it to you then."

Rashid thanks the man. He goes up to his room and gets ready for dinner. He meets Antebe at the restaurant and gets a table in the back. During the meal, Antebe receives a call from Nurlan who informs them they have a ten o'clock appointment with someone to make papers for them. He tells them he will meet them at the back entrance at nine thirty.

The next morning, Rashid picks up his package from Oleg in which one of the "bells and whistles" is a silencer. He explains to Antebe he may need this in the near future. Antebe indicates to him the gun might be useful for their appointment this morning.

Antebe tells Rashid he arranged for tomorrow to have Nurlan drive him to the village of Batpak, which is just outside Bishkek in neighboring Kyrgyzstan. Antebe tells Rashid that he has family there and will stay with them until things cool down and before returning to Dushanbe.

Making their way to the hotel's rear entrance, they observe the blue Lada already there. Nurlan gives him the all clear, and both men walk quickly to the car and get in. He makes his way to their destination, which turns out to be the Kazakhstan Museum of Rare Books. Antebe looks at Nurlan questioningly. "Where have you taken us?"

"Antebe, there is someone who works here that does excellent work. They are expecting us. Please come." Rashid and Antebe exchange worried glances and then get out of the car.

They enter the small museum, and Nurlan tells the receptionist that they would like to speak to Aruzhan. They are told to take the elevator down to the restoration section of the museum. As they walk toward the elevator, they pass a copy of the Koran from the Ottoman era that is under glass. When the elevator doors opened, they are pleasantly surprised this basement is well lit and had good ventilation. They walk along a corridor and reach a door with the words *restoration department* on it. Nurlan knocks on the door, and a woman answers and lets them in. She knows Nurlan but does not like her other visitors. She stands and says nothing, keeping a stern eye on Antebe and Rashid, and they returned the favor. Nurlan breaks the silence, "Aruzhan, these are the men I told you about yesterday who are interested in purchasing new papers. This is Antebe and the other is Rashid."

Looking harshly at Rashid, she finally speaks, "So, Mr. Houtan, we meet again. I am surprised you agreed to meet, given the way we parted company last time."

Glancing sternly at Nurlan, Rashid responds, "Had I known we would be meeting you, I would have not come. The last time we met, I was almost arrested, thanks to you."

"Yes, I also remember our last meeting. I still have the scar from where you shot me. But perhaps today we can put all that aside and conduct some business."

Rashid cocks his head to one side. "Perhaps. We are in need of two sets of identities with complete sets of documents, and we must have them today. Can you accommodate us?"

Aruzhan responds in a demanding tone, "That is a very short turnaround. It will cost you."

"Really? How much?"

"It's $30,000—American!"

"For both?"

"No, for each!"

Rashid explodes in feigned anger, "Are you serious!" He turns to Nurlan. "I did not come here to be robbed!"

"They are the best you will ever find."

Rashid responds sarcastically, "They should be printed on gold leaf for that price! I will give you $15,000 for each."

"No. That does not even cover my costs. I can do $28,000 each and no less."

"I would pay that for both, not each. I can give you $18,000 each. If you cannot, then we do not have a deal."

The negotiators stare at each other for what seems like an eternity. Antebe is enjoying this negotiation, but Nurlan is not.

Aruzhan finally breaks the silence, "Considering I would like the business, I am willing to sell the documents for $23,000 dollars each."

Rashid considers this offer and responds, "I am not as keen to do business with you, Aruzhan, but time is not on my side. Make it $20,000 each and we have a deal."

Aruzhan looks away while making calculations in her head. "Mr. Houtan, you have a deal. Let's take some photographs and let me get started. I will have them ready by four o'clock, so you may want to conduct other business or do some sightseeing in the meantime. I want ten thousand now and the rest when you return. I trust you have the money?"

"Yes, I have it." He fishes out a stack of $100 bills and hands them to Aruzhan. As she reaches for it, he pulls it back and says, "Please be sure my friend that I receive the only copies of the papers you create for us. Eh?"

Aruzhan is slightly smiling. "But of course, you and your friend will receive the only copies. You have my word." Her policy is to create a copy of each identity as insurance. She has no intention of changing that now, especially with Rashid Houtan in the mix.

After the pictures were taken, they leave the museum and get in the Lada. Nurlan, thinking Rashid is angry with him, apologizes for taking them to Aruzhan. "I am sorry for having you meet with her. Had I known you had some bad history with her, I would have gone elsewhere, but it would have been harder to obtain papers."

"Nurlan, I am not angry with you. She is good at what she does."

"But I thought you were angry at me for bringing you here to be robbed!"

Rashid half smiled. "Oh, that. All that was for her benefit, not to scold you."

Laughing softly, Antebe says, "That was well played, my friend."

Rashid, looking out his window, in a darker tone, replies, "I do not trust that woman! She is very ruthless and deceptive." Now wagging his finger in the direction of the museum, he adds, "She has tried to trick me in the past, and she will try it again. We will need to proceed with extreme caution."

As they sit in the Lada, talking, Rashid saw Aruzhan come out of a rear door and go to a car, which he assumes is hers since she unlocks it and takes out a pack of cigarettes and lights one up while leaning on the car. Rashid makes note of the model and color of it and then also checks the museum hours on the front door. He begins to think.

At the appointed hour, the three men make their way back to the Museum of Rare Books and down to the restoration department. They were met by Aruzhan, who had two large manila folders on a table for them. She motions to them, "Here are your new identities."

Rashid opens the one for him and lays out the documents. He produces a loop from his shirt pocket and begins to inspect them, document by document, front and back. After several minutes of inspection, Rashid pronounces them very good. Antebe is also satisfied with his documents as well.

Rashid then produces another stack of $100-dollar bills and hands it to Aruzhan, and as before, he holds on to the money as she grabs it and asks her while looking her in the eyes, "Did you remember your promise? That we would have the only copies of these documents?"

She responds plainly, "Yes, these are the only copies of these papers."

But there it is, it is so subtle and yet unmistakable. Rashid sees the slightest change in her eyes that tells him she is lying. He gives her no indication that he caught it and lets go of the money.

As they gather the documents and place them back into the envelopes, Aruzhan says, "It was a pleasure doing business with you." What she thinks is, *I hope someone comes along wanting to find you and wishes to purchase the second set I made, and maybe I will recoup what I lost in this deal.*

Without saying a word, Rashid picks up the envelopes and turns to go, with the other two men following him. Nothing is said between them until they get back in the car. As he studies the museum, Rashid asks the other two when they plan on leaving the next day.

Antebe responds, "We will leave in the morning, perhaps nine or ten o'clock. When are you planning to leave?" He doesn't bother to ask where Rashid is going because he doesn't want to know.

Before diverting his attention from the museum to answer Antebe, Rashid observes Aruzhan again going out to her car to smoke, and he looks at his watch to note the time. He then responds to Antebe, "I think I will take an afternoon flight, so I will be leaving after you."

The three men drive back to the Hotel Kazakhstan, unaware that they have been followed since this morning by four Asian men taking turns tailing them and using different cars in the process.

CHAPTER 48

Parting

The next morning, it is raining hard, and Rashid, Antebe, and Nurlan have breakfast in the hotel, with two of the four Asian men watching them, pretending to eat a meal. The other two are in a nearby car in case their prey decides to leave. The three men move to the lobby. Rashid says goodbye to the other two, embracing them and wishing them well. The two men then leave the hotel and walk to Nurlan's Lada parked down the street. They make their way through the city to the A-2 Highway and start their five-hour ride to Bishkek.

The two Asian men outside the hotel begin to follow the Lada and decide to take them before they leave the country, if that is what they are doing. The other two remain in the hotel and watch Rashid go upstairs to his room. One of the Asian men makes a phone call to see if they can take him now. The person on the other end tells him no, there would be too many witnesses. So they wait in the lobby for the next time he comes down from his room. They make a phone call to another man they have at the airport to keep an eye out for Rashid.

At two o'clock, Rashid packs his small bag and proceeds to screw the silencer onto the Walther. He then places the weapon in his coat pocket and leaves the hotel room. Instead of taking the elevator, he takes the back stairs down to the first floor, which empties out in the back hallway. Without hesitation, he exits the hotel through the back door into the rainstorm.

Rashid takes a circuitous path to the museum. He walks to the trees in the back of the parking lot, goes behind them near Aruzhan's car, and waits. After a while, he checks his watch and notes that it shouldn't be long until she comes out for a smoke. He reasons that she, in fact, made another set of identities and he cannot allow them to get into the hands of his employers so they can track him. He came to Almaty for a clean break, and she is now a liability. He usually hires someone to handle this kind of work, but today he will have to get the job done. He needs to finish what he attempted to do the last time they were together.

Like clockwork, Aruzhan comes out of the museum and walks quickly to her car, gets in, and slams the door quickly to get out of the rain. She lights up and takes a drag, leans back in the driver's seat, and closes her eyes. She has a headache and is on edge since receiving an answer to an inquiry she put out on the dark web for anyone looking for Rashid Houtan. They had arranged to meet tomorrow. Rubbing her eyes, she contemplates taking a small nap and maybe the headache will go away. She keeps her eyes closed and takes another drag on the cigarette. She is oblivious to the form just outside her window.

Rashid quickly takes two shots—*thuk, thuk*—and the passenger-side window becomes covered in brains and blood. He quickly walks away from the parking lot in the opposite direction than he came from.

Aruzhan's body slumps toward the passenger seat. It now looks like no one is in the car. The cigarette she was holding bounces to the floor of the car, and in a matter of minutes, a small fire erupts. Fifteen minutes later, the interior of the car is engulfed in flames.

Rashid crosses on a bridge over a canal where he throws the Walther into the water. He continues to walk until he reaches a major street. He hails a cab and instructs the driver to go to the airport.

As Antebe and Nurlan continue, the Lada enters the exit to the Bishkek Highway. A man in the trailing car makes a phone call and sets up a surprise when the blue Lada gets to the bridge at Chu River, just before the border with Kyrgyzstan. This bridge spans a very steep gorge with the waters of the river roiling below. It turns out that the guardrails along both sides of the bridge ends about twenty feet short, leaving a gap where vehicles could plunge into the river.

As the Lada approaches the bridge, they notice a truck blocking the road at the other end of the bridge that appears to be broken down with the hood up. They slow down and then stop just short of the truck. Antebe and Nurlan remain in the car, not sure what to do. While they look to go around it, two local men get out of the cab and walk to the rear of the truck, not paying too much attention to the occupants of the car. They pull out two AK-47 machine guns out of the back of the truck, turn around quickly, and begin to open fire on the men in the Lada.

As soon as the men turn around, Antebe knows what is coming and tries to get out of the car. Nurlan is frozen in place by fear, then realizing what Antebe is doing, he tries to get out as well. Both men are too late as the interior of the Lada is torn apart and the windshield obliterated from the gunfire. The bodies of both men are riddled with bullets. The men from the truck stop shooting, and they walk to the car. The one on the driver's side reaches in and puts the car in neutral. Both men push it through the opening in the guardrail and watch it fall quickly into the river below.

The Chinese agents following the Lada roll up to the truck. They engage in a short conversation with the shooters. As they do this, one of the agents gets behind the other two and executes both of them with one shot each to the back of the head. The agents then push the dead men over the edge into the river. They also put the truck in neutral and slowly push it over the edge as well. If the truck and car are ever found, it will look like an accident.

At the airport, Rashid checks the departure screens, looking for flights leaving that afternoon. He has a destination in mind but wants to see if there is still a flight today. He finds what he is looking for and notices it leaves in ninety minutes. Walking over to the Aeroflot ticket counter, Rashid purchases a one-way ticket using his new credit card with his new identity. He walks through security, showing his new passport and boarding pass. He settles in at the gate, unaware of the older Chinese agent following him who sits in a row of seats behind Rashid.

The time comes to board and Rashid gets in line to file into the plane. As he walks into the jetway, the agent takes his cell phone out and makes a call. He informs the person on the other end that Rashid Houtan just boarded a flight to Dagestan.

CHAPTER 49

Intervention

The team's Osprey aircraft touches down at the airport in Marrakesh at about 11:00 PM local time. As the aircraft taxies to the far end of the runway, two white nondescript vans roll up to the rear of the Osprey. The drivers, agents from the North Africa office, get out and stand by their vehicles, waiting for the doors to the airplane open up. Greetings are short, and the team moves quickly to transfer equipment from the plane to the vans. They head north toward their objective and make it to the abandoned building without detection. The team quickly sets up shop, posting lookouts on both floors of the building and placing the snipers on the roof. Echo team leader, Nelson, informs their oversight, Zebra 1, they are in the first position.

The lookouts are joined by one other team member to surveil the area and set up listening posts using parabolic dishes to pick up conversations in other buildings and out in the street. They are watching for potential watchers, those that may be watching them watch the house. At this hour of the night, there shouldn't be a lot of activity, but they still need to look into the shadows for anyone guarding the house on the outside.

The local agents work their phones, talking to their informants to make sure the target is still in the house. After a few phone calls, they are satisfied that Bakkali is in the house and let Nelson know of their latest intel. He, in turn, notifies Zebra 1, who gives him his first green light to proceed.

Nelson assembles the team, except for the two local agents and the snipers, to go over the plan to capture Bakkali.

The plan is to avoid the street in front of the target house and exit out the rear of their building and make their way to the rear. At Nelson's signal, a small-shaped charge will be placed on the rear door. These charges make little to no sound when they detonate. Once inside, they will clear the first floor, making sure opposition does not get a shot off. Any unusual sound will raise the alarm and the target may escape. Their mission is all about stealth, and so no flash bangs will be used tonight. Once the first floor is clear, they will move to the second floor and clear that floor as well. The most recent intel indicates the target is on the second floor at the far end in a room separated by a door. Once they have their target, they will retrace their steps back to the abandoned building, get back into the vans, and head toward the airport where the Osprey is at.

It's now 2:30 AM and Nelson checks in with Zebra 1 to make sure the operation is a go. The overwatch gives Nelson the second green light to proceed. He gives orders to the team to get their weapons and themselves ready to move out.

At 2:50 AM, the team rolls out of the back of the abandoned building and makes their way slowly and stealthily to the rear of the target house and locate the rear door. Nelson radios Zebra 1 that they are in position to enter the house and gets the third green light. He checks in with his snipers if things on the street and the front of the house are quiet. They give him the all clear. With that, he gives a team member a hand signal to breach the door. As he places the charge on the door, two other team members position themselves to fire into the house. Himmel and Johnston are the rear guard and have their attention on the group's flank, ensuring no one surprises them from behind.

At exactly 3:00 AM, Nelson looks over the team to make sure they are ready to go and then nods to the team member that holds the detonator and mashes down on the switch. The door comes off its hinges, and two team members grab it before it crashes to the ground. A split second later, two other team members take out the guard at the rear entrance without him firing a shot. The whole team then files into the rear of the first floor with Nelson and two others in the lead with Himmel and Johnston at the rear facing toward the rear entrance. Team members in the middle peel off to clear rooms as they move forward. The three in front encounter two more guards that are sleeping and woke when the intruders approached. The two guards swing up their assault rifles, but they are dispatched quickly and in silence. Within a matter of minutes, they have stealthily cleared the first floor. Himmel and Johnston take pictures of the guards who were taken out and send them to Zebra 1 for identification. Nelson points upward, indicating to head upstairs.

Lining up as they did when they entered the building, they quietly go up the stairs to the second floor, making as little sound as possible. At the top of the stairs, Nelson holds up his fist, signaling the group to halt. He stays in his crouch and intently listens for any voices, footsteps, or evidence of a TV on. He hears nothing; all is quiet. This might not be a good thing. Perhaps the intel is wrong and Bakkali is not here or he is lying in wait for them. Well, there is only one way to find out. Nelson begins to rise but is frozen by a radio message in his ear from one of the snipers.

"Echo 1, Echo 7. We have an armed tango approaching the front door. Want us to take him?"

In a very low tone Nelson responds, "Echo 7, Echo 1. Do not take him. Say again, don't take him. Let him come in."

"Roger that, Echo 1."

The entire team hears the radio exchange on their in-the-ear comms, and when Nelson is done, he makes eye contact with Himmel and Johnston and points downstairs, wanting them to take care of the late-night visitor.

The two agents make their way back down the stairs but stop before they made it down to the first floor, their assault rifles trained on the front door. In a minute or so, they both hear the front door open and see the man outlined in the doorway. They wait for him to close the door, but as he does so, he notices the bodies of the two dead guards.

The man stops where he stands and raises his weapon, looking around the first floor, noticing also the third guard dead on the floor at the rear door. His attention now goes to the stairway. He sees two dark shadows and brings his weapon up to shoot, but he never gets a chance. He is shot twice in the head and twice in the chest, killing him instantly. The two agents return to the top of the stairs with the rest of the team and give Nelson the thumbs-up.

There is a door at one end of the second floor, and the three lead members of the team keep an eye on it as the rest of the team clear other parts of the second floor. They find nothing and return to the front three team members, the agents keep vigil at the top of the stairs, training their weapons on the first floor. Before they move out, Nelson and Echo 2 take out small red flashlights and begin the painstaking job of looking for trip wires or other booby traps as they slowly advance on the door at the far end. As the pair get close to the door, Nelson begins to think there are no booby traps, but that notion vanishes when Echo 2 grabs his shoulder, stopping him. Echo 2 points to a place on the wall, about two feet up, that looks to have something on it. On closer inspection, it is a laser light that is being used as a trip wire. They look at the opposite wall and see a mirror reflecting the light back. If the light is interrupted, then an alarm or something more sinister may go off. Echo 2 reaches into his small backpack and removes a small flexible mirror and, using duct tape, attaches it over the laser light source, effectively disabling the trip wire.

The rest of the team is beckoned to the door, with some kneeling down and getting low in the front of it as the rest are standing on either side of it. Echo 2 holds out three fingers, then two fingers, then one and drops his hand. At that, one team member mule kicks the door and immediately jumps to the side. After he clears the entrance, the rest of the team pour into the room with their weapons up.

At the sound of the door being breached, Bakkali springs out of bed but realizes that he is outnumbered and raises his hands. Two of the team members move forward and zip-tie his hands behind him, place duct tape over his mouth, and place a black hood over his head. They proceed to push him on the bed, facedown, and frisk him.

As they do that, other team members search the room for anything incriminating but find nothing except for Bakkali's laptop. They put that in a team member's backpack to take with them.

Nelson walks over to the bed and pulls Bakkali into a sitting position, removes the hood and duct tape, and takes a picture with his cell phone. He texts the picture to Zebra 1 and then raises him on the radio, "Zebra 1, Echo 1, we have target in custody and looking for confirmation."

After a few minutes, he gets a response. "Echo 1, Zebra 1. Confirmation is positive. Say again, confirmation is positive."

"Roger, Zebra 1. We're heading to the muster point, then to our primary exit plan." He raises the snipers, "Echo 7, Echo 1. How's it looking out there?"

"Echo 1, Echo 7. All quiet out here. You have a clean exit."

He turns to the team and says, "Okay, Echo team, let's get going." With that, the group heads down the stairs and out the back door.

CHAPTER 50

Reciprocity

Rashid chose Dagestan, thinking neither the Moroccans nor the Chinese would be looking for him there. Dagestan has Chechnya and Georgia as its neighbors. When he got to Makhachkala, the sea-side capital of Dagestan, he obtains a room at the Central City Hotel and lays low for three days, keeping an eye out for anyone following him. During this time, he does not leave the hotel and stayed mainly in his room. After a while, Rashid begins to think he shook the dogs coming after him, and he begins to relax a bit. He ventures out to parks and walks along the shore of the Caspian Sea, initially after dark but began to go out on little excursions during the day. Of course, he dares not turn on his cell phone so as not to give his location away.

On the fifth day in Makhachkala, he ventures out in broad daylight. He visits the national zoo and other sites of the city. Walking down the beach along the tourist areas, he ends up at Café Zolchoi, situated on Pacyna Boulevard, along the shores of the Caspian Sea and just down the street from his hotel. It is a very popular restaurant with the locals and frequented by guests at the hotels. There is a large outdoor eating area with marble-tiled floors, numerous large-potted plants that provides some separation for the guests. Soft Russian classical music can be heard from speakers strategically placed around the open space. Rashid chooses a table in the middle but closer to the street in which he could watch the shoreline or people watch on the street. He decides to sit facing the street, at least for now, thinking he may watch the sunset over the water later. He orders a vodka to start with and plans on having wine with his dinner. His attention is on the menu, deciding what seafood delicacy he could enjoy.

Rashid is overcome by the need to contact one of his informants regarding another pending matter, which he has not been in contact since leaving Wisconsin. He turns on his cell phone and begins texting. After about fifteen minutes of back-and-forth, he finishes. He receives another text from someone he hasn't heard from in a while who mentions a new opportunity. He could certainly go for a new opportunity, especially one in the Philippines, as the text suggests. He becomes engrossed in this conversation, not aware that his phone has been on for over thirty minutes.

Things begin to happen. People seated in the open-air café are now leaving quietly at the behest of a waiter. Pedestrian traffic on the restaurant's side of the boulevard has also stopped. The street isn't so busy now. Soon Rashid is alone but is unaware of this, still engrossed in his text conversation.

A white Russian-built GAZ business van with magnetic signs of the major cell company in Dagestan, Rostelecom, with Chechen license plates, makes its way down Pacyna Boulevard. The driver is going at the posted limit and is not drawing any attention to himself. The man in the passenger seat holds a device that allows him to ping and track cell phones, and right now it is set to Rashid's phone. As the van nears the restaurant, the man in the front passenger seat rolls down his window. The van stops in front of the café, and the side door slides open. The man in the front passenger seat raises an AK-47, along with two other men at the side door of the van who now open it.

The sound of the side door opening gets Rashid's attention, and he immediately realizes he's in trouble. He lurches up to run away, but it's too late. All three begin shooting in his direction, cutting a swath in the restaurant, destroying tables and pots. Chunks of wood and pottery fill the air, along with sprays of Rashid's blood. The men in the van keep firing at him even when his lifeless body slumps to the ground. Once they emptied their guns at him, they speed off.

CHAPTER 51

Divergence

The world is full of perfect plans, but that's not how the story goes. This is a line from a Michael Bolton song which applies to life and also to extraction operations.

As the team is loading up the vans to drive to the airport to meet their plane, Nelson's radio crackles. "Echo 1. Zebra 1. The Osprey is taking small arms fire and is getting out of the area. Abort exfil one. Say again, abort exfil one. Advise me if taking plan 2 or 3."

"Zebra 1, Echo 1. Standby." He now looks at his team. "You heard him, exfil one is off the table. We have options two or three to work with. Any recommendations?"

Himmel speaks up, "If the Osprey is taking fire, then it means somebody is on to us. Getting to the *Stark* means driving all the way across Casablanca and who knows what we will run into. We won't have a tactical advantage in a crowded city. I say we take our chances on exfil three in the desert west of the city. At least we will be able to see trouble coming at us."

Nelson agrees. "Everyone good with that plan?" There are nods all around.

"Zebra 1, Echo 1. We will be executing exfil three. Say again, we are going with exfil three."

"Echo 1, Zebra 1. Acknowledged. Proceeding with exfil three. I will whistle up helos from the *Boxer* for you."

"Roger that, Zebra 1. We are leaving now to the rendezvous coordinates."

The team gets into the vans, leaving the area quietly, heading west into the desert. By the time they make it to the edge of the city, fifteen minutes from the rendezvous point, the captain of the *USS Boxer* is giving the order to launch the helos to the provided coordinates. The skipper of the *Boxer* decides, given the circumstances, to launch a larger Sea Dragon to pick up the team and a Sea Hawk to provide firepower. Both helicopter crews are ready since they are on maneuvers. He gives the orders to launch the helos to Morocco.

The two vans are now speeding through the desert. There is cloud cover, so there is no moonlight; because of that, the drivers cannot see much beyond their headlights. As they bounce down the road, they are getting closer to putting Casablanca behind them. Nelson radios Zebra 1 and finds out the helos are ten minutes out, which is perfect timing. He thinks to himself that, at this rate, they will have a clean exit and be back in Rota in no time.

The driver of the first van notices that the terrain is getting hillier and notifies Nelson that they are getting close to the rendezvous point. What the driver couldn't see is they drove past a highway pirate, a part of the local syndicate that prey on those who travel between cities and towns west of Casablanca. This particular highway pirate is a jeep with a thirty-caliber machine gun mounted where the rear seat would be and occupied by three men—two in the front seats, the one on the passenger side with an automatic weapon, and one standing in the back as the gunner. They hear the two vans coming from a distance and are ready to pounce.

As the vans speed by, they get behind the trailing van and the man in the passenger seat stands up, bracing himself against the windshield and opens fire on the back of the second van. Bullets tear through the metal skin of the van, hitting no one or anything vital to the van. One of the team uses his communicator to notify Nelson in the first van that they are taking fire and asks permission to engage. The driver of the first van looks at his left rearview mirror and tells Nelson highway pirates are attacking. He gives the order to engage.

The four men in the back of the second van devise a plan to see what they are up against, making use of the hatch opening in the roof. Himmel, who is the tallest, moves under the roof hatch and slowly opens it, keeping the opening as small as possible. He peers out and can see the jeep chasing them and the machine gun mounted on the back. He slowly closes it and reports to the others. They quickly come up with a plan to counter the attack.

Himmel grabs an assault rifle and takes up position at the roof hatch; his job is to take out the machine gunner. Johnston and one of the REACT men take weapons and position themselves at each side door. They will take out the driver and passenger. The fourth man wraps ammo belts around himself and each of the men at the side doors to keep them from falling out of the van.

Himmel pops the hatch open and gets himself through it, locating the machine gunner, and levels his weapon at him and pulls the trigger. The gunner doesn't react fast enough, considering the rough ride he is enduring on the back of the Jeep. The first volley from Himmel misses the gunner completely, with the bullets hitting harmlessly into the sand. Fortunately, the highway pirate gunner is having difficulty training the machine gun on the van.

When Himmel opens fire, the team members on the side doors open them, lean out, and open fire on the jeep. They have better luck. Their bullets strike the hood of the vehicle but doesn't slow it down or hit any of the occupants. As the REACT member sends a second volley at the jeep, Johnston waits a few beats before pulling his trigger and is rewarded by the jeep veering into his line of sight to get away from his partner's burst. Johnston squeezes off a burst at the driver, killing him instantly and puncturing the left front tire. This causes the jeep to lurch more to the left and slow down.

With the jeep lurching, Himmel has a good angle on the gunner and opens fire on him, taking him out. He watches the man disappear behind the jeep. With no driver, the pursuing vehicle comes to a stop, and theREACT member takes out the remaining man with the assault rifle. Both men get back into the van and close the door. Himmel drops down and closes the hatch. He then radios Nelson the threat has been neutralized and no one in the van has been hurt.

Nelson is pleased they were able to do that all while they continue to the rendezvous point. Hopefully, there will be no more surprises. Unfortunately, he doesn't get his wish.

The driver of the lead van stops abruptly as he reaches the point where they are to meet with the helos from the *USS Boxer*. He informs Nelson who jumps out of the van and looks to the skies and realizes there are no helos or any kind of aircraft nearby. By the time the second van comes to a halt behind the first and shuts off the engine, they can hear a roaring noise. Nelson turns to the local agents and asks them what is making that sound because it is surely not an aircraft. They say more highway pirates are joining the fight.

Nelson has the local agents quickly move the vans, so they are perpendicular to the road, blocking it, and the nose of one is right up against the back end of the other. He tells his men to pull the equipment bags out of the vans and to set up the four high-volume, tripod-mounted, belt-fed machine guns, affectionately called SAWs. No sooner than they get things ready for a fight, the pirates show up. Four former military vehicles with large machine guns stop some one hundred feet away, not sure what to make of what they are looking at. Nelson doesn't wait for them to start shooting first; he gives the order for the men operating the SAWs to fire. They catch the pirates flat-footed and make short work of the two vehicles closest to the vans. The other two vehicles who hung back now begin to return fire. Very soon, they are joined by a larger vehicle that holds ten men with assault rifles. Within seconds, there is a full-on firefight.

Nelson gets on his radio. "Zebra 1, Echo 1. Where are the helos? I need them now! The LZ is hot." The letters *LZ* are short for "landing zone."

"Echo 1, Zebra 1. The helos are three minutes out. I'll pass along the hurry-up."

The entire team is now fully engaged in the firefight, with the four NCIS agents protecting the flanks. Amid the firefight, another group of six pirates show up and are instructed to attack a flank. They set up on a small ridge on the right flank and begin to fire onto the four agents.

Nelson gets back on his radio. "Zebra 1, Echo 1. Where are the helos?"

"Echo 1, the helos are one minute out."

"Zebra 1, I don't have another minute!"

The pirates on the flank decide to make a charge. Both Himmel and Johnston take rounds in their body armor and legs and go down. The two local agents try to protect the two fallen agents, and they are hit as well. The pirates see their opposition's flank is now wide-open and advances to attack the rest. Just as they come over the ridge they were on, they are cut down by the fifty-caliber machine gun from behind by the Sea Hawk. The helo slides to the right to get a good shot at the advancing opposition and opens up both fifty-caliber guns, mowing them down. The pilot slews the helo to the left and launches a hellfire missile at the small group of opposition vehicles, destroying them in a huge fireball. Just like that, the battle is over. With the Sea Hawk providing cover, the Sea Dragon flies in and picks up the team, including the four wounded, along with the prisoner, and all head back to the *USS Boxer*.

Lightning Strike

Josh and Marsha wake up to five inches of snow that fell during the night, a mid-spring snowstorm typical in Wisconsin. Before getting ready for work, he uses the snowblower and a shovel to clear the driveway and walkways. He gets ready first and has his breakfast, usually checking work e-mails as he eats. Meanwhile, Marsha showers and dresses. When she comes down to the kitchen, he is ready to drive to work. He kisses her goodbye and tells her to be careful on the roads, saying they may not be cleared off yet. He makes a mental note to call her in a little while to see if she made it okay.

Tagger gets to work earlier and plows out where crewmen park their vehicles and cleans off the work area as well. Today will be a busy day. They will be installing the new conductor for the new transmission line. The operation usually takes all day to accomplish, so Josh talks to the crew before they head out to make sure everyone is on the same page on who is doing what and when. As they leave to start work, Josh calls Marsha.

"Hey, girl, how was your trip to work?"

"Oh, the roads weren't too bad, but I almost hit a deer on the way. He just came out of nowhere."

"Dodged a bullet, eh?"

"Yeah. Hey, you be careful today. Don't be slip sliding around."

"Will do, boss! You have a good day. Love you."

"I love you too, bud. Have a good one."

Josh clicks off the call and radios each crew to make sure everyone is in position to get started. They begin the operation, but it isn't long when a problem develops. A rope comes loose off the conductor it is attached to, requiring them to pull everything backward to restart the operation and make sure the rope is secured to the conductor.

By the afternoon, the crew is making progress and well on the way to completing this section before the end of the day. That is, until someone slipped and fell while carrying a piece of equipment. The crewman was passing in front of one of the bucket trucks and whacked his shoulder on the front bumper as he fell. He is writhing in pain on the ground. Josh makes it over to where this crew is working and sizes up the situation. He decides to take the injured man to the hospital given the amount of pain he is in. Josh tells the foreman that he will take the injured worker in his truck since they are in a remote area and would take longer to get the man to the hospital if they waited for an ambulance.

Josh is sitting in the emergency department waiting room at the Wautoma hospital while they work on the injured man. As he sits there, he gets a call from Marsha. He presses the button to take the call. "Hey, babe, how are you doing?"

"I'm doing okay. How about yourself?"

"Well, I'm sitting in the emergency room at the Wautoma hospital."

There is silence at the other end for a few seconds, then, "Did you hurt yourself?"

"No, one of the crew injured his shoulder."

"Is he going to be all right?"

"Don't know. Will know more when the doctor comes out. I'm having a hard time locating his wife to let her know."

"I wanted to tell you that Sarah asked me to come over after work. She said she needed help with something."

"Yeah, no problem."

"There are leftovers in the fridge for supper. Can you start in on the restoration of that old rocker we need to do?"

"Yeah, I was thinking of doing that tonight anyway." What neither of them are aware of is that it will be a very long time before that project gets started.

At the end of the workday, Josh comes home to a dark house. Before putting his truck into the garage, he retrieves the day's mail delivery from the mailbox. Once he gets into the garage and closes the overhead door, he sheds his work clothes. He strips down to his long underwear and socks, making a mental note to start some laundry after he eats but before he starts in on the rocking chair. He enters the kitchen, carrying the mail and his lunch bucket and sets them on the counter by the kitchen sink. The house is quiet, and the only illumination in the house now is coming from the kitchen light. He grabs a glass out of the cabinet and pours himself a glass of water out of the tap. He is looking at a piece of mail as he drinks the water. He consumes most of the water in the glass and sets it to the left of the sink, and that's when he notices something odd.

To the left of the sink is a wooden block that holds kitchen knives, and he notices that one is missing. He wonders why a kitchen knife is missing from the block. He cleared out the dishwasher before he left this morning and there shouldn't be any dirty dishes, at least not a kitchen knife. He quickly realizes that he is not alone and whoever is in the house has the kitchen knife. He tries not to show a reaction, and a knot in his stomach tightens as he feels a sense of dread overtake him.

As calmly as he can muster, he moves over to the edge of the counter where there is a drawer. As he leans on the counter with his left hand, pretending to read the piece of mail, his right hand moves into the drawer where he keeps a loaded small handgun. It is a Colt Cobra Classic, a small six-shot handgun that Marsha wanted there in case of intruders.

Just as he gets his hand on the gun, a Chinese operative springs at him from the other end of the kitchen. The attacker holds the kitchen knife to the side of Josh's neck and, with his free hand, grabs Josh's right shoulder so he is right up against Josh, demanding the envelopes. The attacker doesn't see Josh's right hand or where it is and tries to pull Josh away from the counter, but Josh is a bigger man and resists the smaller man.

As the operative tries to take him to the floor, Josh pulls the gun out of the drawer. The assailant momentarily loosens his grip on Josh's shoulder to try again, and Josh regains his footing. At that exact moment, Josh brings up the Cobra between his body and his left arm and fires into the man's chest twice. The attacker lurches back with a surprised look on his face and drops to the floor like a stone. As he falls, he deeply slices Josh's shoulder with the knife, who screams out in pain.

The other operative comes after hearing the shots and screams. Josh sees movement from the direction of the living room and spins around and starts to bring up the Cobra. The second attacker fires a shot that slams into Josh's upper chest on the other side of where he was sliced. The impact of the shot and slipping in the pool of blood from the first attacker drives Josh down to a sitting position on the floor. As the surviving operative gets ready to fire again, Josh uses all his strength now to raise the Cobra and fires the remaining four bullets at his assailant.

The first bullet goes wide, destroying a lamp in the living room before embedding itself into the couch. The next two bullets come close to the assailant, causing him to move away, and slam into the far wall of the living room, spraying chunks of sheet rock in all directions. The fourth shot obliterates the left eye of the operative and exits out the back of his skull. He's dead before he lands on the floor.

Josh is in a sitting position, leaning against the lower cabinets under the counter, rapidly losing blood. He reaches for his cell phone in his shirt pocket, using all the strength he has, and dials 911. As he tries to communicate with the 911 operator, he can't hold the phone any longer and it skitters to the floor into a pool of blood. Josh notices he is very cold, and everything looks gray. He can faintly hear the 911 operator but does not have the strength to retrieve the phone or even move for that matter. The kitchen is spinning now, and his world is getting more and more gray and wonders if this is how it's going to end for him. He can hear a loud crashing noise as his world fades to black.

EPILOGUE

A hard rain falls on a chilly spring evening in Madison, melting the snow that fell the night before. The small group of family and friends hastily gather in the university hospital emergency waiting area, sitting anxiously to hear some good news from the doctors about Josh. They sit and wait, oblivious to the rain pouring down outside.

The DCI agents assigned to watching Josh tell Marsha what happened at the house. They were parked outside the house and heard the gunshots. Kicking in the front door, they found Josh in the kitchen with the two attackers. They determined Josh was still alive and had him flown to the hospital. The agents tell Marsha that Josh killed both of his attackers and police are processing the crime scene in their home. They tell her not to expect to go back home for a while. As it turns out, she never steps foot in the house again.

The surgeon comes out to the waiting room to tell Marsha that Josh survived the attack and required surgery to remove the bullet lodged between his lung and the spine. With the damage to the lung and muscle in the area, the recovery will be long. He will also require another surgery to repair his shoulder from the knife wound. She asks to see him, and the surgeon tells her Josh is unconscious but could see him for a few minutes. She is led upstairs to an ICU room and sees Josh with tubes and wires everywhere, connected to all sorts of instruments.

Marsha takes his hand and kisses him on the forehead, then speaks to him even though he can't hear, "For crying out loud, Josh, can't I leave you home alone for a while? The doctor says you're going to pull through this, so you better follow doctor's orders. I'm not ready to let you go just yet." She pulls up the chair by the bed and begins her vigil to sit with him until he awakens.

Several months of recuperation and rehabilitation have taken a toll on Josh. He is thinner and lost his muscle tone. Badger Power welcomes him back with open arms, but his happiness to get back to work is short-lived. They give him a new job, sitting at a desk, looking at construction plans made by others. His new younger boss tells him that they need his experience and expertise to make sure these plans are right, which pegs the needle on the BS meter. Badger has given his general foreman job to a younger guy who isn't apt to be an independent thinker. Josh can tell right away he drank the Kool-Aid and a lot of it. After a month of this, he tells Marsha that he wants to retire early and do something else, anything but sitting around looking at someone else's plans. Marsha knows he is unhappy and tells him to make that call whenever he wants to and that she would retire too.

Whenever he thinks about his good friend Roger, his thoughts usually gravitate to a line in the song "Against the Wind" by Bob Seger: "I wish I didn't know now what I didn't know then." *Was it worth digging in Roger's past? Look where it got me.* But how else could the case be solved? Surely the evidence he gathered greatly helped the investigation and bring the people responsible to justice. Could it have been solved without him, sparing him all this pain? Yes, but it would have taken longer. Besides, that's not how he's wired. It's in his nature to jump in and help a friend, even posthumously.

Marsha can't get over what happened in her house, a place she felt was their sanctuary, a place where they could get away from the world. That feeling has now been shattered, and the home she loved is violated, no longer bearable, and vows not to live there again. Sarah opens her home to them and tells them they can stay for as long as they want.

Josh and Marsha always talked about living in a somewhat warmer climate and opening a furniture-recycling business, pretty much what they do now on the side. After a month back at work, Josh announces his retirement two months hence and puts the house up for sale, and he and Marsha take a trip to Tennessee to scout a place to live. They had vacationed down there before, and they liked the eastern side of the state, with its mountains and forests. Not only did they find a home; the property also has a barn to house their furniture reclamation business.

Sarah feels lonely in her home, especially since the kids are out on their own and have their own lives. She tried to work after the funeral, but her heart was no longer in it. When they were younger, when the kids just started high school, they took a driving vacation out west. Roger and Sarah loved it so much that they thought they would retire somewhere near the Rocky Mountains. Putting the house up for sale, she moves west with no particular destination in mind. She hops around the Rockies, spending time in Cody, Frisco, Cheyenne but ends up in Estes Park, working in a coffee shop close to the mountains with a quaint duck pond. She also works as a substitute teacher at the nearby Colorado Mountain School. She is learning how to enjoy her new life, but her kids are worried and want to keep track of her.

Josh, Marsha, and Sarah keep in touch, the ladies more so through social media. Once a year, in the summer, they meet in the Black Hills of South Dakota, sometimes with their kids but most times it's just the three of them. All three learned, through their kids, how to use Skype, and so on holidays, they connect that way.

*****

As they usually do when they successfully close a case, Agents Tuganov and Dempsay drive to a favorite seafood establishment, The Log Cabin Restaurant, in Stafford, Virginia, for drinks and dinner. It is a fifty-minute drive to the restaurant, and the rules are, by the time they get there, all shop talk ceases. As Dempsay drives, she is in a good mood, but Tuganov seems a little quiet, which doesn't go unnoticed by his partner. She asks him, "What's wrong, Toog?"

"I don't know, Demps. I think this case kinda got to me. I've known you for a long time but don't really know your past that much."

"I'm not interested in talking about my past boyfriends or what I allegedly did at the senior prom."

"Allegedly did at your senior prom? What did you do?"

"Nope, that is locked away. Hey, I thought we're going to celebrate. We knocked out three open cases at once."

"I hope Himmel and Johnston heal up quick and get back to work. You know, that could have been us." They are both aware that Himmel and Johnston could have career-ending injuries. He continues, "The two field agents didn't fare as well, receiving injuries that are life-threatening and certainly career ending."

"Well, it wasn't us, Toog. Just be happy about that. When we signed up for this gig, we knew that could happen and so did Himmel and Johnston."

They make it to the restaurant and get a booth with an ocean view. They settle in and order their food. Sensing there is something else going on, she asks, "Okay, Toog, what's really bothering you?"

He hesitates, then says, "I just wonder what I'll do if I meet someone I want to settle down with. I don't know if I would still be an agent or not. I don't want to put someone I love through what Himmel and Johnston's wives are going through."

"Toog, what would you do? You're a very good agent, and I like you as my partner, so don't get any ideas about leaving. Otherwise, I'll have to hunt you down and make your life miserable." The last thing she emphasized with her fork.

With a wry smile on his face, he says, "Well, who says you have to hunt?"

ABOUT THE AUTHOR

 Marko Sans is a masterful writer of thrillers and mysteries. He has spent his life crisscrossing the globe, in not so fun parts of the world, working in various capacities. Some of them cannot be mentioned. He has seen many things over the years and he skillfully weaves these experiences with fiction to create riveting stories of international intrigue. The backdrop of his stories are those people and places not on the beaten path. The rich tapestry that makes up his books, leave the reader wanting more. Marko lives and writes, with his wife, in central Wisconsin.